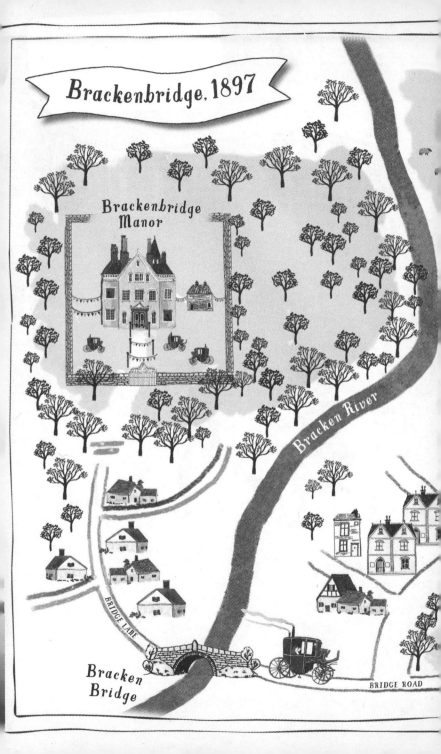

To Mum and Dad

First published in the UK in 2018 by Usborne Publishing Ltd., Usborne House,
83-85 Saffron Hill, London EC1N 8RT, England. www.usborne.com

Text © Peter Bunzl, 2018

Cover and inside illustrations, including map by Becca Stadtlander
© Usborne Publishing, 2018

Photo credits: Clockwork key © Thinkstock / jgroup; Border © Shutterstock/ Lena Pan; Stripes ©
Tippawankongto; Grunge/halftone © Shutterstock / MPFphotography; Crumpled paper texture ©
Thinkstock / muangsatun; Circus lettering and decoration © Thinkstock / Shiffarigum; Clockface
© Shutterstock / Vasilius; Coffee ring stains © Thinkstock / Kumer; Wood texture © Thinkstock /
NatchaS; Plaque © Thinkstock / Andrey_Kuzmin; Newspaper © Thinkstock / kraphix; Old paper
texture © Thinkstock / StudioM1

Published in the United States by Jolly Fish Press, an imprint of North Star Editions, Inc.

First US Edition
First US Printing, 2020

Library of Congress Cataloging-in-Publication Data (pending)
978-1-63163-431-4

Jolly Fish Press
North Star Editions, Inc.
2297 Waters Drive
Mendota Heights, MN 55120
www.jollyfishpress.com

Printed in the United States of America

SKYCIRCUS

PETER BUNZL

JOLLY
FiSH
PRESS

*M*ost people who fall in their dreams wake before they hit the ground.

She never did.

Instead, she dreamed of flying.

In that split second before she crashed to earth, she would throw her arms out wide, stretch her fingers like feathers, and swoop like a bird.

Drink the air.

Kiss the clouds.

Swallow the sky in one great glorious gulp.

Before an angry red sun burned her from the heavens...

And she tasted only ash in her mouth.

Afterwards she would wake alone and disorientated on her hard pallet bed in the attic of the Camden Workhouse and, with a pencil, mark the date next to all the others on the crumbling plaster. Then she would huddle beneath her rough blanket and think of all the things she had missed before getting up.

Breakfast was leftovers from the meager food that had been sent up to her the day before. She fed the stale scraps from her tin plate to the brave birds who came to perch on her windowsill, pushing her hands through the bars to offer them crumbs.

When they'd finished she would watch them wing their way across the rooftops, wishing she could soar as high. But she could no more fly than she could set foot outside this room. She'd been imprisoned for so long she'd forgotten how the weather tasted.

The only person she ever clapped eyes on was the kitchen boy. Each afternoon he would saunter across the yard and haul on the creaking pulley to raise her basket of food; sometimes, he would send a message too. When it came time to return the plate, she liked to add a present for him and a note in reply.

In spring she sent down empty eggshells from the nesting house sparrows; in summer, feathers from molting pigeons; in autumn, conkers gouged from the green spiked shells that dropped on the roof slates. In winter it was bones picked white by scavenger crows.

She enjoyed his look of surprise when he received these gifts. His tiny eyes sparkling beneath his dark fringe of hair and the amused grin that lit up his tanned face. His was the sole smile she ever saw.

Until the day the visitor came.

A creak on the stair and a jangle of keys in the lock announced the arrival.

Then the workhouse proprietress, Miss Cleaver, opened the door and strode into the room, beckoning her to rise from her bed.

The visitor brushed a silver cloud of hair from her face and stepped out from behind Miss Cleaver, across the attic floor.

"Good morning, Angela. I've come a long way to see you."

Angela, yes, that was her name. It had been a long time since she'd heard it. She wanted to say hello, but when she opened her mouth to reply, she could find the words neither on the tip of her tongue nor hidden away deep inside her. She didn't mean to be rude, but sometimes when she was scared, speech would not come. It had been an age since she'd last talked to anyone, and she barely knew where she kept her replies.

The visitor came closer, smoothing out a fold in her sky-blue dress, and stopped at Angela's bedside. Soft rays of sunlight filtered through the barred window behind her head, lining her gray locks with angelic streaks of gold.

"Can you walk?" the visitor asked.

In answer, Angela threw her itchy blanket aside, reached for her stick, and struggled to her feet.

The visitor proffered a hand. "Would you like to go on a little journey with me?"

Angela hesitated. She'd often longed to leave this attic, but now that freedom had been offered up so plainly, she felt scared. Surely this stranger couldn't be worse than the workhouse or Miss Cleaver? She didn't *feel* worse, but feelings sometimes lied.

Angela rubbed her eyes and stared unblinkingly at the visitor, who gave her the vaguest of smiles in return.

"Take my hand. I promise we are going somewhere special. Somewhere safe. Then, when we get there, I will help you find your wings. Would you like that?"

Angela nodded. Yes, she would. She would like it very much indeed. It was as if the visitor had seen straight into her dreams.

But how could this lady, who looked as if she'd never stretched or strained for anything in her life, teach her, a brittle orphan girl, how to fly?

To find out, she would have to risk everything.

She glanced one last time around the dusty room, then reached out and grasped the visitor's hand, holding it tightly in her own.

CHAPTER 1

Have you ever listened to your heart beat and wondered what makes you tick?

Lily Hartman had. Many times.

On the outside she resembled an unremarkable young lady, with flame-red hair, rosy cheeks, and eyes the color of the deep green ocean. But on the inside she was as different from other people as chalk was from cheese or cog from bone.

This was because Lily had the Cogheart—a heart made entirely from clockwork. A machine of springs and mechanisms that nestled inside her chest. Ever since she first realized she possessed it a year ago, Lily had often wondered about the Cogheart's unique qualities.

By every account it was indestructible—a perpetual motion machine. Lily was not entirely sure what that was, but there had been some suggestion, from Papa, that it meant she—or at least the heart—would carry on forever. To live forever was not an idea she was entirely enamored of. The thought of outlasting everyone she'd ever known and loved was not a pleasant one. It made Lily feel less a natural human, more a freak of design…

At least, that was how she thought of herself when she dwelled on such things—though she tried not to, because often there was so much else to contemplate. Today, for example, was September the twenty-third and her fourteenth birthday.

Lily was relieved to be banishing her unlucky thirteenth year to the past. It had been a time of sticky scrapes and perilous situations, and she would never have survived it without the help of her friends. Its departure was definitely something to celebrate.

The trouble was no one *was* celebrating.

Not her best friend, Robert, nor Malkin, her pet mechanimal fox, nor Papa, nor the mechanical cook and housekeeper, Mrs. Rust. Not even Captain Springer, Mr. Wingnut, or Miss Tock—the rest of Brackenbridge Manor's brigade of clockwork servants. Not a single one of them!

That felt criminally unfair and downright outrageous! And the worst part of it was that Papa had postponed her birthday party until tomorrow, which was tantamount to canceling it altogether.

Instead, later this evening, there was to be a grand gathering in the formal dining room, which was not to celebrate her fourteenth year—as one might expect—but rather to mark the fact that Papa was due to receive some sort of lifetime achievement award from the Mechanists' Guild for his work on mechanicals or mechanimals… or some such.

To be honest Lily wasn't quite sure which, because she'd stopped listening at the point where he'd told her the presentation would preclude the celebration of her birthday. He had, of course, offered his most sincere apologies, but the date was fixed. Prearranged. Set in stone. And, as such, could not be changed.

So Lily had found herself moping around all day. The difficulty was finding a satisfactory place to do the moping, since the entire house was filled with the clanking preparations for Papa's "special" event.

At ten past five, Lily had finally settled on the stairwell. She had even changed early into her bright red evening dress—her favorite because it was the only one with pockets and because it helped her stand out against the hall's somber wallpaper. (That way the entire household might finally notice her bad humor and what a martyr she was.)

Yet, still, no one paid her any attention.

Through the open doors of the dining room she observed Papa in his white silk shirt and smart black tailcoat, nervously touching his slicked back hair. He was instructing Mr. Wingnut, one of their mechanicals, in some last-minute adjustments to the table setting.

Miss Tock, the mechanical maid, stood nearby, fastidiously polishing the cutlery that was laid out on the sideboard. Her arms moved quickly in repetitive clockwork motion, and the chipped paint of her brow furrowed in concentration.

At the far end of the hall, the kitchen door stood ajar, and Lily could hear Mrs. Rust, the mechanical cook, juggling pots and pans and cursing the dishes she was preparing as if they were alive and could understand her.

"*COGS AND CHRONOMETERS, BOIL, WILL YOU, YOU BLASTED TROUT!*" she shouted. And then, "*CLANKING CLOCKWORK, ARE YOU CABBAGES NEVER TO BE SAUERKRAUTED?*" This was only marginally worse than her usual turn of phrase.

As for Robert, who'd lived with them nearly a year since his da's untimely passing, Lily hadn't seen or heard a peep from him all day. She imagined he was in his room getting changed into his smart suit for dinner. Malkin, that furry red-faced rascal, was more than likely with him. Either that or he was up to no good, digging holes in the lawn again.

Lily had just decided she might take herself off somewhere to be even more alone, so she could have a good sulk about things in peace, when she heard a strange little knock at the front door.

A slow and rhythmic *rat-a-tat-tat*.

The knocking was quite insistent.

Lily looked about to see if there was anyone else who might answer it, but there was not, so finally she stood and walked through the vestibule.

As she reached for the door handle the knocking stopped, and when she pulled open the door there was no one there at all. Only a small red-and-white striped hatbox tied with a twirl of multicolored ribbon, which sat on the doorstep.

Tucked beneath the box's ribbon was a cream-colored envelope addressed to:

Miss Hartman, of Brackenbridge Manor.

Lily bent down and picked the hatbox up. A present!

How exciting! She hadn't been expecting anything from outside the house. She looked around eagerly for the mysterious phantom who must've delivered it, but whoever they were, they seemed to have entirely vanished.

So instead, she pulled the envelope from beneath the ribbon and took out the card. It featured an etching of a striped hot-air balloon hovering over a red-and-white striped circus tent. On the back of the card in the same scrawling handwriting as on the envelope, a poem was written:

Dear Lily,
We have a simple question, and it's one that's
    not a trick:
Some of us are wondering what it is that
    makes you tick?
Two clues may solve our riddle, if we may
    be so bold –
One is something spanking new, and the other
    something old!
We hope that you enjoy both gifts and dearly
    want to say:
We wish you many happy returns on this, your
    fourteenth birthday!

Lily considered who this rhyme could be from and what it could possibly mean. One line gave her particular pause for thought:

What it is that makes you tick.

The phrase made her ill at ease. It felt a little too close to the bone. As if whoever'd sent the card was aware of her mechanical heart…and yet nobody knew of that save for Papa, Malkin, Robert, and the house-mechanicals…Oh, and Anna and Tolly. But surely none of them had sent this, had they?

And anyway, why such a cryptic riddle, with all its hints and winks? Because what else could "tick" mean in this context but the sound her heart made? The question was not only about who she was, it was about *what* she was… Unless she was reading too much into it? Could it be an accidental turn of phrase? Perhaps she'd become too paranoid about the Cogheart, too worried about its discovery…

The mystery was made more absurd by the fact that this was the first and only gift Lily had received today.

She undid the ribbon, lifted the lid of the hatbox, and peered inside.

A sliver of vermilion flashed in the sunlight.

Lily took the lid off completely.

Inside was not a hat or any item one might reasonably

wear on one's head. Instead, nestled in a cloud of green tissue paper, was a thin book bound in soft, port-colored leather. The cover was stamped with a curling gold ammonite.

Lily took the book out of the box. It was barely bigger than her hand. The pages were buckled out of shape, overflowing with stuck-in scraps that protruded from the edges. A notebook, then?

She opened the cover and flicked past the flyleaves. In the center of the first page, printed in ink, were three initials:

Lily knew at once who the notebook had belonged to: her mama, Grace Rose Fairfax. Fairfax had been Mama's maiden name, before she'd married Professor John Hartman, before she'd had Lily, and before she'd died on that tragic snowy night nearly eight years ago.

This was her notebook. A notebook Lily had never known existed.

Lily was so wrapped up in that thought that she completely forgot her qualms about the accompanying message on the birthday card. She felt as if she was holding a slice of the past in her hand.

Her fingers shook as she turned the pages, her eyes skimming odd images and phrases. The notebook seemed to be an attempt to document the various characteristics of flight. It was filled with diary entries, drawings, collages, diagrams, and sketches of birds. Scattered charts of weight-to-wing ratios were mixed with graphs and maps plotting the wind currents in the skies over England and tinted images ripped from magazines and newspapers, depicting angels, sphinxes, and harpies. On one page there was even an illustration ripped out of a children's book of Icarus and Daedalus with their wax-and-feather wings, flying too close to the sun.

She would need some time to take it all in. And she needed to find out who'd sent it. Surely no one in the house would trouble to deposit a present on the doorstep, would they? But where else could Mama's notebook have come from? It couldn't have been left by someone local, because no one in the area had known Mama—she had died before they'd moved here. What's more, Papa made sure they kept to themselves, so it seemed unlikely there were any neighbors or villagers who would even have known it was Lily's birthday. Two gifts, the card had said, and yet this was only one. Perhaps there was another clue in the box? She searched among the green tissue paper, but there was nothing else.

Still pondering these conundrums, Lily descended

the porch steps and stared out along the length of the driveway, hoping for some sign of where the mysterious delivery may have come from. But all she saw was Captain Springer, the mechanical odd-jobs man and driver, raking the front lawn. The cogs and springs of his arms and legs were jittering and chugging as he gathered leaves into one big, neat pile. The peeling paint on his metal chassis was almost the same rusty red color as the autumn trees.

Lily put her fingers in her mouth and whistled her loudest wolf whistle to get his attention.

Captain Springer stopped his raking and turned his head, the rims of his large goggly eyes whirring around as his pupils focused on her.

"Did anyone just call at the house?" Lily shouted.

Captain Springer shook his head. It rattled loosely on the gimbal joint in his neck. "Bless my bolts, no. Not for the whole afternoon. Why? Has something happened?"

Lily wondered if she should tell him about the present, but then decided against it.

"Nothing in particular," she said.

Captain Springer tutted and returned to his task.

Lily picked up the hatbox and went back inside, shutting the door behind her. She stood in the front hall for a good few seconds, stroking her fingers across the box's lid and pondering the notebook and card.

She should probably find somewhere to look at them properly before dinner. The grandfather clock beside the door to the front parlor read 5:35. She had until six, when people would start to arrive for the party.

If she really wanted to get some reading done, it would have to be somewhere private, where no one would look for her—and she knew the exact spot!

With the hatbox under one arm, Lily ascended the grand staircase and made her way along the landing. She passed the library and then Papa's office, where the portrait of Mama stared down at her from over the fireplace.

She crossed in front of the closed door to Robert's room and heard him arguing with Malkin inside.

"I'm trying to perform a delicate operation here," Robert was saying.

"Then let me help," Malkin replied.

"No, you'll only get fox fur in the workings. Or chew something valuable."

"I will not."

"You're gnawing at my trouser leg right now!"

"Well, I do need to keep my teeth sharp. And I think you should know you positively reek of mothballs."

Lily didn't hear Robert's reply, for she continued on her way, past the back bathroom and the linen closet. At the end of the passage, she reached for a glass doorknob set at hand-height into the wallpaper. Turning it, she stepped into a secret servants' stairwell that ran up the back of the house.

Lily climbed the steep staircase, avoiding the mechanicals' quarters on the highest landing, before finally reaching a set of wooden steps that led under the eaves of the roof into a tower room at the very top of the house. There, dusty wooden floorboards stretched out beneath four big arched windows that faced out to the north, south, east, and west.

Set before the eastern window was a telescope attached to a tripod, which Lily, Robert, and Papa sometimes used for stargazing. At the opposite end of the room, a sun-faded rug spread across the floor beneath the western window. On it sat an old armchair with upholstery that looked like it had survived a vicious squirrel attack, but had actually only been mauled by Malkin. Next to the chair was a steamer trunk that Lily and Robert used as a coffee table. Its top was crowded with stacks of books, half-drunk cups of tea, and an old oil lamp.

When Lily and Robert had first made this room their den, Lily had busily decorated the walls with copperplate etchings from her most gruesome penny dreadfuls, pinning them onto the bare bricks around the chair. There were four illustrations from *Varney the Vampyre Versus the Air-Pirates* and six from *Spring-Heeled Jack Battles the Spider-Monsters*—a particular favorite series of Lily's since she'd learned her friend Anna Quinn had penned a few issues.

Each grisly page had been liberally doused in blood-red paint to make them even gorier. Lily had used a whole tube of red from her Young Lady's Watercolor Set to paint them and most of the pins in her Goodly Seamstresses' Sewing Kit to fix them to the wall—those past birthday gifts from Papa had come in useful after all.

The illustrations flapped in the wind as Lily opened the nearest window to let in a little air.

She dropped the hatbox beside the armchair and sat down. Cradling the red notebook in her lap, she opened it to the first full page of writing.

On the top line her mama had scribbled the day and date, and an opening entry:

Sunday, 1st September 1867,
the Fairfax residence

A new Flyology
This notebook is inspired by the writings of Ada Lovelace—
mechanist extraordinaire. Specifically, her innovative

study Flyology, in which she first proposed the creation of clockwork-powered, winged creatures—ornithopters that mimicked the flight of birds.

Within these pages, I intend to expand on her theories, shepherding my own ideas into fruition so that they might soar to the great heights enjoyed by Ada before the end of this most marvelous century.

Not only will I record my day-to-day progress in this endeavor, but I will also document the trials I face as one of the first women studying in the mechanical field—an arena dominated by men.

My name is Grace Rose Fairfax, and this is my story...

As Lily read, a lump formed in her throat. At points her eyes blurred, and she lost focus. It was almost too much to bear to think she could meet Mama again through the pages of this red notebook. Each sentence felt like an invitation she hadn't expected to receive to a conversation she'd never known she could have.

How long had Mama worked on the Flyology project? Had she ever managed to make it a reality? Papa had certainly never mentioned it, nor this notebook. So who had sent it? Perhaps the second clue the riddle mentioned would offer an answer when it finally arrived.

Come to think of it, Papa hadn't said much about the

fact that Mama had been a mechanist either. He had alluded to it in passing, but he'd never gone into detail. Lily longed to ask him about his and Mama's life together, but she was afraid talk of the past might upset him, and she never seemed to hit on the right moment.

Now here, between the pages of this red notebook, she might find the answers she'd been searching for to the questions that burned so strongly in her heart. A heart that broke on that cold October day seven years ago when Mama died.

Lily's hand strayed to her chest and felt for the soft outline of her scars—cuts she once thought had been made by shattering glass during the accident that had gravely injured her and killed Mama, but were in actual fact from the transplant operation when the Cogheart had been knitted into her body.

Those raw wounds had healed over long ago, but the ghostly pain and loss they'd ushered in still ached within her, and Lily didn't feel like reliving those emotions right now. Not on her birthday.

She took her hand from her chest and closed the notebook. As she did so, a single sheet of scalloped card fell from the endpapers, fluttering to the floor like a feather and coming to rest at her feet.

She bent down to pick it up, turning it over to examine it.

Etched on its front in silver and gold was an image of a girl. From the picture it was hard to tell the girl's age, but she looked to be around fifteen years old. Her long, languid arms were spread wide above her head, and stretched out behind them was the most enormous set of mechanical wings.

The wings flowed from the girl's back as if they were part of her body. Their every feather, cog, and wire was picked out in ink, and around them a set of curlicued words was arranged:

SLIMWOOD'S STUPENDOUS

SKYCIRCUS

presents...

Miss Angelique Airhart — the world's only winged aerialist!
Witness a unique feat of soaring aerodynamic entertainment!

★ Show also includes outstanding acrobats, animals, funambulists, freaks, and clowns! ★ One night only. One-hour-long performance. 7.30 p.m., Thursday 23rd September 1897.

*This VIP ticket entitles Lily Hartman and three
friends to visit us and receive answers.*

PS Angelique would like to meet you after the show!

Could this be the second clue? Strange, Lily knew no
one named Angelique, nor any circus performers, and she
was entirely unfamiliar with Slimwood's Stupendous
Skycircus—whatever that was… But to discover a hybrid
girl with wings wanted to meet her—right after learning
about Mama's Flyology project, and to find the promise of
answers in the same invitation—that was just too
intriguing.

Hybrids weren't common, and Lily had never
encountered one her own age before. In fact, the truth
was, she'd only ever met two: horrible eyeless men named
Roach and Mould who'd tried to kill her. Otherwise,
she'd no idea how many more existed in
the world. The rest, she imagined, were in all likelihood
hidden away: kept closeted from sight, as she was, so as
not to disturb the "normal" populace.

That being probable, it was nice to see a girl who, at
least in this picture, was displaying her difference and
seemed proud of it. Lily hoped her wings were real and
not just fancy-dress or fantasy. How had she ended up in

the circus in the first place? And was there a connection between her and Mama?

She peered closer at the girl's picture, but her face held no answers; it was merely a mystery dissolving into print marks. There was only one way to discover the truth—she would have to go to the Skycircus tonight. It would be her only chance to speak with Angelique.

From its rather unpromising start, this birthday was turning out to be far more interesting than she'd expected. She scanned the ticket again.

The address was a mystery, but the sun had barely started to set—if the circus was in Brackenbridge, she would probably still be able to see it from her tower window.

She stood and pressed her eye to the end of the telescope; her heart ticked loudly as she swung the lens around, scanning the countryside.

In the sky, the gray scudding clouds were rimmed with gold, like sweat-stains on the silk lining of an old hat. A thin yellow fog rose from the waters of the River Bracken and wound its way through the village, where the crowns of the trees, blazing a bright autumn red, interrupted the jagged lines of the rooftops.

In the meadow at the far end of the village, half-hidden by the scrub and woodland, a strand of gold flashed in the quickening twilight.

Lily focused in on it.

It was a winged figurehead on the front of a tethered sky-ship.

A hot-air balloon bobbed above it. The red-and-white striped silks pulsed softly like a glowworm in the gloaming, spilling out strands of light over the top of an enormous canvas tent and a high, spiked circular wooden fence plastered with colorful posters. Crowds of people were already wading through the knee-high fog to line up outside the kiosk and gated entranceway of what had to be the Skycircus.

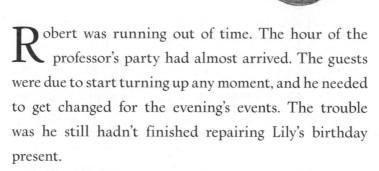

CHAPTER 2

Robert was running out of time. The hour of the professor's party had almost arrived. The guests were due to start turning up any moment, and he needed to get changed for the evening's events. The trouble was he still hadn't finished repairing Lily's birthday present.

He'd always intended to have the pocket watch mended by her fourteenth birthday at the very latest and to give it to her as a surprise. But here he was, still working on it at the eleventh hour. And here the watch was, still not working.

At least Malkin had stopped gnawing at his trouser leg—that was one less distraction. Though the threadbare old clockwork fox was still curled up beneath his desk, getting under his feet.

"What's taking so long?" Malkin asked, blinking his black eyes. "You said you'd be finished by now."

"One more piece…"

Robert peered down through his magnifying glass at the watch's interior. The hairspring, gear train, balance wheel, fork pin, and escapement mechanisms were perfectly balanced and aligned, like a miniature landscape. On the top edge of the case, beneath the crown, was the maker's mark: *T. T.*—for his da, Thaddeus Townsend.

The pocket watch had been made by Thaddeus years ago, and Lily's papa had bought it and given it to her on her ninth birthday. But the caliber inside the case had stopped when he, Lily, and Malkin had fallen into the Fleet Ponds on Hampstead Heath after jumping from a moving airship, and since that day Robert had taken it on himself to repair it.

He'd spent months cleaning every interior element of the watch, and now he had only to replace one last jewel bearing that balanced the pivot wheel. He took up his tweezers and carefully picked the tiny glinting gem up from his desk.

His hand shook as he held it over the watchcase and teased it into place.

"What've you got Lily?" he asked Malkin, more to distract himself than anything else.

The fox drew back his lips, revealing yellow teeth. "I shan't tell you. It's a surprise."

Robert wondered if that surprise was the dead mouse he'd seen Malkin nudging around the dusty corner of the hallway the other day, but didn't dare ask.

The bearing slipped smoothly into its fixing, slotting in with the other parts. Robert closed the watchcase over it. There. His work was complete.

His belly fluttered with excitement as he wound the watch for the first time and brought it up to his face. He could hear the tick of the parts in the caliber, and the hands moved smoothly, just as they should.

He set the time by his new mantel clock, then slipped the watch into an envelope, which he tied with a red ribbon.

Now he could give it to Lily as soon as he saw her.

He stood and changed quickly into his outfit for the evening: a dress shirt, sharp black trousers, and shoes that shone bright as buttons.

He tucked away his ma's silver Moonlocket that he always wore beneath his shirt collar, before tying his bow tie and finally adjusting his cog-shaped cuff links.

Then he pulled on a long-tailed, silk-lined suit jacket

and put the envelope containing the watch in its pocket, before stepping over to the full-length mirror next to the washstand to admire himself.

He didn't scrub up half bad. The suit still fit, just about. He'd worn it to the Queen's Diamond Jubilee in July and for his own birthday last month. Though it had gotten a little short in the sleeve since then, he observed. And his reflection now grazed the top of the mirror.

With delight he realized he must've grown. Perhaps he was destined to be the most statuesque one in his family? His da hadn't been particularly tall when he'd been alive, and his ma and little sister, Caddy, who he'd first met over the summer, had both turned out to be rather dainty in stature. Currently the pair of them were traveling the world, performing in their spiritualist show, and though they'd promised to return soon, Robert wasn't sure how long that would be. He wished they could see him now. Fourteen years old and looking practically a man in his smart suit…carrying on Da's work an' all—how proud they'd be of him!

Though his hair was still a mess… He reached over to the washstand for a glop of pomade and ran a hand through his tangle of curls, trying to straighten them out.

It didn't work. The hair sprang back almost immediately, its unruly spirals twirling round the tips of his ears like overenthusiastic ivy. He gave up and, after washing his hands in the basin, straightened his bow tie instead.

When he'd finally finished, he did up the breast button on the front of the suit.

"How do I look?" he asked Malkin, who was now rustling the tissue paper in the suit box that lay on the bed, trying to make a nest with it.

The fox gave a black-lipped sneer and wrinkled his threadbare nose. "Like a penguin who's just lost a job as a waiter."

"Thanks." Robert contemplated trying to wrestle a ribbon around Malkin's neck. Partly in honor of the evening's occasion, and partly in revenge for his snide comment. Then he remembered how sharp and snappy Malkin's teeth got when he was angry and thought better of it.

"I think Lily's hiding from us," Malkin said. "Or sulking. You know how bad she gets when she thinks no one's paying her any attention, and that's when it's not even her birthday. Clank knows what she'll be like tonight, with a party where she's not the main event. At least we've got our gifts to cheer her up. You'll carry mine for me, won't you, Robert?"

Malkin jumped off the bed and nudged something

small and furry toward him along the floor. It was the very dead mouse Robert had feared. "I've no opposable thumbs, you see."

"All right." Wearily, Robert picked up the deceased rodent and put it in his pocket. He found it best not to argue with the fox in cases like this.

At least Lily would be pleased with his present. He was pretty chuffed himself with how it had turned out. His clockmaking skills were improving, and one day he would be a master horologist, just like his da. He was, he realized, gradually becoming the sort of person who could put anything back together. No matter how broken it might be.

Downstairs in the hall, all the lamps were lit and the front door was open. Lily was nowhere to be seen, but in the foyer the first few visitors had already materialized. Outside, in the glowing sunset, a line of hansom steam-cabs waited to disgorge the rest of the guests onto the front steps.

Professor John Hartman, Lily's father, was standing in the vestibule, shaking hands and bowing politely to each and every new arrival as they entered the house. When he glimpsed Robert and Malkin at the base of the stairs, he surreptitiously beckoned them over.

"Have you seen Lily?" he asked.

Robert shook his head. Malkin shook his snout.

"That's a shame," John said. "She's missing out on all the fun."

What fun? Robert wanted to say out loud, and he was surprised that for once Malkin didn't say it for him.

By now the entire hall and front parlor were packed with fusty, dusty-looking professors from the Mechanists' Guild. Robert knew they were from the guild because each wore a single golden cog insignia—the guild's symbol—pinned to their coat lapel. And he knew they were professors because they looked professor-y—which was to say, rather rumpled, eccentrically dressed, and a little wild round the edges. He searched for a friendly face among them, but there was no one he knew.

John observed his look of skepticism. "I invited some of Lily's pals—that reporter, Anna Quinn, and her assistant, Bartholomew Mudlark."

"Where are they then?" Malkin queried.

"I don't know," John replied, "but they promised to put in an appearance. This lot have flown in on the evening transport zep, but Anna's probably bringing Tolly in her own airship."

"You mean *Ladybird*?" Robert asked.

"That's the one." John nodded. "After they've arrived,

and when the presentation part of the evening's over, I'm going to give a little speech for Lily at around nine and give her her birthday gift in front of everyone."

He pulled two small packages from his pocket and showed them to Robert and Malkin. They were both beautifully wrapped in colorful paper and red ribbon. "They're a surprise. So if you wouldn't mind keeping them a secret until the big moment arrives? You too, Malkin—I know what you're like."

"Of course," Robert said.

"No matter what," Malkin yapped.

"Thank you." John smiled. "In the meantime, go see if you can discover where Lily's got to. Try to cheer her up a bit and get her to come down, eh?"

"I'll do my best," Robert said.

"As will I," Malkin agreed. But as they wandered off, he added, "I imagine she'll need a great amount of cheering when she hears the quality of the guests who've arrived so far."

They decided to start the search for Lily in her bedroom, but when Robert knocked and put his head round the door, he found that, apart from the clothes thrown across the floor and the stacks of gothic novels that adorned the bookshelves, the room was empty. He checked under the bed, in case she was hiding from them there, but she wasn't.

As he stood up he knocked the bedside table, toppling over a small fossil. He set it carefully right as best he could. The fossil was an ammonite of fool's gold embedded in a stone that Lily's mama, Grace Hartman, had found on a beach and given to her daughter. Robert knew it was one of the last gifts Lily had received from her, and as such, it was extra-special. Lily had told him that Grace had been a keen amateur geologist, as well as one of the first female mechanists in Great Britain.

The library was next, because Lily sometimes liked to sit in there and read, but it too was empty. As were the other upstairs rooms, and the servants' quarters, which they hadn't really expected her to be in anyway, seeing as Mrs. Rust and the others weren't there for her to talk to.

Finally, Robert suggested they try their den at the top of the tower.

Malkin complained loudly as the pair of them climbed the stairs to reach the topmost room. "There's too much winter damp up here. It rusts my insides. Seeps into my springs."

"John's asked that we find Lily, Malkin," Robert said. "And anyway, it's either this or talk to those boring professors for hours—which would you prefer?"

"Well, when you put it in those terms…"

They stepped into the tower room, and there was Lily, sitting in the scruffy old armchair. Her long shadow stretched across the dusty floor in the last yellow slivers of fading sunlight. In her hand she held a red leather-bound book, which she must've been reading, but she slammed it shut as soon as they arrived. From the look on her face, Robert guessed she'd overheard everything they'd been saying.

"What're you doing up here?" he asked.

"Sulking," Lily said. "D'you want to know why? Because it's my birthday, and everyone's ignoring me. Rushing around after Papa, who's behaving as if he were the Queen of Sheba. And now the house is full to the brim with those awful old mechanists, who are no fun at all. There's no one for me down there."

"That's not true," said Malkin. "If you'd bothered to ask, instead of moping around, you'd realize there *are* guests coming for you."

"Who might they be?" Lily asked.

"Anna and Tolly," Robert replied.

"Really?" Lily leaped from her seat.

"They're not here yet," Malkin said.

"Oh." She sat back down on the arm of the chair and hugged her book despondently.

The gold pattern embossed on the cover glinted. It looked like an ammonite, Robert thought. "What's that book?" he asked.

Lily opened her mouth to reply, but then seemed to think better of it. After a moment she said, "It's either nothing or you'll-have-to-be-a-lot-nicer-to-me-before-I-tell-you." She hid the red notebook behind her back. "The choice is yours."

"In that case," said Robert, "you won't be wanting the birthday presents we've brought you."

"I didn't say that, did I?" Lily replied with a wry smile. She leaned back in her seat and folded her arms, waiting to be impressed.

"What've you brought me?"

"Give her my gift first, Robert," Malkin commanded.

Robert reached into his pocket and apologetically handed over the perished rodent.

Lily took it in her palm and gave it an unsavory stare. "It's certainly…different. I mean, it's not like anything I've been given before."

"I thought you'd like it." The fox ran his long pink tongue round his whiskers. "Keep it safe. A lot of thought went into that."

Lily shrugged. Robert watched as she reluctantly put the dead mouse away in the pocket of her dress.

"Where's your present, Robert?" Malkin yapped.

"I have it somewhere." Robert made a show of searching through his jacket. "I'm just not quite sure where… While I'm looking, d'you want to see a new trick I've learned?"

"You're certainly dressed for it," she retorted. "You look like a proper stage conjurer in that outfit." She checked herself. "I'm sorry. I didn't mean…"

"That's all right," Robert said. Half his family—the bad half—had been magicians. He didn't really like to think of them. But his ma and sister, who'd given him his Moonlocket, were theatrical mediums. They wrote letters sometimes, telling him about their enchanting escapades as they traveled and performed alongside conjurers and the like, and ever since he'd started corresponding with them, magic was an interest that had grown in him.

"Oh, I know where it is!" He tapped Lily's dress pocket on the opposite side from the dead mouse. "Have a look in there."

Lily put her hand in her pocket and pulled out an envelope tied with red ribbon. "How did you do that?" she asked, astounded.

Robert grinned. "A little bit of sleight of hand. It's the same as picking pockets, except you put something in instead of taking it out."

"What's in the envelope?"

"Open it and see."

"It feels heavy." She tore along the side of the envelope and tipped the pocket watch into the palm of her hand. "You fixed it?"

Robert nodded.

Lily examined the watch, her wide, excited eyes reflected in the brass case. "You've stamped my initials on the front. And it's ticking again!" she exclaimed, putting it up to her ear. A broad smile burst across her face. She pressed the crown switch, and the case flew open to reveal a second hand sweeping round the clockface above the slower minute and hour hands.

"There's something else," Robert said.

Taking the watch from her, he twisted the crown three times. A fourth hand appeared from behind the hour hand and swirled around the watch. He stopped it over the minute hand, and the watch chimed loud as a bell.

"I added an alarm," he explained. "I thought it might come in useful."

"I bet you had to rejig the entire workings to get it to do that," Lily said.

"Not the entire workings, just a few cogs and levers here and there. I learned a lot of it from your pa's teaching: he's been showing me how to move mechanical workings about to change the way a thing functions."

"Well, it's the best present ever." Lily looked so proud of him.

"What about my gift?" Malkin asked haughtily.

"That was good too, but this is even better. Thank you." She kissed Malkin on the snout and Robert on the cheek.

"It's a pleasure," Robert mumbled, fiddling with his cuff links as a wave of heat flushed through him. "Now you have all the time in the world."

Lily laughed. "And I shall keep it always. In my pocket."

"We ought to go downstairs and join the party," Malkin suggested.

"Perhaps."

Lily picked up her book and stepped toward the door. Then she stopped and turned mischievously toward the telescope and the east window. "I thought we might only stay at the party for a little bit—there's somewhere else I wanted to go."

"Where's that?" Robert asked.

"Take a look." She tilted the telescope toward him.

Robert bent down and squinted through the eyepiece. The twilight countryside was swathed in patches of fog, thick as fallen clouds. "What am I looking for?" he asked Lily.

"Beyond the last house on the left, in the meadow by

the bend in the river, at the far end of the village." Lily pointed for him, and through a gap in the mist, Robert spotted it…

A red-and-white striped hot-air balloon and ship-shaped wooden gondola, tethered beside an enormous Big Top that had been erected inside a high white wooden fence. The balloon's silks flickered like an oil lamp, illuminating a long queue of excited-looking villagers running all the way down from the lane at the edge of the field to the kiosk and spiked gate set into the high fence around the circus.

"Let me look! I can't see a thing!" Malkin bounced about at Lily's feet and scraped at Robert's leg.

"Foxes don't do telescopes." Robert shifted his focus to the sign above the entrance way. "'Slimwood's Stupendous Skycircus,'" he read.

"That's where we're going."

Lily handed him the birthday card.

"It's an odd poem," he said at last, when he'd read it. "What does it mean? And what are the two clues?"

"This is the first one." Lily showed him the ticket.

Robert was dumbfounded by the drawing of the winged girl and the message. "And the second?" he asked.

"This." Lily pulled the red notebook from behind her back. "It belonged to my mama. It's about a project of hers to design mechanical wings," she explained as Robert flipped through pages of amazing drawings and sketches of winged figures.

"You've no idea who sent these?" Malkin asked.

"Maybe this winged girl, Angelique. She's asked to see us. I think she might be a hybrid too, like me. She looks nice."

"I'm not sure, Lily. How would she have got hold of your ma's notebook?" Robert tapped the red cover. Something about the notebook's sudden and unexpected appearance made his head itch with worry. "It could be a trap. Why else would whoever had this book send it to you, rather than to your father?"

"Because it's my birthday." Lily snatched the notebook back and shut it with a snap.

"But how would they know that?" He handed her back the ticket and card as well. "Don't you think it's odd for a circus to come to Brackenbridge? There's not been one before. Such grand shows never normally visit such tiny villages."

Malkin stuck his tongue out of the side of his mouth. "Robert has a point," he said. "For them to arrive on your birthday, of all days…then there's these clues and presents, and the invite… I mean, what on clunking earth…?"

"Oh, I don't know, Malkin—that's why we should go

and find out." Lily looked at the pocket watch. "It's almost six twenty now. We can probably arrive at the circus before it starts at seven thirty. See the show, meet Angelique, and be back by nine, before the party's even halfway over."

"We can't just disappear without speaking to any of the guests." The fox wrinkled his nose disapprovingly. "Your father's expecting you to put in an appearance."

"Then we shall greet everyone briefly, before we sneak off," said Lily. "What do you think, Robert?"

Robert wasn't certain they should be going at all. He wondered if he should mention the fact that Lily's da was planning a surprise speech and present-giving at nine? But then he remembered he'd promised to keep that a secret. Did such promises apply if you were running off to see the circus? He thought he'd best keep his mouth shut, just in case they did. If it looked like they weren't going to be back in time, he might mention it to Lily then—to be sure she'd get a wriggle on.

Besides, he did love a puzzle, and this one was very intriguing. The circus could be fun, and this might be his only chance to see it...

"Fine," he said at last. "Let's do it."

"But if we get into trouble," Malkin added, "it was your plan."

Lily ruffled his ears. "We won't get into trouble. When have we ever got into trouble?"

The fox sighed deeply. "I'm not going to even dignify that with a response."

Lily picked up the ticket, card, and notebook. She was glad she had a new mystery to solve. At last she felt as if she was doing something exciting and worthwhile on her birthday.

"Don't worry so much, both of you," she said, shutting the window. "We'll be back before Papa's even missed us."

CHAPTER 3

Lily, Robert, and Malkin crept down the grand staircase to the front parlor, where a gaggle of guests were milling around, talking before dinner.

Lily glanced about the crowd, searching for Papa, and though she couldn't see him anywhere, she recognized a few faces in the room.

There was the mayor of Brackenbridge, talking to the parson of nearby Brocklebridge Church and Mr. Chantry from the secondhand bookshop. There was Inspector Fisk from Scotland Yard, who'd helped Robert, Lily, Malkin, and Tolly foil a plot by Robert's grandfather, the infamous escapologist Jack Door, to steal the Queen's diamond. He was talking with Papa's lawyer, Mr. Rent, who'd been a partner in a firm called Rent and Sunder, before Mr. Sunder had run off with their old housekeeper Madame Verdigris and a ton of Papa's patents and papers, never to be seen again.

And there was Mrs. Chivers, whose clockwork canary Robert had once repaired. It was sitting on her shoulder now, chirping incessantly.

The rest of the room appeared to be filled with mechanists and professors from the guild. Lily noticed that there were no ladies among them and remembered that, on the first page of her notebook, Mama had mentioned how hard it was for female scholars to become mechanists.

There'd certainly been no talk of such career opportunities at Miss Scrimshaw's Academy—the awful finishing school Papa had attempted to force Lily through last year. The life of a young lady, according to that place, was meant to be an endless parade of polite tea parties, cluttered with doilies and bone china, or else a stream of embroidery, etiquette, and deportment classes. If Mama had truly altered things and gone against the grain of those ideas, why was it no one else had followed her example?

Anna was the only other woman Lily knew who took exception to those kinds of rules. She looked for her among the throng of guests, and Tolly too. She was sure Robert had mentioned they'd been invited, but she couldn't see them anywhere. She wanted to at least speak with Anna before they snuck off, and perhaps she could persuade Tolly to accompany them to the circus—they did have four tickets, after all.

Finally, she spotted the stout figure of Anna in the far corner. The journalist and aeronaut looked rather incongruous, for, unlike the rest of the guests who were in evening dress, she was wearing her best bloomers and leather flying jacket. Although, in a concession to the formality of the occasion, she had taken off her hat and goggles, and had pinned her hair up in a neat braid around the top of her head.

Lily wanted to ask her where Tolly had got to and maybe tell her about the card, ticket, and red notebook, but as she approached she saw that Anna was deep in conversation with someone—a tall professor with bulbous ears and a bald patch. The professor had his back turned to her, and so did Anna, but their discussion was so interesting that Lily couldn't help but eavesdrop.

"I'm writing a piece on hybrids," Anna was saying, "and I need some facts and figures for my article. I hear you worked at the Mechanists' Guild for a time, so I wondered if you might be able to help... How many hybrids are there in England, would you say?"

The tall professor laughed and took a swig of champagne from the long-stemmed glass in his hand. "A good question, Miss Quinn. But, honestly, I've no idea. They're not my specialty. If I had to make a guess, I'd estimate probably only half a dozen or so. The hybrids that were created were...experiments. Many of the early incarnations did not survive more than a few years, and those that did aren't seen by the world at large... For obvious reasons—I mean, the sight of them is frankly unacceptable." The professor gave an involuntary shudder. "But, fortunately, such work is no longer being undertaken. The only mechanist I know who dealt in such things—apart from our poor deceased colleague Professor Silverfish—was a Dr....Droz, I think the name was. A thoroughly unpleasant and discredited character." He leaned in closer to Anna and whispered theatrically, his eyebrows wiggling like hairy white caterpillars, emphasizing each word. "Thrown out of the guild years ago. Though the details of that are not for me to divulge."

Lily was about to interrupt him when he continued, "Legend has it that Hartman and his wife were involved in hybrid research too, you know! The gossip was of some corrupted creature with a clockwork heart."

Lily felt a horrible shiver of panic.

"Of course, we at the guild disavow hybrid study entirely," the professor continued.

"Why?" Anna asked.

He shrugged. "Turning humans into hybrids is unethical; it changes who they are. Creating mechanicals is a different thing. But creating hybrids—half-and-halfs—it's against the laws of nature. It contaminates us. People should be left as they are. I mean, why meddle with what the great maker himself intended?"

Anna put her empty glass down on a side table. "Even if helping them means they're happier and healthier?" she asked. "Even if it saves someone's life?"

"Especially if it saves someone's life," the professor said. "If you change someone with clockwork, turn them into a hybrid, how are you saving them? Would you want them to have to deal with *that* stigma? It's worse than being a mechanical. No, better they remain normal and a little damaged: a pure human who meets their fate with dignity, rather than a transformed *freak*."

Lily gasped and felt the air knocked out of her. Did people really believe such things? Her blood boiled just to hear his little speech. He knew nothing of hybrids—if it wasn't for her clockwork heart, she wouldn't even be here, alive, on her birthday. She was no freak! Why did he think he had the authority to spout such vile opinions, the oaf!

"How could you possibly understand what it feels like to be a hybrid?" she asked, stepping between him and Anna and thrusting herself into their conversation. "Who are you to say what's good or bad?"

The professor's eyes widened in alarm. He was obviously rather surprised to be interrupted in full flow. "My dear young lady, it's common knowledge that hybrids are problematic, which is why we at the guild banned their creation."

"Lily!" Anna cried. "It's so good to see you." She kissed Lily on both cheeks.

"And you," Lily replied. But she was still fuming about the professor's remarks.

"Do you know each other?" Anna asked.

Lily shook her head.

Anna introduced them. "This is Professor Manceplain—a noted expert on mechanical studies. Professor, this is Miss Lily Hartman, John's daughter."

"A pleasure, young lady."

Lily shrugged. It was certainly no pleasure for her to meet such a horrible man. For a moment there was an awkward silence, of the kind grown-ups sometimes fall into at parties when nobody knows what to say.

"I'm so glad you're here, Lily," Anna said at last. "Your father told me it was your birthday, and we've a present for you. Only I left it with Tolly, and I can't seem to see him anywhere... Perhaps we should go find him?"

She took Lily's arm and led her away from the tall professor, the pair of them pushing through the sea of bodies.

"How could that man hold such idiotic views?" Lily asked. "Why were you talking to him? Are you investigating something to do with hybrids?"

"Thank goodness you came over," Anna said, not answering any of her questions. "The conversation was getting onto rather shaky ground. I don't know what I would've said if it had continued! But I really need to speak with your father," she went on, spotting him and pointing him out. "Why don't *you* find Tolly? He's got your gift, and we can catch up later..." And she vanished into the crowd.

Someone tapped Lily's shoulder. It was Robert. "You'll be pleased to know I've seen Tolly," he said. "He's hiding in the kitchen."

The sideboard downstairs was laid out with Mrs. Rust's various replaceable tool-hands. Preprepared dishes lined the table, awaiting their delivery to the dining room.

There was a large boiled salmon with cucumber and lobster cream perched in a grand blue-and-white serving dish, alongside veal croquettes and a leg of lamb on a bed of blanched spinach and roasted potatoes. Then, for pudding, there was a gooseberry tart with whipped cream and orange jelly, and a lemon cake. And cheese and biscuits. It all smelled amazing, and it felt almost a shame to go out and miss such a feast.

Tolly sat alone among the platters of food, his chair turned toward the hearth. His tanned face, with its thatch of chestnut curls, looked sad, but then he glanced up and saw Lily and pasted on a smile. "Happy birthday, Lil! Hello, Robert! Are you having a good party?"

"It's not really her birthday party," Malkin said. "More a stuffy event for mechanists."

"That's why we stepped out," Robert explained.

"Too right!" Tolly leaned back in his chair. "I didn't fit in there neither. It's full of blimmin' professors—the crème de la crème of the mechanist community, supposedly. Anna was talking to some awful fella about her article, so I decided I'd come in here and sit by the fire on me own for a bit." Tolly leaned forward in his chair and straightened his jacket. "Oh, I almost forgot, Lil. Me and Anna brought you a gift."

He felt about in his pockets and pulled out a leather

wallet. When Lily opened it, she discovered it was full of tiny implements—miniature lockpicks, each one barely longer than a match.

"We thought they'd come in handy on your adventures," Tolly explained. "Might have better luck with them than hairpins."

"Thank you." Lily laughed. "It's truly what I've always wanted." And it was.

"I brought some firecrackers an' all," Tolly said, pulling a handful from his pocket to show them. "Just to liven things up," he explained. "But I don't think it's that kind of a do."

"No, it doesn't seem to be," Lily said sadly. Then she perked up. "I know something that might cheer you up, Tolly. And it's far more fun than this dull party."

"Oh, what's that?"

Lily and Robert showed Tolly Mama's red notebook and explained how it had arrived with the bizarre birthday card and circus invite. Tolly flicked through the book as they told the tale, taking in all the wonderful drawings and illustrations of flying creatures.

"It's a proper mystery," he said when they finally finished. "Just how did Angelique and the rest of these circus folk get hold of your ma's notebook in the first place?" He handed it back to Lily.

"That's what we intend to find out," Robert said.

"As well as catching the show," Malkin added. "I'm hoping there'll be fire-eating, juggling, and some hummable tunes. But obviously no mimes—they're the worst."

Lily put the book away and checked her pocket watch. "It's seven now," she said. "We should probably get going. Why not come with us?"

"Spit and sawdust!" Mrs. Rust said as she bustled in to pick up trays of food. "Did my metal ears deceive me? Are you going out?"

"We thought Tolly might like to take a turn around the garden, Rusty," Lily said. "He hasn't seen it before."

"Dough-hooks and dishcloths! What the tock for? It'll be dark out."

"A bit of fresh air. He's feeling a little sick, actually."

"I am?" Tolly looked confused. Then, when he saw the frown on Lily's face, he clutched his stomach and played along. "Ooh, yes, I'm afraid I am."

Mrs. Rust gave a loud tut. "Well, wear a coat."

"Of course, Missus." Tolly clasped Robert's arm and hobbled toward the cloakroom that led to the back door.

"And, Lily," Mrs. Rust added, "before you go wandering off—"

"We aren't!"

"I know you better than that." Mrs. Rust put down her tray. "Make sure you've a scarf. It's cold out. In fact, I wasn't going to give you this till later, but it seems as if you could use it now."

She opened a drawer in the kitchen dresser and took out a rather rumpled-looking package. "Steam-fountains and stockpots! It's got a bit squashed." Mrs. Rust placed the package in front of Lily on the scrubbed table. "That's from us mechanicals, my tiger." She gave a wheezy cough. "Well, that is to say, mostly it's from me, as I'm the one who made it."

Lily's heart soared. From a day when it seemed everyone had forgotten her, she'd ended up with a whole armful of presents.

She kissed Rusty on her dented metal cheek and set to opening the package. Inside was an orange-and-black striped scarf. The longest scarf she'd ever seen. She wound it round her neck, but even after she had done so a number of times, the end still trailed on the floor.

"It's lovely," Lily told Mrs. Rust. "If a spot on the large side."

"Fulcrums and fenders! Sorry about that," Mrs. Rust said. "I'm not the best at knitting. Thing is, I can cast on, but I've not quite fathomed how to finish. So I keeps going until the wool runs out. Never mind, I'm sure you'll grow into it."

"If she turns out to be a giraffe," said Malkin, who'd returned from the cloakroom.

"Maybe I will, Malkin." Lily hitched up the end of the scarf and stuffed it into the pocket of her dress. To Mrs. Rust she said, "Thank you, Rusty, I shall treasure it forever and never take it off, not even indoors!"

Mrs. Rust gave a bolt-filled grin. "Gridirons and girders! I should think not! You be careful out there. Don't step on any of Springer's begonias, and mind you're back in time for your father's big speech at nine!"

In the cloakroom the back door was open, spilling out heat and letting in the dark and a chilly breeze. Just beyond the last rectangle of light, Malkin and the others stood on the bottom step in the gathering fog, waiting for her.

Lily took her coat from the rack and thrust her gifts into its pockets, glancing back into the kitchen as she did so.

Mrs. Rust stood framed in the doorway, bent over a tray that she was filling with food. Lily's stomach rumbled. She felt suddenly famished. She wondered if she should go back and steal a croquette or two for later, but then realized they'd only get squashed in her pockets. Anyway, there was sure to be plenty of leftovers when they returned.

She was glad to be leaving the party. She hoped by the time the four of them got back that dinner would be over and all those stuffy professors would've retired to the smoking room or, better still, gone home. Papa probably wouldn't even notice they were missing.

In the meantime, she'd had enough of duty for one evening. It was time for her birthday treat…and to get some serious investigating done! They were off to see the circus!

CHAPTER 4

The air was damp and chilly, and through the patches of fog, Robert glimpsed the first stars already out in the night sky. As he followed Lily, Tolly, and Malkin along the path that wound round the side of Brackenbridge Manor, a sudden thought struck him.

"How are we going to get to the circus and back before nine?" he asked. "It'll take at least forty minutes to the village each way—or more, considering we'll get lost in this weather—and then the show lasts an hour, and we need to be back in time for your da's speech at nine. We can't possibly make it."

"We can if we're not on foot," Lily replied.

"What are we going to do, fly?" Malkin sneered.

"No." Lily led them onto the front drive. "We're going to take one of those." She pointed at the long line of steam-hansoms sitting wheel-deep in the mist and waiting to take Papa's guests back to the Brackenbridge Airstation.

Robert wondered why he hadn't thought of that as they clambered aboard the first machine.

"Budge up!" Tolly said, climbing into the passenger compartment beside Robert and Malkin as Lily negotiated with the driver. When she'd finished, she climbed in as well, slamming the door behind her and settling into a seat. Then she banged on the roof to signal they were ready to depart. In a moment the steam-hansom had chuffed to life, and they set off at a rattling pace. Malkin jumped onto her lap and lay down, resting his front paws and snout across her knees. Lily stroked the top of his head.

They barreled through the open gates at the end of the drive, the night mizzle thickening and rolling across the fields toward them.

Robert wedged his cap on straight, his fingers fumbling with its brim. Then he shoved his hands deep in his pockets and wrapped his coat close around him, snuggling into the soft collar.

The coat had once belonged to his da. Its thick wool felt warm and cozy, and far more comfortable than the smart suit he had on beneath it. A few flakes of old tobacco lined the pockets. They must've fallen from Da's pipe, which he'd kept in there sometimes.

For years the coat had hung on the rack in the back hall of their old shop, Townsend's Horologist's. Da would scoop it on whenever he went out to deliver a clock he'd repaired. He'd been gone almost a year now, and Robert still missed him every day. The coat was one of the few things that remained of him.

"I ain't never laid eyes on a proper circus before." Tolly shifted about excitedly in his seat. "I seen a few street *arteeestes* round Camden Town and some music-hall turns in the penny gaffs, not to mention that spiritualist show of your ma's, Robert—but none of that's the same as the whole Big Top number, is it? What do you think this Skycircus is going to be like?"

Lily cast a glance at Robert. His face looked flush with nervous excitement. She too had a few anticipatory butterflies in her stomach—or was that the lurch of the cab?

Robert shrugged noncommittally. "I've no idea. These kind of shows never normally come to Brackenbridge."

"I can't wait to see the girl with wings," Tolly chattered on. "I wonder if she'll fly for real, or whether it'll be some kind of swing-and-wire trick?"

Malkin's ears pricked up, and he shifted, his claws digging into Lily's lap. "Human bone density makes it highly unlikely she'll actually take off," he told them.

"Seems a lot of effort to make mechanical wings if they don't work," Robert said.

"Chickens," Malkin replied.

"What about them?" Tolly asked.

"They have wings but can't fly."

"You think she might be like a chicken?" Robert asked.

"Chickens are a bit clucking stupid, aren't they?" Tolly said. "That'd be odd if she ran around like one of them."

"I disagree with all of you," Lily interrupted. "This girl's going to be a marvel!"

She got out the red notebook, pulled the ticket from beneath its cover, and flipped through some of the strange diagrams and drawings of winged creatures held within its pages.

Would Angelique turn out to be a real winged hybrid like these drawings? A hybrid like *her*. And was there some link between Angelique and Mama? Lily couldn't be entirely sure, but a small part of her felt that the connection wouldn't just be coincidence. She couldn't wait to meet Angelique and ask her. In the meantime, she would have to content herself with reading more of the notebook.

Monday, 9th September 1867,
Histon College, Cambridge University

My first day studying Mechanics, specializing in ornithopters. Histon is the first ladies' college in the country. They have a Latin motto on their crest, which I recognize as the same one that was above the door at my old school:

VINCIT OMNIA VERITAS.

Truth conquers all.

I feel it's an auspicious beginning. One should always strive to be authentic, especially to oneself.

Lily scratched her head. How curious. *Truth Conquers All* had been the motto of her school too—Miss Scrimshaw's Finishing Academy. Had she and Mama studied at the same place and she hadn't even known it?

Tuesday, 10th September 1867,
Histon College

Last night, to celebrate our arrival, I and some of the other girls from the dorm on West Quad decided to visit a circus that was in town.

Lily pursed her lips and stopped reading again. This was even stranger. She was on her way to the circus, and here was Mama talking about one.

I saw the most amazing trapeze artist! It was almost as if she was flying through the air on her swing. It made me think about my thesis—to make someone fly with mechanical wings. In all honesty, it will be difficult to bring to fruition.

That's not to say it's an impossibility, and I am willing, above everything, to give it a try.

That was the end of the entry, but the coincidences were such that Lily could not resist turning the page and reading the next one too.

<u>Tuesday, 17th September 1867,</u>
<u>Histon</u>

I had my first tutorial today. My tutor says we can discover the universal truth of things in science, numbers, and equations, just as we can in the fossils of the past or in the written word. My mother used to say something similar: "What would you do if you weren't afraid?" Back then I never knew the answer, but now I do: tell my truth.

And today my truth lies in the Flyology project.

The Flyology project… Had Mama really gone on to create a winged person in the years before her death? Lily had never heard tell of such things, not from Papa or anyone, so it seemed unlikely. Then again, before tonight she hadn't even entertained the idea that a flying hybrid girl could exist. And yet, here they were, perhaps on their way to see one.

It was possible, she supposed, that there were others, who were kept secret—hadn't the professor at the party told Anna such experiments were banned?

Lily wondered whether the rest of the pages would reveal the whole story… If not, Angelique might know more.

She closed the red notebook and replaced it in her pocket, then glanced over at Robert and Tolly, who were both staring out of the window.

The interior of the cab had filled with condensation. Robert wiped the window glass with his handkerchief so they could see better, but outside was only darkness.

A bump made Tolly jump in his seat.

"What's that?" he asked.

"It's all right," Robert said. "We're crossing the Bracken Bridge." And, indeed, his words were accompanied by the chatter of water as the river ran beneath them.

They swept on up Bridge Lane and onto the High Street, where Robert pointed out five small halos hanging in the air that illuminated the clumped silhouettes of buildings submerged in the mist.

"Those streetlamps mark the edge of the village green," he explained to Tolly. "And there's my shop—where I used to live."

Tolly stared out at the blackened carcass of Townsend's Horologist's, sinking into the fog like a shipwrecked galleon. "You were lucky to get out of a place like that."

"It wasn't so bad before it burnt down," Robert replied. "Besides, I've got plans. Sometime soon, me and John are going to start fixing it up." Though the reality was that since their meeting with Jack Door there at the start of the summer, he hadn't had the heart to return to Townsend's.

As the hansom left the green and proceeded up Brackenbridge Hill, Robert had second thoughts about this evening's adventure. But he figured if things looked bad at the other end, he could make Lily turn the cab around and take them home. He was just contemplating how to broach the subject when they jerked to a stop.

They'd arrived.

THUD! The driver leaped down from his seat and crunched around the side of the cab to pull open the door.

Eerie music and flickering colored lights drifted through the fog from behind the hedgerow of the nearest field. Pinned to the slatted wooden gate in front of them was a wooden arrow-shaped sign painted with bright white letters:

Robert scrunched up his eyes and jumped down from the footplate behind the others. The spectral foggy emptiness of the lane made his belly flutter with anxiety. Where were all the people he'd seen lining up through the telescope? Had they gone in already?

For a second, he considered the possibility that they had come to the wrong place and wondered again if sneaking out of the party had really been such a good idea. If something went wrong John would have no idea where they were.

"We should get the cabbie to wait," he mumbled, but it was too late—the hansom had already turned round and was trundling off up the road through the thick fog. "Now how are we going to get home?" he complained.

"Robert's right," Tolly said, watching the steam-hansom vanish into the night. "It's too dangerous to walk back in this weather."

Malkin looked at them crossly. "Why didn't you say anything sooner?"

"I didn't think," Robert said. "It was Lily's plan, and I assumed—"

"Never assume anything," the fox said snootily. "Assumptions are always a mistake. Look at Lily—not one of life's planners, and yet she assumes everything will turn out rosy because—"

"Quiet!" Lily snapped. But the truth was Malkin was right. She hadn't thought her plan through, and already it was going wrong. She had expected at least a few hansoms and steam-wagons belonging to the earlier crowds to be parked here, and she had hoped that one of them might offer them a lift home later. But there was no chance of that. The place was deserted.

Beside her, Robert and Tolly shrunk into their coats, and even Malkin was on high alert, his hackles raised. She took a great gulp of air to try and calm herself, but her fear still fizzed and fizzled in her. She couldn't let her sudden sense of dread distract her from her earlier excitement over the chance to find out more about Mama's work. Someone at the Skycircus—maybe Angelique, maybe another act—had sent Mama's notebook, and they must be able to tell her more about it. She took out her pocket watch and checked the time.

"It's already 7:29. We'd best hurry, if we want to catch the start of the show." She pushed open the gate and stepped into the foggy field beyond.

"Wait for me!" Malkin cried, rushing behind her with his tail down.

Tolly glanced at Robert. "Come on," he said apprehensively, and together, they both followed the others through the gap.

A narrow path lined with flickering candles in glass jam jars led them down into the dell they'd seen earlier from the tower, where the high circular wooden fence of whitewashed slats stood, plastered with bold posters of circus folk. Behind it was the striped canvas Big Top, and behind that was the gigantic red-and-white hot-air balloon—big as a harvest moon and twice as bright.

Lily was relieved to see through the mist that a last handful of villagers were standing beside the ticket booth and a gated entranceway in the fence, paying for their tickets. She and the others joined the line behind them. When they'd finished, they pushed through the high spike-tipped iron gates one by one and disappeared beyond the fence.

Then Lily found herself at the front of the line.

Inside the kiosk was a man in clown makeup and a frilly collar. His ghostly face was white with powder. A black makeup snake squiggled round one eye, and a painted teardrop fell from the other, making him look positively frightening.

Lily smiled at him and got a grimace in return. Then he reached up and began pulling a metal grille down over the window. "Sales are closing," he explained through the bars. "The show's about to start—if you want to join the crowd, you'll have to be quick-smart."

"We've a VIP ticket. A personal invite." Lily placed their ticket on the counter in front of him. The clown examined it.

"So you do. This looks fine! And since you're in line, you're most assuredly on time!" He ripped the ticket into tiny pieces and giggled, throwing them over his head like confetti. Then, leaping out of a side door of the booth, he tipped his triangular white hat at them and bowed so low that the red pom-poms on the front of his polka-dot clown suit squashed together about his tummy. Coming up he was all smiles, which was disconcerting, as there was already a sharply outlined grin painted on his lips.

"Come along, good fellows, follow me. Outside the Big Top there's nothing to see!" He ushered them through the iron gates, locking them behind him, and was only slightly taken aback when Malkin slipped through the bars and joined the rear of the line.

The mist had yet to penetrate beyond the fence. A red carpet, edged with more glass-jar lanterns and furry as a tongue, had been unfurled across the grass and between the taut guy ropes. It ended at a wide-mouthed archway hung with lanterns, where the last few stragglers they had just seen were making their way into the Big Top. A jingle of accordion, drum, and fiddle music accompanied them, mixed with a chatter of expectant voices that drifted from the tent.

"My name's Joey the clown," Joey said. "I smile more than most, but sometimes I get down." He pointed to a painted teardrop on his cheek and gave a leering approximation of a sad face.

Robert thought Joey very odd indeed. The clown's singsong jabbering was not putting him anymore at ease. It had an awkward nervous quality to it beneath the light jokey tone. He wondered if everything the clown said was always in rhyme. Surely that would drive him crazy, if he wasn't so already?

As they neared the canvas entrance, a mechanical

man lumbered into view, his limbs creaking like the screech of unoiled brakes. He was about eight feet tall— taller than any human, and bigger and wider too.

The mechanical man turned his head and stared at them as they passed, and his neck joints made a horrible crunching sound. His eyes were as big and dead and empty as the round headlamps on a steam-wagon, while his mouth ran straight across his face in a flat expression that was neither a smile nor a frown. His bulky body looked like it was made from discarded parts of heavy machinery, and his arms clanged as he folded them across his chest. Robert shivered. They were as thick and square as brick pillars, with hands that looked big enough to crush a skull. Lucky that mechanicals were programmed not to hurt humans.

"That's the Lunk," said Joey. "He stands guard. Guards the stand. He's our mechanical strongman. He creaks the whole time because he never uses an oil can."

Lily and Tolly stared worriedly at the Lunk, but they didn't have the opportunity to consider the mechanical anymore, for Joey was guiding them down a short canvas tunnel into the Big Top, where the smoky aroma of roasting chestnuts and burned cotton candy mixed with a smell of canvas, wood shavings, and stale sweat.

They passed a gaily painted cart in the entranceway, behind which stood a second clown, whose face looked entirely different from Joey's. White rings surrounded his eyes, red lipstick splurged around his mouth, and his hair, which stuck out at every angle from beneath a battered bowler hat, was dyed a bright orange color that reminded Lily of a raw carrot. To top it off he wore a suit of loud, mismatching checks draped over his squat body like an oversized tablecloth. It looked like it had been assembled from the remains of an explosion in a tartan factory.

"Roll up! Step right this way!" he called out, waving at the jars of sweets laid out on the counter of his cart. "Tracks and sneats! Gine wums, shemon lerberts, stickerish licks, drocolate chops, fandycloss, and choast restnuts—you too can taste these trondrous weats…"

Robert didn't know what any of those were, but they sounded quite disgusting!

"This is Auggie," Joey said. "He's a bit of a spoonerist, gets his words all mixed up, but if you listen carefully you'll get the gist."

"We don't have money," Lily told the clowns.

"That's ferfectly pine." Auggie reached out one big-gloved hand, plucked a small red-and-white striped heart-shaped box from beneath the wagon's counter and passed it to Lily. "Another gift yor fou."

"Oh, I forgot to say..." Joey added, "compliments of the house, since it's your birthday."

"Thank you." Lily's grin couldn't quite hide the confusion she felt inside. She took the box of chocolates and handed them to Robert. She didn't recall telling the clowns it was her birthday, but somehow they seemed to know. Could they be the ones who'd sent the first present?

Joey led them past rows of tiered wooden benches, which were arranged five deep around the tent and filled with everyone from the village who hadn't been invited to Papa's party. Lily recognized various local faces among them. The schoolmistress, out with the butcher's boy from the High Street, was trying to ignore a gaggle of her pupils sitting directly behind her. The baker and his wife and their two children were sharing a box of popcorn, the littlest one dropping half of his on the floor. Beside them, the old man whose job it was to light and snuff the five streetlamps around the village green was busily puffing on his pipe.

Other notable local faces filled the rest of the stands. People who nodded to Lily and Robert, but then immediately turned to their neighbors to gossip about them when they'd passed. Lily imagined they were probably wondering why she wasn't at Papa's party scoffing platefuls of the food Mrs. Rust had been out purchasing in their local shops all week.

"Here we are!" Joey stopped at a handful of empty wooden chairs beside the central sawdust ring that had been cordoned off by a red ribbon. "The Vee–*EYE*–Pee area!" he said, pulling his left eye wide with one finger and rolling the eyeball about. Then he blinked. "Sorry! Feeling a bit sick—bit of a tick… Tick-tock! Ha-ha… Wondering what it is that makes you tick…"

Lily stiffened. He'd said exactly the words from the card, that had rhymed too. She was starting to suspect he'd written it, and she was beginning to have terrible misgivings about this whole adventure, but Joey was already whisking the ribbon from the aisle and ushering them into their seats.

While they were taking off their coats, he pointed out the red velvet curtains on the far side of the ring. In the shadows stood the four-piece band—three men and a woman dressed in patchwork suits—who were playing their jangle-sharp warm-up tune on their instruments as the last of the audience settled in for the show.

"This spot might not look like much to you," Joey explained, "but rest assured it has the best view. Happy birthday, Lily, on our behalf and look for me in the very first half." With that, he saluted and was gone.

Lily looked anxiously around, uncertainly trying to determine what they'd gotten themselves into. One thing the clown had said was true: they were in the best seats in the house. She could see everything from where she sat.

A quartet of poles around the ring held up the roof. From them radiated swathes of canvas hung with black, white, and yellow bunting. Smaller side-poles around the edges were hung with individual oil lamps. Gradually, the babble of the crowd died away as the two clowns, Joey and Auggie, moved among them, laboriously and with much slapstick, snuffing out each of the lamps.

Finally, there was only one flame left. It guttered and died, and the entire tent was plunged into darkness. The band stopped playing their jittery tune, and Lily found she was holding her breath.

She wondered if the next hour would give her the answers she hoped for or if coming here had the makings of a grave mistake.

CHAPTER 5

Lily's eyes were still adjusting to the inky insides of the tent when a single limelight flickered to life, illuminating the sawdust ring with a lurid glare, accompanied by a strong smell of burning calcium. The soft bowing of the fiddle cut through the air. Soon it was joined by the beat of the drum, then the squeezed wheezings of an accordion, and finally the plunk of the double bass.

As the jaunty fanfare became louder, the velvet curtains parted, rising in swags from the center, to reveal a black backcloth sewn with tiny fragments of mirror that caught the light from the auditorium and twinkled like little stars.

Two figures—a man and a woman—paraded out onto

the sawdust. They set off walking in opposite directions around the ring. The man wore a high top hat with a broad brim, which shaded his gaunt clean-shaven face and a pair of dark, deep-set eyes, and he carried a black horsewhip. His red swallowtail tuxedo flapped with each stride, while the woman's loose blonde hair bounced with every gliding step. She wore a vermilion dress and twirled an open red-and-white parasol about her head. Her face was painted with brightly colored makeup, and she had a long blonde beard that matched the color of her hair.

The two met at a point directly in front of where Lily and her friends were sitting, and threw their arms up in the air in unison.

The man swept off his top hat and bowed to the assembled crowd, flashing them a sparkling smile crammed with gold teeth. "LAAAAAADIES AND GENTLLLLLEMEN! Welcome to our Big Top! Tonight, in our ONLY BRACKENBRIDGE SHOW, you will witness MAGNIFICENT ESCAPADES of UNIQUE QUALITY!"

"Blimey!" Tolly whispered. "He's got the patter, hasn't he?"

"It's almost as stale as the smell in this tent," Malkin sniped.

"My name's Slimwood," the man continued. "I'm the

ringmaster of this circus of ROUSTABOUTS that you've the pleasure of witnessing this evening, HEREABOUTS and THEREABOUTS! Allow me to introduce MY BEAUTIFUL ASSISTANT—MADAME LYONS-MANE, our bearded lady and ringmistress." He threw a white gloved hand out to his companion. "We have come to RELIEVE YOUR SUFFERING! Create a little AMUSEMENT in your dull lives… Our acts will perform the MOST OUTRAGEOUS tricks of DANGER and DARING for your DELIGHT and DELECTATION!" He waved his hands at the crowd as if these wonders were already visible.

Madame Lyons-Mane stepped forward. "Before we begin, one of my clowns has told me that tonight is someone's birthday!" She glanced at Lily. "Would you please join me in the ring?" she asked in a melodious voice.

Lily stood and obliged, feeling an odd pull in her stomach.

"A big hand for Miss Hartman!"

The crowd applauded, and Madame Lyons-Mane opened her parasol in front of the pair of them, leaning in to whisper in Lily's ear, "Happy birthday, Lily. I've another present for you." She motioned to Auggie, who dashed over and handed Lily a bunch of wildflowers wrapped in newspaper.

"Font dorget to water them," he chirruped as Lily took the bouquet, and he sprayed her with a squirt of water from a fake silk carnation in his lapel.

After that, Madame Lyons-Mane indicated she should return to her seat.

Lily sat back down and put the wilted flowers on the floor beside her.

"Don't go chewing those," she told Malkin as she wiped her face on the end of her scarf.

"It couldn't make them any blooming deader," Malkin muttered from under her chair. "By the by, that woman shouldn't be opening umbrellas indoors. It's bad luck. Everybody knows that. You'd think circus people would too."

Tolly tapped Lily on the arm. "Did you ask her about Angelique?"

"There wasn't time," Lily said. "I'll do it later. Maybe she'll—"

But their conversation was interrupted by a loud drumroll as Madame Lyons-Mane flipped her open parasol in the air and caught it by the handle, balancing it on her palm before finally snapping it shut.

Then Slimwood shouted, "Remember—THERE ARE NO RULES OR REGULATIONS, AND NO

SAFETY NETS! Merely the GREATEST SHOW ON EARTH... And now, LET THE EXTRAVAGANZA BEGIN!"

Lily settled back in her seat, distracted by the thought of Madame Lyons-Mane. Something about the sharp scent she wore had seemed familiar. When she'd leaned in close to whisper, the aroma had cut through the sawdust and animal smells of the circus ring. It lingered like a memory Lily couldn't quite place, faint and out of reach.

But she didn't have time to contemplate it, for the show was now in full swing. They saw plate-spinners, tumblers, jugglers, and dancers, and Lily found herself drawn more and more into the drama of each act.

"PRESENTING THE FABULOUS BOUNCING BUTTONS!" Slimwood announced as the show reached its halfway point, and a family of three dark-haired, tanned-looking acrobats entered the ring. He pointed at them one by one: "Bruno, Gilda, and Silva!" Silva was the youngest, about Lily's age, and Lily thought she had to be the daughter or the sister of the other two. "See them jump like tiddlywinks! See them shine in their astounding acrobatic act!"

The Buttons sprang about, performing backflips and cartwheels to the tunes of the band. Meanwhile, with much screeching, the Lunk brought out a seesaw.

Carrying it as though it was as light as a matchstick, he placed it in the middle of the ring and lumbered off again.

Silva Buttons stood on one end of the seesaw, while Gilda climbed onto Bruno's shoulders to create a human tower. Silva nodded to them and slapped her hands to her thighs, and as one, they hopped onto the other end of the seesaw, sending Silva flying through the air, so that she landed atop their tower.

Silva wobbled momentarily, and it looked like she might fall; she glanced nervously offstage at Slimwood and Madame Lyons-Mane, waiting in the wings. Behind them lurked the great square shadow of the Lunk, shifting from foot to foot. The sight seemed to make Silva sway even more, almost as if she was more worried about getting the trick wrong in front of them than she was about the audience.

Then Gilda threw her arms around Silva's legs to steady her, and she seemed to regain her confidence and balance. The music swelled in encouragement, then dropped into a drumroll.

Silva pasted a nervous smile back on her face and, throwing her arms up, leaped from the top of the human tower...

She bounced onto her hands, somersaulted across the sawdust and landed with a flourish, closely followed by Gilda and Bruno, who vaulted into place beside her. Then the three Buttons lined up, opened their arms, and gave big extravagant bows to each corner of the tent, exiting to applause.

The Fabulous Bouncing Buttons were followed by Dimitri Grai, the Youngest Horseman of the Apocalypse, who wore a Cossack riding outfit and rode two stallions, one black, one white, round the ring simultaneously.

Then came an ancient-looking man who ate four flaming firebrands, which he washed down with tea straight from a teapot, before polishing off an entire set of crockery from the same tray as if each piece of china were merely a cream bun.

At last, Slimwood appeared again. "And now WHAT YOU CAME HERE FOR," he called. "The FREAKISH and UNNATURAL portion of our show!"

The crowd's mutterings became filled with a kind of electric excitement, and the music accompanying Slimwood took on an edgy, scrambled tone.

"LADIES AND GENTLEMEN, PLEASE GIVE A WARM HAND—OR PREFERABLY TWO, HE COULD USE THEM BOTH—FOR LUCA THE LOBSTER BOY!"

A boy with mechanical clawlike hands appeared in the gap between the curtains. He wore a linen shirt and woolen breeches, and had blue eyes and blond hair, scruffy as a haystack. He seemed ill at ease, but he snapped his claws on cue. Lily guessed he was about fifteen, though he was barely taller than her.

"Take note of his gruesome appendages," Slimwood advised, pointing at Luca with his whip from the edge of the ring. With a shudder, he leaned toward the audience and held up his free hand, whispering theatrically from behind it. "Each claw can cut through six inches of steel like paper!"

Luca had a bandy-legged gait and his shoulders stooped low. Lily noticed he could barely keep his heavy-looking claws from dragging in the sawdust. She fidgeted in her seat, balling her fists. She didn't appreciate the sneering grandiosity of Slimwood's words or the way the boy was being treated. She wondered if Slimwood spoke to Angelique that way too, and found herself grinding her teeth at the idea of him exploiting hybrids like her for entertainment. Displaying their idiosyncrasies as things to be gawped at and feared.

While she was thinking all this, the Lunk had creakily dragged a pair of dangling chains along a suspended roof rail and hung them directly over Luca's head in the center of the ring.

"Tonight," Slimwood explained, as Luca began to

climb, "Luca will ascend these chains unaided and swing from them using only the strength of each hooked hand. Don't get too close or anger him, ladies and gents, for he can tear off your nose with a single snap of his claw!"

"LAWKS ALMIGHTY!" shrieked someone in the row of seats beside Lily. "HE'S A MONSTER!"

Lily waited for Slimwood to come to Luca's defense. He wasn't a monster. Why couldn't they see that? But Slimwood merely confirmed the woman's opinion. "In the circus we call them FREAKS, Miss!"

At that, the woman fainted dead away, and her companion made a big scene of fanning her back to life. Luckily, Madame Lyons-Mane, who was still standing near the edge of the ring, was on hand to administer some smelling salts. She plucked a little glass bottle from her pocket and hurried over to wave it beneath the woman's nose.

The sharp and pungent stink wafted across the row of seats and made Lily feel quite dizzy. Auggie the clown helped the woman to her feet, and her friend escorted her outside for some fresh air. Meanwhile the entire auditorium, including Luca, had paused to watch this strange sideshow. As she exited, the woman was still muttering about what a horror he was.

Lily glanced at his sad face, and her heart went out

to him. Robert and Tolly looked disgusted by the scene too.

"Why do they behave that way?" Robert whispered. The audience's attention had returned to Luca as he started to climb the chain.

"People despise what's different," Tolly said. "They're scared to death of it." He nodded at the ringmaster and Luca. "But if I had to guess who was the rotter out of them two, I would put my money on that Slimwood fella."

Lily remembered when she'd told Tolly about the Cogheart and how it made her feel she didn't fit in. Tolly had admitted he often felt the same. He was an orphan selling newspapers back then, and people often looked down on him because of that. He knew what it was like to be seen as different or lesser than others. And he was right, Lily reflected. Most people never gave you a chance to prove yourself their equal, especially if you didn't look quite like them.

Luca had nearly reached the roof by now.

"No one knows how he lost his hands," Slimwood narrated as Luca completed his climb. "Perhaps they were severed in a threshing accident or mangled in a loom? Maybe they were snipped off with scissors when he was a tailor's apprentice as punishment for sucking his thumb? Not even he can recall… But none of that's important. What matters is this freak's claws are as TOUGH AS IRON!"

Luca swung back and forth from the top of the chain, holding his body at a right angle to it, exhibiting unnatural strength.

Then he scrambled back down to the ring and bowed to end his act. His face was filled with disdain as he stared at the audience, and he clacked his claws together distractedly to accompany their uneasy round of scattered applause.

Lily was beginning to feel hugely uncomfortable about the whole Skycircus setup. After all, what was the difference between people like Luca, who everyone paid to goggle at, and her, with her own hybrid nature? The only real distinction was his oddness was self-evident, whilst Lily's was hidden deep inside.

"UP NEXT IS DEEDEE LONG-LEGS, THE WORLD'S WEIRDEST AND MOST WONDERFUL WIRE-WALKER!"

A young girl with dark brown hair wearing a pink tutu waltzed out across the ring, teetering on stilt-like mechanical legs that whirred and fizzed with her every step and made her look like a clockwork flamingo.

Once again, the audience screeched and caterwauled. But Deedee ignored them. Instead, she climbed gracefully up a rope ladder to the wire that was suspended high over the ring, only visible now that the spotlight was on it. Then she took up a long pole that was balanced on hooks beside the platform at the top of the ladder, and holding it out for balance, she began to walk the wire, putting one foot carefully in front of the other, her mechanical toes grasping the rope with each step.

Soon, as swiftly as she had stepped onto the wire, she was running along it, skipping back and forth, performing flips and handstands on the rope—tricks that Lily had never seen or even heard of before, not even in the penny dreadful circus stories she'd read. When Deedee had finished she climbed down to the ring and bowed distractedly to the audience with a look of studied indifference, before slipping away through the curtain.

"NOW, WITNESS THE LARGEST MECHANICAL MAN EVER BUILT. HE LITERALLY DOES HAVE MUSCLES OF STEEL! OUR RESIDENT STRONGMAN—THE LUNK!"

The Lunk stomped into the ring. His humongous square body squeaked as loudly as an unoiled steam engine, his square metal feet sending up puffs of sawdust and shaking the ground beneath him.

He approached a cage being wheeled on from the other direction by a group of four heavyset men, and his long square shadow fell across two mangy-looking lions, one tiger, and a bear, all stalking about inside it.

The Lunk demonstrated his superhuman strength by bending an iron bar, before shutting himself in the cage with the dangerous animals. But somehow neither feat was particularly impressive. There was nothing the carnivores could do to him, given that he was made of metal. In fact, Lily felt more afraid for the animals when the Lunk threateningly waved a chair at them. It wasn't fair to put such an indomitable iron man up against these poor scraggy wild beasts. They didn't even try to come near him.

As the Lunk's act ended, a vague and uneasy atmosphere floated over the ring like oil on water. Surely they must be nearing the end of the show? Lily wondered if they were making a mistake staying until its conclusion. Would it be better to leave now—after all, they still had to work out how they were going to get home? Or should she still wait? She dearly wanted to see Angelique—to witness her performance and speak with her.

In that instant the band started up again, the fiddle bowing and swooping, and the accordion and drums getting faster and faster, rising in apparent anticipation of something astounding still to come. Then Slimwood reappeared and spoke over the music: "LADIES AND

GENTLEMEN, YOU ARE ABOUT TO EXPERIENCE OUR GRAND FINALE AND SHOWSTOPPER!"

Lily sat forward in her seat. This had to be it, surely? What she'd been waiting for…?

"Watch the Skycircus's most FANTASTIC FREAK perform on the FLYING TRAPEZE! A monster so MAGNIFICENT, a hybrid so HYPNOTIC, that they call her THE FAIRY-PRINCESS OF ENGLAND! Daedalus's daughter! THE BEWITCHING BIRD-GIRL OF GREAT BRITAIN! A creature of the earth and air! A hybrid miracle of our modern clockwork age! A ONCE-IN-A-LIFETIME VISION!" He waved his whip at the audience. "See her SOAR ABOVE THE SAWDUST in a feat of FANTASTIC FEATHERED BRAVERY! Observe her fly from trapeze to trapeze, performing the impossible quadruple somersault in PLAIN SIGHT, from the astounding height of ONE-HUNDRED-AND-ONE PERILOUS FEET! I give you OUR VERY OWN ACROBATIC ANGEL: MISS ANGELIQUE AIRHART!"

The spotlight swept across the ring and paused halfway up a long rope ladder. And there, hanging from a rung, suspended between heaven and earth, was the girl with wings.

CHAPTER 6

Lily's eyes were pinned to Angelique, who was framed in the spotlight. Glass beads twinkled in her thick, fuzzy braids of hair, which wound about the top of her head like a halo, and her wide chestnut eyes were highlighted by the shimmering colors of her costume that stood out against her brown skin. The dark feathers of her wings, pinned to her back, wavered as if blown by a soft breeze.

This was who they'd been waiting for.

Lily was so entranced by Angelique, she barely heard the loud, low gasp of Tolly in the seat beside her.

"I recognize that girl," Tolly said. "I didn't realize before from the invitation—the picture was too small and blurry—but she used to live in the Camden

Workhouse. Her name was Angela in them days, not Angelique, and she never had them wings." He shook his head in marvel. "We were friends back then, her and me—although we hardly talked. I used to send her food up in a basket and messages too, sometimes, to the attic where she lived. One day she went missing. I asked the other orphans what happened, but none of them knew. She'd just disappeared."

The music gradually built as Angelique hauled herself up the ladder, rung by rung. Her body was tall and straight and regal, but beneath her smile was a slight wince that suggested she found the ascent painful, and Lily observed that she used her left leg more than her right to climb.

Tolly had noticed too. "She broke that leg working for Miss Cleaver."

"Who's Miss Cleaver?" Robert asked, watching Angelique with bated breath.

"The woman what ran the orphanage," Tolly explained, his rapt eyes following Angelique. "She told us she was sending Angela to be looked after in a hospital for a while. Then a lady came and took her away, and we never saw her again. But in all my days I would've never imagined she'd end up here, working in the circus. And with wings an' all—who'd have thunk it!" He whistled softly to himself.

Lily felt the scars over her heart itch. "When was all this, Tolly?" she asked.

"Five years ago. Angela weren't half brave then," Tolly replied, jiggling nervously in his seat. "Still is, it seems."

Lily saw that he was right. The higher Angelique rose from the ground, the more buoyant she became and the more she seemed to swell with confidence. It was as if being up in the air made her more herself.

By now she had reached the edge of the platform, and she threw out one hand, waving to the audience, giving a bright, confident salute to match the beaming smile radiating from her face. "You're sure Angela and Angelique are one and the same person?" Robert asked Tolly.

He nodded. "Sure as eggs is eggs. I'd remember her anywhere. Seared into my memory, she is. Face of an angel."

Angelique leaped nimbly from the top of the ladder onto the hanging platform. With a dreamy air, she dipped her hands in a tin box attached to the platform and then clapped them together, spraying white chalk like fairy dust through the air. She grasped the trapeze and flipped onto the bar—then she opened her wings and flapped them wildly until the trapeze began to sway back and forth.

As the rhythm of its movement became faster, Angelique sprang to her feet on the bar. On the next forward swing she let go with her hands and fell backward, hooking her feet around the corners where the ropes met the bar. Hanging upside down, her wings streamed behind her like a cape of feathers.

Lily watched, entranced. She was so busy following the girl's flowing movements that she forgot all about the questions in her head.

Angelique beat her wings hard and fast.

The trapeze swung ever higher, reaching the zenith of its arc.

Fifty feet away was another trapeze that sat empty and entirely still.

Angelique had it in her sights. It was clear that she was going to jump between them. An impossibly dangerous distance. A daredevil deed.

On the ground, Slimwood waved up at the empty trapeze. "Ladies and gentlemen, don't take your eyes off Miss Angelique Airhart for ONE SECOND. She's about to attempt the impossible quadruple somersault with NO SAFETY NET. Drumroll, please!"

The drum played a steady pitter-pattering beat.

For one last time, in the tent's star-spangled heights, Angelique swung forward on her bar... And made a leap

      of

             faith.

Whirr-tick went her fluttering wing-rotors.

Whoosh! went her feathers.

Lily's heart screamed in anticipation. Her scars itched. A lump lodged in her throat.

Angelique somersaulted through the air, her wings streaming behind her. The spotlight following.

It seemed for an instant as if she wasn't going to make it.

She was a second too long in free fall, her plumage a mere decoration, incapable of keeping her up.

She tried to grab for the other trapeze, but missed...

Lily gasped. Robert wrung his hands together, and Tolly let out a horrified yell, joined by the cries of the audience as Angelique tumbled toward the ring.

Then suddenly, a second from hitting the sawdust, she sprang to life, flapping her wings and swooping upward to circle around the edge of the tent. It had been a pretense.

"Wow!" Tolly gabbled. "I ain't never seen the like! She can really fly!"

Robert wanted to reply but he had no words, he could only yelp in relief.

Then the entire audience were on their feet, whooping ecstatically and laughing in maniacal release.

Lily felt a bubble of joy burst inside her, and she stood and joined in the rapturous rounds of applause. Angelique was astonishing. She had performed her own dazzling hybrid miracle.

Every head turned to follow her as she soared through the air. Swooping about the canvas rooftop and basking in the adulation, she looked entirely relaxed. Her flapping wings beat slower with each twirl, until her movements became leisurely, as if she was gliding through water. She frolicked through the air, like a fish swimming in the sea, a butterfly drunk on pollen, or an eagle soaring in the sky—hovering on the strength of her wings, an angel in flight.

Finally, she dived down and alighted, with a perfect puff of sawdust, at the edge of the ring, where she bobbed low and picked up a walking stick that must've been left there for her. She pulled herself up to her full height, chin lifted and proud, and leaning on her stick, she stretched her wings out wide and took a bow.

The crowd cheered crazily as Angelique hobbled to the center of the ring, smiling and waving to everyone, but within moments the cheers began to die down, and Lily heard the return of the gossipy chat. The applause had become a mere smattering. It seemed to Lily as if Angelique's smile didn't quite reach her eyes, and as she reached the backstage curtain, Lily saw her mask of joy fall completely.

Angelique stepped from the spotlight and was smoothly replaced by Slimwood and Madame Lyons-Mane.

"That was our last act of the night!" Slimwood shouted.

Every eye was on him now but Lily's. So only she saw that outside of the spotlight, framed between the closing curtains, the Lunk appeared at Angelique's side.

"Please could you make your way quietly to the exits as soon as the house lights come back on," Madame Lyons-Mane added.

Lily watched Angelique shrink back as the metal man grasped her arm. Her shoulders hunched and her wings drooped, their tips grazing the ground. She stared desperately out through the closing velvet drapes, and her eyes widened in alarm. Lily followed her darting gaze and realized she must have caught sight of Tolly.

Then the Lunk pulled her back, and the curtains swished together, and they were gone, leaving only Slimwood and Madame Lyons-Mane in the ring.

None of the other acts returned to take a bow, but

Slimwood and Madame Lyons-Mane seemed happy to accept the applause on everyone's behalf.

"Did you see that?" Lily cried, when the pair had finally finished bowing.

Tolly nodded. "I think she recognized me. And that mechanical was hurting her."

"It can't be," Robert said. "Mechanicals don't hurt humans."

"Where'd you hear such stories?" Tolly asked.

"My da told me," Robert said. "It's the first law of mechanics: a mech can't kill humans or seriously harm them. It's part of their design, built into their valves and circuits."

"I'm not so sure," Lily said. "I think Tolly might be right. Angelique didn't look happy."

Joey and Auggie the clowns were trundling round the ring, relighting the oil lamps. The crowd stood and began filing toward the doors.

Robert, Tolly, and Lily put on their coats and buttoned them. Robert wedged his cap back on, and Lily wound Mrs. Rust's long tiger-striped scarf around her neck. She left the wilting flowers and took out her repaired pocket watch to check the time.

"Eight thirty-two," she told the others. "I know Rusty said we should be back by nine, but the party's bound to go on until midnight, and I really think we should find Angelique and see if she's all right. Maybe get some answers about all this too, like we were promised."

"But how are we going to talk to Angelique if the Lunk's guarding her?" Tolly asked.

Lily shook her head. "I don't know."

"Lily, I've got a bad feeling about this place," Robert butted in. "The atmosphere's creepy, and we should be getting back for your pa's speech. If we go now we can still get home in time to make it seem as if we were never away. We could leave Angelique a letter. Find someone here we trust and ask them to give it to her? Perhaps the ringmistress?"

Lily remembered Madame Lyons-Mane had told her to come look for her after the show. She glanced about and spotted the bearded lady clutching her parasol next to Slimwood by the tent's exit, shaking hands and waving goodbye to the crowd. Madame Lyons-Mane seemed to feel Lily's gaze, for she turned and stared back across the dimly lit tent, and to Lily it felt like the woman's eyes were boring straight into her soul.

"Maybe it's not such a good idea to ask her for help," she muttered.

"Personally, I didn't like the mugs on any of them," Tolly said. "And now I've seen her, I don't think I can leave Angelique in this place without checking she's not in trouble."

"I'm not sure it's safe to go behind the curtain," Robert said. "Who knows what we might find."

"Best if we sneak out round the back among the crowds?" Tolly suggested.

"Is it me," Lily said, "or are the circus folk watching us?"

Robert flicked a glance around the ring from under the peak of his cap. "They have been the whole evening," he muttered. "Something's up with this place. With all of them. It's almost as if they're waiting for a big occurrence to happen."

A throng of villagers were still making their way to the exit, while some rough-looking heavyset men, dressed in regular clothes, had appeared from behind the curtain and began to upend and fold down the empty benches to cart them away.

Lily still couldn't work out who'd sent Mama's notebook and invited her here. If it wasn't Angelique then was it one of the others? Madame Lyons-Mane or Slimwood? Even the Lunk? Or those two stupid clowns who'd made a big fuss of her when she arrived…and who seemed to be keeping an eye on her now as they went about helping to dismantle the show.

She thought again of the rhyme on the card that had arrived with the ticket and red notebook:

We have a simple question, and it's one that's not a trick:
Some of us are wondering what it is that makes you tick?

The answer—*the Cogheart*—felt suddenly fraught with danger. The professor at the party had said there were only a handful of hybrids in England—three of which, including Angelique, Lily had just seen being treated badly in the show. With an overwhelming rush of nausea, Lily realized it could mean only one thing: She'd been invited here tonight because she was a hybrid too and somehow—she wasn't quite sure how—the circus folk knew it and had made plans for her.

"MIND YOUR BACKS!" said one of the men, loudly ripping up the bench at her side.

Lily glanced round and saw they were the last three members of the audience left in the tent. "Where's Malkin?" she asked suddenly, for they had been getting ready to leave for quite a while and he'd been remarkably quiet. It wasn't like him not to give a running commentary on everything. Maybe he'd wound down and fallen asleep beneath the bench? She bent down to look for him, but he wasn't there.

"Malkin's gone!" Lily cried hoarsely, her throat constricting in alarm. Panic twisted like a broken glass wind chime in her chest. Where could he be? She felt ill thinking of him wandering round this suspicious place on his own—anything might've happened to him.

All of a sudden, she wasn't sure what to do. Part of her still wanted to find Angelique, but if they didn't recover Malkin and get home in time for the end of the party, Papa would discover they were missing and they'd be in even more trouble.

"MALKIN!" she called out.

Then she put her fingers in her mouth and gave a piercing whistle.

"MALKIN!" Robert yelled, squinting across the dark tent.

"MALKIN! HERE, BOY!" Tolly brushed his hair out of his face with the back of his hand.

Robert wasn't sure the fox would respond to a call like that, but it was worth a go. They waited, listening for Malkin's shrill bark… But it never came. And his bright red brush was nowhere to be seen.

The worry was suffocating; Lily could barely breathe. She loosened her scarf. Her eyes darted desperately about the tent, scanning the blurred silhouettes of the heavyset men who were busy pulling up benches, ignoring their cries of alarm.

In the same instant, Slimwood dropped the flap across the exit, while Madame Lyons-Mane held up her parasol and let it fall sharply to the ground. At which signal, the men all turned ominously toward Lily and her friends, dropping what they were doing and coming for them. Lily's heart beat loud as a drum. They had been tricked.

CHAPTER 7

Malkin had bored of the performances quite early and decided that he would take a look around and do some solo investigating instead.

While Robert, Lily, and Tolly were watching the dreadful antics of the show, he'd slunk away beneath the rows of seats and fidgeting feet. Avoiding the scattered popcorn droppings and the half-eaten toffee apples stuck to chair legs, he crawled to the edge of the tent and shimmied under a loose flap of canvas.

Outside in the field, the candles in their jam jars flickered like fireflies in the mizzle, guttering. Mice and rats scampered around them, and moths flittered above, attracted by the light. Malkin growled and snapped his teeth at them, and they scattered.

The haze cleared momentarily, and he saw that the fencing and ticket kiosk had already vanished. The rest of the signs and stands had been taken down and folded flat and were being carted away by a gang of men toward the big Skycircus balloon floating behind the Big Top. Soon, the whole site would be dismantled and ready to be transported off, along with the crew, to the flying circus's next stop.

The gray murk descended again. Malkin set off after the men, taking care to keep to the shadows as he followed their path. The ground beneath his paws felt soft with the damp of the field. He shivered at the cold slimy feeling of it against his footpads.

The big striped Skycircus balloon bobbed above a huge wooden gondola at least three stories high—almost as tall as Brackenbridge Manor itself—and shaped like an old galleon. Its keel ground into the grass like a beached boat at low tide; it was anchored to the field by taut ropes, and the mist had left raindrops hanging from them, like dewy spiderwebs. Rows of portholes curved round each floor. Malkin tried to count them, but lost his place after twenty or so. He guessed that each one represented a cabin. The gondola must have contained enough rooms for the whole circus troupe to live in as they moved from place to place.

Why had this Skycircus ship come here? Malkin wondered. *And how had this Angelique and the rest of them got hold of Lily's mama's notebook?* Lily would be so pleased with him if he found out. Unlike those other clanking mongrel-pups gawping at the show, he was out here investigating—sniffing out the truth beneath the facade, searching for clues and answers. Pretty soon, he'd solve this mystery and get to the heart of what it was about!

He snuck closer to the gondola and hid behind a colorful pile of discarded signage. He would be safe here for a while. He watched four large men carrying bales, props, and fencing into the sky-ship's cargo bay. The Skycircus wasn't like any other type of circus Malkin had heard of. They usually traveled by train or in a caravan of wagons. But this troupe seemed to float about in this strange bulbous sky-ship. Perhaps the answer to all Lily's riddles lay inside it. In there…

Malkin approached the ramp cautiously and then ducked underneath it, snuffling at a bag of wooden pegs that had tumbled down behind a stack of cutout figures painted on thin wooden board. The figures smelled old and rotten, and looked like they were falling to pieces. Only the paint seemed to be holding them together. He'd noticed that the tent and the sky-ship—in fact this whole place—was the same. Something about it felt stale and fishy—and not in a good way, like the fishmonger's in the village.

Malkin poked his head out from beneath the ramp and stared up into the dark interior of the ship. One of the men was just disappearing inside, leading a pair of horses up the gangway and into the cargo bay. There was a shout of "MIND YOUR HEADS!" and a big cage with two lions, a tiger, and a bear inside was wheeled on board.

Malkin heard horses' hooves from deep within the sky-ship and a whinny of alarm. One of the big cats gave an angry roar. Then there were creaks and clanks as the cage was stowed away in the hold and made good.

He wondered if he should really risk climbing aboard and looking inside or if it was better to go back to the Big Top and rejoin Robert, Lily, and Tolly and make a plan together. But they didn't even know where to start. Perhaps talking to the animals for a few minutes would help—surely those creatures would know what was going on?

He shimmied up the ramp and into the darkness of the gondola's loading bay.

The wild animals' cage was parked in the center of the space, secured to cleats on the floor with ropes. The lions and tiger and bear inside looked mangy and mournful.

"Good evening," Malkin said to them pleasantly.

But they didn't respond. It seemed they were not mechanimals but wild beasts and consequently couldn't understand a word he said. They looked dumb as a box of rocks and twice as dolorous. It would be no use trying to get any inside information out of them. The best he could expect was a bunch of disappointing squawks and growls—that's if he was lucky, and if he was not, then probably a few farts and burps as well!

He was about to give up his quest and beat a hasty retreat when he heard two voices at the base of the cargo ramp.

He dipped down on his belly and inched to the edge of the loading bay, then peered out. The figures, leaning together in such a conspiratorial way, were a bit of a blur in the mist, but Malkin recognized the voice of Slimwood and the shape of Madame Lyons-Mane. He slithered closer and pricked up his ears to try and catch their conversation.

"...the ticket and book must've drawn her as we'd hoped," Madame Lyons-Mane was saying.

"It worked then, our flytrap?" Slimwood replied. "She really does think the winged girl has something to do with her mother?"

"*Oui.*" Madame Lyons-Mane laughed a cut-glass

laugh. "*Mon Dieu!* If only she knew the facts. But I guarantee that she'll wait until after the show to speak with Angelique. When that happens, I want you and the Lunk to grab her."

Malkin jumped to his feet. He had to get back to warn Lily, Robert, and Tolly right away. They must flee, and quick!

Behind him, the lions and tiger and bear in their cage growled softly, and the horses whinnied and shifted in their stalls.

As soon as the bearded lady and the ringmaster returned to the Big Top, he stepped from the cargo bay and ran to the end of the ramp. He was just about to jump down when an enormous figure loomed up in front of him through the mist.

He tried to dodge away from it, but its hand shot out and grabbed him in a self-assured grip. "What's going on?" Malkin cried, his voice wavering with shock. "Unhand me, you fiend!"

The figure laughed, and the creaking cackle emanating from its mouth sounded like fingers scraping down a blackboard.

The Lunk! Malkin's alarmed barks were silenced by the mechanical's large fingers grasping his snout. The Lunk shoved a dog muzzle over Malkin's face and drew the straps up tight, slicing into his fur. Then he stuffed the fox unceremoniously into a sack. The drawstring swooshed shut over Malkin's head, grazing the tips of his ears, before he was bundled up like an unwanted cat and thrown over the Lunk's shoulders with a loud and painful clang.

Pins and needles jarred through the cogs in Malkin's legs. What an ignominious end to the evening! He hadn't been wound since this morning either. How could he be so stupid as to wander away from the others, and without his key?

The Lunk creaked back up the incline of the loading ramp, and Malkin realized he was being returned to the cargo bay. The cogs in his stomach fizzed with regret. What a fool he was to be so easily fox-napped! His friends were in trouble, and now he had no way to warn them that Lily was about to be kidnapped too.

CHAPTER 8

An air of menace wafted through the tent, accompanied by the sweaty stench of the approaching men. Robert counted them. There were at least ten, if not more. Eager, heavyset fellows with bulging tattooed arms and dark eyes in shadowed sockets.

"We need to get out of here fast," he told Lily and Tolly, glancing at the exit.

Slimwood and Madame Lyons-Mane still had it blocked. They'd barely reacted to Lily's cry of alarm—in fact, they might've even been smirking.

Slimwood had his arms folded as if he was waiting for the children to be brought to him, while Madame leaned on her parasol and watched as the men split apart and tried to surround them.

"There must be another way out!" Robert exclaimed. He picked up a chair and threw it at the men, but one merely batted it aside, and another caught it in his hand like he was performing a circus trick, while the rest of them laughed.

"We gotta find Angela," Tolly said.

"And Malkin," Lily snapped. She pulled at Robert's sleeve and pointed in the direction of the artists' entrance, where the curtains had been taken down. "There!" she cried. "We can slip through there."

They ran in a scrambling panic, the men following. The end of Lily's scarf dragged behind her in the dust, and she hiked it up from round her heels.

They'd almost reached the far side of the ring when a horrible caterwauling emanated from behind the artists' exit, and with an awful wrenching sound, the Lunk appeared in the gap, blocking that way out.

His neck screeched slowly as he turned to watch them with hardened interest. Headlamps glowed behind the brights of his eyes, flickering with evil malice.

The men chasing them stopped and gathered round, throwing little broken-toothed grins and tips of the head to each other as they drew in from every side, making a ring around the children with space for the Lunk to step through. The Lunk ground forward with his arms outstretched.

Lily stopped in her tracks and looked desperately about. The three of them huddled together, trying to keep an eye on the Lunk and the men all at once.

Robert's hands trembled as he groped in the pocket of his da's coat for his penknife and pulled it out, unfolding the blade.

"You can't fight a metal man with that," Tolly hissed.

Robert shook his head. "I'm going to cut a hole in the tent," he whispered.

"Where?" Lily asked.

"Anywhere will do, but we need a distraction!"

"I've just the thing." Tolly put his hand in his pocket and pulled out the firecrackers and a box of matches. "Screw up your peepers!" he shouted.

Robert and Lily closed their eyes tight as Tolly lit a cracker and threw it at the men.

BANG!

The men ducked and cowered away as it went off. Tolly threw another.

BANG!

Lily blinked and spotted a gap in their line. She pulled Tolly and Robert by the hand, and they ran through it, toward the canvas wall of the Big Top.

The Lunk saw what they were doing and let out a loud squeal of alarm, but Tolly lit another firecracker and threw it at him. "Hurry!" he cried.

Robert jabbed his knife through the canvas of the tent and began sawing downward, the explosions still echoing in his ears—or was it the Lunk screeching as he ambled toward them?

BANG!

Tolly threw a fourth firecracker at Slimwood and Lyons-Mane, who were rushing at them from the other side.

Slimwood covered his face with a hand as his red tailcoat flew out behind him. "STOP THEM!" he cried.

Robert realized the bangs had gone quiet.

"You'd better get a move on," Tolly said. "I've run out of crackers."

Robert pulled the knife from the slit in the tent and ripped the two halves of the canvas apart to make a hole. "You first," he said, thrusting Lily through. Tolly went second, and Robert third. As he scrambled through the slit, Slimwood gripped his leg. Robert winced in pain and slipped, but Lily and Tolly seized his arms and yanked him until he tumbled out onto the grass.

Quick as a flash, the three of them were up and running. Drizzle folded around them. A few feet away the dim shape of the gigantic Skycircus balloon pulsed like a glowworm. Robert kicked over an empty jam jar. The candle lights that had marked the path were gone and so were the fence and kiosk. The rest of the audience had long since left. There was no one about to help them.

They skirted a patch of flattened grass and ran toward a copse of trees that stood at the edge of the field.

There, they stopped and caught their breath. Robert heaved in great lungfuls of air, trying to cool the panic flooding through him. Beneath his coat and jacket, his shirt clung cold and damp to his back.

He could hear the men nearby, searching for them.

"Why are they hunting us?" he gasped, agitated.

"I don't know," Lily whispered hoarsely. "Perhaps Malkin does. They could've captured him already. He might be in grave danger. We must find him."

"And Angela…I mean, Angelique." Tolly wiped the sweat from his face. His hands were shaking from throwing the firecrackers. "D'you think they've trapped her an' all?"

Whatever Lily was about to reply was interrupted by one of the men shouting, "THIS WAY!" Then two glowing headlamps turned toward them, and the Lunk was coming, along with other figures holding lanterns above their heads.

"MISS HARTMAN!" a deep booming voice called out. Robert recognized it as Slimwood's. "Come out, come out, wherever you are. No point hiding in an open field. We've got your mechanimal, and we have you surrounded."

Lily's mouth fell open. She rubbed her eyes. "W-what do they want from me?" she asked, her voice shaking.

Robert thought she might cry, but she bit her lip and held the fear in.

Suddenly there was a whooshing sound, and the ghostly shape of the Big Top collapsed. Through the mist they saw flashes of its candy-colored canvas folding in on itself like the rippling waves of a patterned ocean.

"We have to scarper," Lily said, pointing along the hedgerow. "That way."

They made a dash for it under cover of the chaos. Now that the tent was down, the anchored Skycircus balloon seemed to loom even larger. The silhouette of the gondola's big wooden hull was like a beached wooden whale.

"If they've caught Malkin," Lily said, pointing at it, "he'll be in there. We have to sneak aboard and get him. We can look for Angelique too."

"Definitely," Tolly said, squeezing in beside her. "She's a good person. She ain't involved in all this. We can't leave her behind."

"They're after you, Lily," Robert said, staring despairingly at the gondola. "Going aboard might be exactly what they want you to do."

"Or," Lily said, "it could be the last place they'd expect to find us."

"Let's do it!" Tolly said, but his eyes looked wide with fright.

They hunkered low so their shapes wouldn't be spotted in the fog and ran in short bursts along the hedge. When they reached the hot-air balloon, they stopped a few feet away and crouched in the tall grass.

Robert glanced back to where they'd just been, and his heart jumped. A few of the men were searching that very spot. Best not to think about it. They had to keep moving—find Malkin and Angelique and get away.

A great carved figurehead loomed above them—an angel with chiseled wings thrust back, the wooden feathers spreading out along either side of the three-deck gondola, lit portholes streaming behind her, making pinpoints in the fog like sparkling stars.

Skirting round the hull, they passed a gangplank and platform on the far side leading to a hatch locked with a large padlock. Farther on, at the stern of the ship, the loading bay was open and the rear ramp was down.

As they reached it, Tolly almost tripped, but he

righted himself before he fell in the mud. A rudder and large propeller blade stretched above him.

The mist cleared for a second, and beyond them, Robert glimpsed the collapsed Big Top. Figures crossed the tent's striped surface or crouched low to the ground, pulling apart the seams. The Top was being stripped, picked apart, the pieces folded up and forced into waiting bags.

"We probably don't have much time to get in and out before they stow the last of their stuff," he said to the others.

Tolly looked like he was about to reply when a harsh whine echoed down the cargo-bay ramp. For a second Robert thought it might be the scream of a human child, but there was a rough edge to it that could only mean one thing: it was Malkin.

"D'you hear that?" he whispered to them both.

"It was coming from inside," Lily said.

The three of them slunk up the ramp and peered carefully in.

The cargo bay looked empty of people, but the noises and the sour scents of the animals cut through the air. A cacophony of growls, snarls, roars, huffs, grunts, and whinnies that made Robert shiver.

"What an awful earful!" Tolly said. "If they don't

simmer down they'll have those men on us again. And they'd best not bite. I'll tell you, I'm not a fan of biters."

"Me neither," Robert said. "Just don't get too close to the cages. Malkin!" he called out quietly into the dark. He worried that they might not find the fox at all—at least not before the circus folk arrived to load up the last of their stuff. What if their friend had been imprisoned elsewhere?

Something large in the oversized cage in the center of the bay shifted. Forgetting his own warning, Robert peered in to see what it was.

With a *ROAR!* a tiger threw itself against the bars.

A spike of terror soared in Robert's chest. He jumped back, almost leaving his skin behind, while Tolly yelped and stepped on Lily's foot as she stumbled aside.

The tiger paced restlessly, uncurling its long tail and shaking its huge fearsome head. Two lions and a bear lurked behind it, but of the four of them, the tiger seemed to be the leader. It arched its back and licked its chops, scratching in the sawdust with its claws and making jagged lines in the boarded floor of its cage. If they'd been any closer it surely would've got its teeth into them. It was a wonder they hadn't eaten each other.

Robert was about to say as much to Lily and Tolly when they heard the noisy clump of boots outside.

They ducked quickly behind a stack of boxes. Robert held his breath as a long line of men brought in bags of canvas and piled them against the far walls.

Some of them looked like the group who'd chased them.

"This is the last of it," one said.

"We'll be off soon," another added.

"After we find those kids."

"Forget about them. They're one of Slimwood's stupid ideas."

"Hardly worth it."

"Nor for all that running about," said another. "Still, best do as he says if we don't want to get a beating from that creaking metal monster of his. Let's try outside again."

When they were gone, Robert let out a sigh. "That was close!"

"Too close," Tolly whispered. "We can't take anymore chances. Why don't I wait by the door? I'll whistle if they return."

"All right," Lily said quietly. "But if we get caught now you're to run home and fetch Papa at once."

"Right you are." Tolly disappeared along the length of the cargo bay, taking up a position just outside the doorway.

Robert heard a faint yelping coming from behind a nearby stack of shelves.

Hrrmmm. Hrrmmm. Hrrmmm.

It was accompanied by a low and persistent scritchy-scratching noise that seemed to match his own heartbeat. He tapped Lily on the shoulder, and they stepped toward the noise. It was coming from a small cage about the size of a doghouse, inside which a thin, red, angry thing was scrabbling about.

"Malkin!" Lily cried, and Robert's chest flooded with relief at the sight of him.

"Mmmm!" Malkin whined from inside the cage. "Mmmm." He stepped toward them, thrusting his face between the bars.

A muzzle strapped around his snout was stopping him from speaking properly.

"Mmmm," Malkin said again.

"Don't worry," Lily said, stroking him through the straps. "We'll have that off and you out of there in a jiffy."

The fox's big black eyes rolled worriedly up at her as she pulled at the muzzle, but she couldn't reach far enough into the cage to get her fingers around to the back of it.

"Keep him still," she told Robert.

Robert grasped Malkin's snout. The fox's dry tongue

darted through a small gap in the leather muzzle and licked his palm with a sandpapery slurp. It felt warm against his skin, a balm of relief.

Lily drew her hand back through the bars. "I can't undo the strap like this; I still can't reach. We'll have to try the cage door first instead." She pulled out the lockpicking kit Tolly had given her. "Hold out your hands," she said.

Robert held both palms out in front of him, and she unrolled the leather scroll onto them. "Will these get it open?" he asked, staring at the tiny lockpicks in their pockets.

"I don't know yet. The lock looks rather complicated." Lily selected a pick from the set and stuck it into the keyhole. Then slowly, steadily, she flicked the pick to the side.

There was a grinding noise as the lock's cylinder began to turn.

The animals in the other cage, and the horses in their stalls, shifted restlessly, whinnying, growling, and snapping. Robert clasped the leather wallet and tried to quiet the unease rushing through him as he watched Lily fiddle with her pick, peering at the lock.

She jiggled the pick one last time, and the lock rattled loosely.

Then, with a *click*, everything dropped into place.

"You did it!" Robert whispered, the tension easing from his face.

Lily opened the cage, and Malkin leaped into her arms. "MMMM!" he whined in alarm as she pulled on the muzzle strap at the back of his head. Finally she got the buckle undone.

"It's a trap!" Malkin barked. "They haven't given up on you! They know you're here!"

But it was too late. Tolly gave a desperate warning whistle and then a worried yelp from outside as the cargo-bay door clanged shut. Then, with a horrible grinding clank, they heard the bolts being slipped across the door hatch, securing it in place. They were trapped!

Robert stuffed the lockpick set into his pocket and ran to a porthole along the side of the ship. The men were releasing the anchor chains that kept the ship secured to the ground. With a whirr, the prop started up, clearing the ground fog. The last of the men ran up a gangplank and through the hatch in the fore of the ship, the hum of the engines began, and the animals growled and complained as the entire vessel lifted slowly off the ground.

They were already ten feet in the air when Lily stuck her face into the porthole beside Robert's. "Where's

Tolly?" she shouted over the noise. "I can't see him."

As if on cue, Tolly jumped up from behind a clod of grass, sidelit by the ship's headlights. He was the only thing left in the empty field; everything else was gone. It was as if the ticket booth, the canvas outhouses, the Big Top, all of it had never existed. The Skycircus had been awaiting their capture, waiting to skyjack them, and now it was taking off with them aboard.

"TOLLY!" Lily screamed through the glass. "Don't let them take us!"

Tolly waved his arms above his head and shouted something in return, but they couldn't hear it above the engine's roar. They tried to make out the words he was mouthing, but the sky-ship was rising fast now, and his little face was getting smaller and smaller as they lifted higher into the sky. Soon he'd diminished to the size of a matchstick, then a pin, and then, as the glow from the sky-ship dissipated from the field, he disappeared altogether.

A terrible dread crept over Robert at the thought of what might lie ahead, and when he looked to Lily and Malkin, standing beside him in the cargo bay full of wild animals, he knew they felt the same.

The very last they saw of Brackenbridge and their home were the five lampposts illuminating the tiny fog-shrouded village green. But soon those shrank away too, becoming no more than one part of the patchwork of darkness as they were spirited into the night sky by the enormous red-and-white striped circus air balloon.

CHAPTER 9

Lily clasped Malkin in her lap and huddled close to Robert. The cargo bay was remarkably chilly. She looped her scarf twice more around her neck, then handed the other end of it to Robert to wind around his. She was grateful now that Mrs. Rust had not been able to stop knitting, for the scarf was easily long enough for both of them to wear.

A dim light set in the ceiling glowed at regular intervals, revealing brief glimpses of the wild beasts now cowering in their cage and the horses shifting in their stalls. The groan of the engines as the sky-ship chugged along, full steam ahead, mingled with the animals' intermittent yelps and cries.

Lily felt like crying too. Some birthday this had turned out to be. Madame Lyons-Mane, Slimwood, and their accomplices had used Mama's notebook, the birthday poem, and the tickets to entice her to the show, then caught her unawares and snatched her away like a prize, along with Robert and Malkin.

But why? And what dreadful scheme did they have in store for her and the Cogheart? For she felt sure now that it was the very reason they'd kidnapped her. She racked her brain, trying to think of what use it might be to them, but could come up with nothing. Instead, she kept circling back to how idiotic she'd been to fall for their tricks in the first place. And to get Robert and Malkin kidnapped too. She chided herself for such blatant stupidity. Would she never learn? She seemed to repeat her mistakes endlessly, like the hours on a clockface. Only Robert's chattering teeth interrupted her self-recrimination.

"I hope Tolly makes it back to Brackenbridge," he muttered. "And tells everyone what's going on."

"Me too." Lily pulled her coat tight around her.

"And please let help come before we die of hypothermia." Robert rubbed his hands together and pulled down the brim of his cap. "My face is froze. My bones are froze. My nose is froze. Even my toes are froze. I feel like I've got icicles in my hair!"

"I'm not surprised," Malkin replied darkly. "I swear, by Noah himself, there's no heating on this ridiculous, balloonatic flying ark." His eyes were practically slits. He stood and shook out his fur. "We should've stayed at the party, Lily."

"Stop complaining, both of you!" Lily snapped. "I need to think."

She closed her eyes, searching once more for a solution... Even if she were able to pick the lock on the cargo-bay door, they were miles in the air—too high to jump. Besides, hadn't they heard the sound of bolts on the outside being pulled across? She'd never get through those. And when they'd first taken off she'd probed the rest of the room to find there was no other way out.

It was no use. Any plan she made would have to factor in those problems, and right now the worry of where they were going, or what might happen when they got there, was busily worming its way inside her, taking up all her brainpower.

"I suppose being kidnapped on your birthday is marginally better than being ignored," she said at last, more to try and cheer herself up than for any other reason. "You shouldn't have come with me, either of you. I've been far too foolish. Got you both abducted, and Tolly in trouble to boot."

"Nonsense," Malkin yapped. "Now you're clanking well grousing."

"It's true." She stroked his ears. "If I hadn't brought us on this wild-goose chase to meet Angelique, we'd be at home with the fires lit and the rooms bright and cheerful…" She felt like she might burst into tears. "What do these people even want from me?"

"You weren't to know it was a trap." Malkin nuzzled his nose into her hand.

"Whatever they want," Robert said, "we won't let them have it. We'll fight them together, like we always do. In the meantime, Tolly'll get home and explain everything to your father."

"And if anyone knows how to find us it'll be John," Malkin added.

"I hope you're right," Lily replied. "Papa's probably worried sick. I wish I hadn't been so difficult with him."

"I've something to tell you on that account." Robert leaned in toward her. "I wasn't meant to, but I reckon it doesn't matter now, all things considered. The thing is… your da, he was planning a surprise. He'd a present he was going to give to you at the end of the party after he'd made a special speech."

"And Mrs. Rust was going to bring out a cake with

fourteen candles," Malkin added. "She baked it yesterday and hid it in the larder."

Even Robert was surprised by this news. "How do you know that?" he demanded.

Malkin licked his nose proudly. "I sniffed it out this morning."

"Why didn't either of you say?" Lily asked. "Half the reason I suggested we skip out this evening was because I thought he'd forgotten my birthday."

"John made us promise not to," Robert said. "It was a secret."

Lily felt a sudden flush of guilt. Papa ignoring her birthday had been nothing but a ruse. By now everyone was probably wondering where they'd got to, if a panicked Tolly hadn't already rushed in with the bad news. Then perhaps Papa and the police could pick up their trail before the Skycircus flew too far away?

That thought faded and her chest convulsed as, with an uneasy flurry of fear, she realized they'd probably already passed the point where they could be tracked. They truly were in trouble, and it was all her fault. She glanced at the faces of the others, cold and miserable, and hoped that the three of them would be all right. Home was a long way off.

Half an hour passed, and the silence was only interrupted by the odd sputter of the engines or the occasional snarl and shriek of the animals, while each of them remained lost in their thoughts.

"We'll take it in turns to rest," Malkin suggested. "One of us needs to keep watch at the porthole, in case we pass a clue to where we're headed."

Robert shook his head. "It's pitch-black outside, Malkin. We won't see a thing. It's more important to cheer ourselves up." He squeezed Lily's shoulder. "What time is it?"

Lily consulted her pocket watch. "11:25."

"Then it's still your birthday—let's do something to celebrate. I, for one, am starving." Robert took out the box of chocolates and opened it. Twelve truffles in frilly white paper cups nestled in the box. Each was topped with a colored jewel of candied fruit—they reminded Lily of the costumes of the circus performers.

She picked one and popped it in her mouth. It had a soft praline center.

"Mmmm!" she mumbled through her mouthful.

Robert ate one too. It was nougat-y and stuck to his teeth in chewy chocolate lumps.

Lily chose another—candied ginger, and another—rose cream. She was relieved to find that none of them tasted of stickerish licks or any of the odd flavors Auggie the clown had bandied about when he gave them to her.

In fact, the chocolates tasted so good, and they were so hungry, soon they were gorging their way through the whole box. When they finished the first layer, they discovered a whole extra one underneath and ate those too, smushing them together into glorious sugary lumps in their mouths and stuffing the empty paper wrappers into their pockets.

Malkin didn't partake. He was a mechanimal after all, and mechanimals never ate, not even in dire circumstances, and certainly not chocolate.

Lily took out the notebook and read from it to cheer them up. Reading aloud reminded her of the bedtime stories Mama used to tell her.

<u>Thursday 21st September 1867,</u>
<u>Histon College</u>

I am one of the first female students to declare my intention to become a mechanist. I'm attending classes in science, engineering, and mathematics. If I can complete those courses, I may be able to work at the Mechanists' Guild in London. Not as a mechanist, of course—those jobs are only available to men currently, so my professor, Dr. Droz, tells me. Although I intend to see about that.

Lily tapped the page with a finger. "Droz," she said. "Why does that name ring a bell?"

Robert yawned through his last mouthful of truffle. "I've no idea."

"Neither do...I," Malkin stuttered, his eyes flickering. He was running out of ticks. If they didn't wind him soon he'd be asleep.

"Never mind." Lily read on.

Dr. Droz intends to put in a good word for me at the guild and suggested I might obtain a position there as an assistant or a punch-card operator in the Department of Mathematical Engines.

It would be a good start, a chance to work with world-famous professors and to see the machines of Charles Babbage and Ada Lovelace up close. I would love to learn something of Ada's work, not only on the original Babbage Engine (though I was furious to discover Ada's part had not been given due credit here), but on her Flyology project as well.

Lily remembered the conversation Anna had been having earlier that evening with that mechanist from the guild. *That* was where she'd heard the name Droz. He'd mentioned Dr. Droz alongside Papa and Professor

Silverfish—something to do with hybrids and having been kicked out of the guild.

But Droz had taught Mama too. And Mama's words seemed so wise. Before she'd received the notebook, Lily had barely thought of Mama as anything other than, well…Mama. But now, reading the pages aloud, she realized there was a whole other side of Grace Fairfax that she'd missed. Mama had had her own life, separate from Lily's and Papa's. Her own dreams she'd wanted to achieve. And here she was, telling them to Lily as if they were in the same room together.

It was funny how someone who'd been gone so long could be brought back to life through their words. Lily was finding Mama could still surprise her, even though she wasn't there to do it in person. She wished her mama really *was* there. To tell her how brave she was and to offer encouragement for the predicament they were in. To tell her not to stop asking questions until she found the right answers. Answers that would help them get out of here.

Lily realized her mind had drifted far away from the book. The others hadn't even noticed. She glanced at Malkin and saw he'd wound down. Robert had dozed off. The empty chocolate box lay tipped to one side in his lap.

She was starting to feel a little woozy herself…

Not quite…

all…

there…

One of them had to stay awake—that's what they'd decided, wasn't it? In her sleepy state she couldn't quite remember. Suddenly Lily felt more tired than she had been in her entire life. She rubbed her eyes and tried hard to concentrate, squinting at the next diary entry. The words crawled spiderishly across the paper. She tried to corral them together, but they would not become sentences, and when she looked up from the page, the room was swaying.

She closed the book and lay her head on her arm.

And then, just like that, she was somewhere else.

No longer stretched out in the cold cargo bay, but sprawled beneath a chair in the parlor of her old house at Riverside Walk, Chelsea.

The ammonite stone was clasped in her hand, and a flickering fire in the grate warmed her socked feet, which were propped on the edge of the hearth.

If she put her chin on her hands and looked upward, she could glimpse Mama's feet. Her satin slippers poked out from beneath her long dress as she paced to and fro across the carpet, holding the red notebook open in her hands and reading aloud from it.

Lily tried to call to her, but when she opened her mouth to speak no words came out. She could find them neither on the tip of her tongue nor hidden away deep inside her. So she closed her eyes and fell into a deep, uninterrupted slumber.

CHAPTER 10

Robert woke with a splitting headache. His right arm —the one he'd slept on—felt dead. He fancied he could still taste the sugary grit of the chocolates in his mouth. A sickly, sticky feeling filled his belly, like greasy stones grinding together.

The ripe tang of the animals wafted through the cabin, along with their whinnies, growls, and grunts, which made Robert think of some strange interspecies conversation.

The hard wooden floor beneath him was no longer shuddering, and the hum of the engines had ceased. That could mean only one thing: the Skycircus was no longer moving. They'd arrived at their destination.

He shifted onto his back and took up his cap from where it had fallen on the floor. Then he rubbed the pins and needles from his arm until it came back to life.

When he sat up, the heart-shaped chocolate box slid from his lap, and a second rancid wave of biliousness hit him like a runaway steam-wagon.

He tossed the empty box aside and gagged. He felt awful. The last thing he recalled was a sudden unnatural heaviness in his head and a sensation like being dropped down a well. He looked back at the box suspiciously. Was it the truffles? Had they been drugged? He remembered the clown giving Lily the special box in the Big Top and the men crowding in afterward to capture them—they'd probably been expecting a slower target. But Slimwood and Madame Lyons-Mane had caught them anyway in the end, he thought angrily.

He got to his knees and looked around. Lily and Malkin were sleeping on the far side of the cargo bay. Lily had passed out with her coat open and her scarf draped oddly across her body. Malkin had wound down and was curled at her feet.

Robert shuffled over and gently shook Lily by the shoulder.

"Wake up," he whispered.

"I feel terrible," Lily moaned, opening her eyes a slit.

"You look it," he retorted.

"Thanks a lot. Where are we?"

"I've no idea. We appear to have landed."

"How did we sleep through that?"

"I think there might've been something in the chocolates."

"Really?" She rubbed her eyes with a palm. "Everything's spinning."

"It will for a while. Take deep breaths."

He put a hand on her back and helped her sit up.

Eventually, she started to feel a little better. She brushed her hair from her face, then found Malkin's winding key around her neck and, leaning forward, started to wind him. The fox's gears tightened and clicked into place with each turn of the key.

When Lily had finished, the cogs inside him fizzed and ticked into movement, and he came to life, blinking his coal-black eyes and staring at the cage of wild beasts and the horses in their stalls.

"I forgot about this balloonatic ark of misfits," he chirruped. "You were halfway through telling a story, Lily. I thought we were going to take it in turns to stay awake. What the clank happened?"

"You wound down," Lily said, "and Robert and I passed out. We think the chocolates were drugged."

"They'd have to be for you to sleep through such a

stench," Malkin said, sniffing the air. "This place stinks worse than a dead rat's smelly socks. What time is it?"

Lily fished around in the pockets of her coat and took out her pocket watch, flipping open the lid. "Nine fifteen." She fiddled with the fob. "Unless it's lost time overnight."

"It shouldn't have." Robert stood and peered out through the porthole.

A low sun hung in a white sky flecked with slate-gray clouds above a clearing surrounded by autumnal trees. In the distance, higgledy-piggledy tall stone buildings clustered together as far as the eye could see.

Beneath the porthole, a group of men were throwing out mooring ropes, fixing the gondola to the ground. Others were busy erecting the kiosk and the site's exterior fence.

The Lunk pounded around everyone in creaking circles, his arms clasped behind his back like a jailer, while his dim headlamp eyes swept the workforce, keeping everyone in line.

Robert watched him nervously. "It really is an odd circus," he said at last. "What d'you think they want from us?"

"Me. Or at least my Cogheart." Lily's scars itched. She buttoned her coat across her front.

Robert dragged himself away from the window. "Why so?" he asked.

"You saw the way Slimwood and Lyons-Mane used the other hybrids in the show. Playing on their differences. Distorting their natures. They exploit hybrids, and I am one. So all I can imagine is that they must have similar plans for me. The pair of them were definitely the ones who sent this." Her fingers traced the pattern of the ammonite on the front of the red notebook. "Goodness knows how they got hold of it."

"It's a clanking conundrum to be sure." Malkin scratched at an ear with his back foot.

Robert nodded anxiously. He couldn't help thinking Lily was right. He feared for her safety in a place like this; horrible visions of what might happen to her, to both of them, swirled around inside him. "What should we do?" he asked at last.

"There's nothing we can do," Lily said, "except wait." She opened the notebook and flicked past pages of technical drawings and scribbled records. "Shall I read another diary entry from the notebook?" She took a breath and, over the growls of the animals, began at the top of the next page.

Tuesday, 23rd September 1884,
Riverside Walk, Chelsea

"That's seventeen years from the last entry!" Malkin squealed.

"And the day of my first birthday." Lily bit anxiously at a fingernail.

"Which means Grace would've been thirty-seven and married by this point," Robert said. "What could possibly have happened to her that meant she stopped writing in her notebook for seventeen years?"

"Who knows." Lily read on…

I found this book whilst going through my old papers. I've been examining its pages to reacquaint myself with my ideas for the Flyology project I dreamed once of creating.

But my most important creation is not represented here, and so I've decided to remedy that by writing about my darling daughter, Lily.

Today is Lily's first birthday; we have decided to throw her a party. This afternoon, in fact. We've recently installed ourselves in a rented house on Riverside Walk. The house is barely decorated, and we've no servants to speak of, so we'll have to make do. It will be a simple affair: myself, John, and a few friends and family. Simon Silverfish is invited. Lily will be baptized soon, and he is to be her godfather. He and John have become firm friends since they set up their business together making mechanicals.

Lily is so beautiful. She has strands of flame-red hair thin as cotton, rosy cheeks, and a smile that lights up my heart every time I see it. We will do our utmost to make this birthday special for her. And every one hereafter.

Lily paused. The edges of the words were blurring. It was true, Mama had always tried to make her birthdays special—often taking her to places she would never normally see.

She recalled a treasured photo of her third birthday, when they'd visited the London Zoological Gardens and she and Mama had ridden on a live elephant, a bit like the Elephanta.

Another time they'd gone to see an exhibition with Papa about the amazing electrical work of two famous American professors, Nikola Tesla and Thomas Edison.

On a third occasion they'd visited the Babbage Engine at a special lab near the Mechanists' Guild and seen the machine in action, computing complex problems.

Lily had always thought the majority of these outings had been Papa's idea, but she could see now that many of them were Mama's choices.

In the last year Mama was with them, Lily remembered, they had gone to watch the airships taking off at Counter's Creek Moorings, and Mama had tried to explain to Lily a little of the science that lay behind their flight.

She wondered what Mama would say if she knew of her predicament right now.

But she hadn't any time to consider this, nor to read the notebook's next entry, for her thoughts were interrupted by the clatter of chains and the turning of cogs as the cargo-bay door began to open.

"Quick!" she told Robert, waving the notebook at him. "We can't let them take this back. We need to hide it. Push it under my belt," she suggested, hitching up the back of her coat.

Robert wedged the notebook between the belt of her dress and the curve of her back. Its red cover was almost camouflaged against her vermilion silk party dress.

She dropped the back of her coat over the book as the cargo-bay door opened with a *CLANG* to reveal two figures.

It took Robert a moment to become accustomed to the glare from outside before he recognized the silhouettes of Slimwood and Madame Lyons-Mane.

They were both wearing the same clothes as last night. Slimwood, in his red riding jacket and dress coat, grasped a black horsewhip in his right hand, and under his left arm he carried a lumpy-looking laundry bag. His gold teeth flashed in a thinly sliced grin.

Madame Lyons-Mane twirled her striped parasol.

The pointy tip glinted. It looked sharp enough to poke out an eyeball.

"*Bienvenue à Paris!*" she said gaily.

Paris! They'd been taken to another country!

Robert felt a jagged pang of panic course through him, and Lily clasped her hands behind her back to stop them shaking. Malkin raised his hackles and bared his teeth, letting out a low, threatening growl.

"If you want to survive this encounter," Slimwood advised, coming close enough for them to see the whites of his eyes, "then you'd best muzzle that mechanimal."

"Do as he says," Robert whispered to Lily.

"Behave for a bit, Malkin," Lily said quietly, retrieving the muzzle and strapping it back around Malkin's nose. "We'll get out of this, I promise."

"This must be some sort of terrible mistake," Robert said to Slimwood. The words squeaked timorously out of him.

"Oh, no mistake." Madame Lyons-Mane stroked her hairy face with four long fingers and stepped into the shadowy interior of the cargo deck. "Everything's gone perfectly to plan."

Suddenly she grasped her beard and mustache and, in one smooth movement, ripped them away, wincing with pain as her skin puckered and snot-like strands of glue stretched between her fake hair and her skin. "*Bon anniversaire, ma chérie.* I hope you enjoyed your birthday surprise."

Lily scrabbled backward as bile rose in her. She knew she'd recalled that scent—it was lily of the valley. And now she recognized the beardless face of that betrayer too…it was her one-time governess and Papa's old housekeeper.

"Madame Verdigris," she gasped.

"*Exactement*," Madame replied.

"You look better with a beard," Lily blustered bravely. "Being hairy suits you."

The ringmistress gave a jagged, glassy laugh. "Very well, *ma petite*."

"Don't think you fooled us for one second," Lily bluffed. "We knew it was you. Your stinking perfume gave you away a mile off. You smell as bad as your mangy animals. I could work out your stupid tricks in my sleep."

"*Vraiment?*" Madame said. "Then how is it we caught you so easily, eh?"

She signaled to Slimwood, who grabbed Robert's arm and twisted it sharply behind his back until he cried out in pain.

Madame, meanwhile, seized Lily, gripping her shoulder so hard Lily felt like it was caught in a vise.

Malkin tried to slink off, but Madame blocked his path with her parasol, jamming the hooked end of it into the back of his muzzle like a lead.

The fox growled, his eyes bright with anger.

"Enough!" Madame cried. "*Silence*. Hold your tongues! Creating a scene will only make things worse."

"Don't tell me to be quiet," Lily spat, struggling against the woman's vicious grip. "I want to know why we're here."

The corners of Madame's mouth tweaked up into a mocking, malicious grin. "I came back for you, Lily, and I brought the whole circus with me. We've been planning your kidnapping for months."

"We?" Lily's face went pale.

"Of course, *chérie*. Did you actually think I was going to let you expel me from your life forever with not a thought of revenge?" Madame's fingers tightened even further. "When I found your mama's notebook among your papa's papers, I knew it would whet your interest. You were always whining on about her."

"Papa trusted you!" Lily said. "You *stole* those papers. And Mama's notebook."

"And look what I've caught with her words," Madame said. "I was sure, along with the birthday card and the tickets for the show, they would be enough to reel you in… I was right, wasn't I, Lily? You never could resist a mystery."

"*What it is that makes you tick*," Lily spat. "Your pathetic riddle."

"You like it?" Madame asked. "A friend came up with it."

"I don't even know what it means."

"Of course you do, *chérie*. I must say, it took me some time to guess the answer myself. But I was foolish not to see it long ago. Your mama's notebook was no great use to me in that regard, but your papa's papers—they explained everything. Why everyone had been after his perpetual motion machine, where it had ended up, and how valuable it was."

"There's no such thing as a perpetual motion machine," Robert said. "They don't exist."

"Oh, but they do. There's one right here." Madame unbuttoned the top of Lily's coat and knocked on her breastbone. Lily's chest made a horrible, low *tock-tock* sound.

"I don't know what you're talking about," Lily bluffed, balling her hand behind her back, pressing her nails into the skin.

"It's called the Cogheart, *n'est-ce pas?* Professor Hartman stole it from Silverfish to save your life. That's why everyone was looking for it. Why Silverfish's henchmen, Roach and Mould, promised to pay me if I kept an eye on you and brought you to him. When they never came through on that pledge, I had to get away quickly with the one thing of value I could lay my hands on: your papa's papers."

"I hope they've brought you nothing but trouble," Lily said.

Madame chortled until her cut-glass earrings shook and tinkled like little bells.

"They did. And now they're destined to bring you trouble too, *ma petite*." She leaned in until the stench of her perfume was almost unbearable. "Let me explain something…and I'm only telling you this because you will never *ever* leave this place. Those papers contained valuable information about the Cogheart. They would've recompensed me for the hours I worked looking after you for pathetic pay." Her voice hardened. "It's a pity we couldn't sell them, but we risked arrest. They were stamped with the Hartman Silverfish Corporation logo, you see, and your father had offered a reward for their safe return."

"By 'we', I take it you mean yourself and Mr. Sunder?" Lily said. "Whatever happened to him?"

"That useless fool!" Madame sneered. "He refused to cooperate with my schemes. Threatened to go to the gendarmeries—the police. But I had him disposed of. My friend Slimwood saw to it."

Robert couldn't believe his ears. He glanced up at Slimwood, who gave a loud guffaw, revealing his mouthful of flashing gold teeth.

"Sunder was an idiot!" Slimwood said. "We sure did a number on him, didn't we, Hortense? It's how we deal with anyone—inside or outside the circus—who doesn't agree with us." He ran a finger slowly across Robert's neck. "Same way we'll get rid of you, if you give us any trouble."

"At first I was going to use the papers for blackmail," Madame continued, "but when your papa put the word out against me, I couldn't even ditch them on the black market." She tutted, as if her thieving and the subsequent fallout had all been just a minor inconvenience. "Then Slimwood said he knew someone—an old friend— making illegal hybrids, and we thought the papers might interest him."

"Who?" Lily asked.

"A certain doctor who was only interested if I could provide you as part of the deal. And so I came up with the kidnapping plan. A perfect crime as it means I get my revenge on you too."

"What doctor?" Lily demanded. "What do they want?"

"All in good time, *ma petite*," Madame said. "First, we visit Room Thirteen."

She hustled Lily and Malkin out of the loading bay, Lily twisting desperately to look back over her shoulder at Robert as she was dragged away.

Robert moved to follow them, but Slimwood's grip didn't waver.

"No, boy. You're with me. And if I have anything to do with it, you'll not be seeing your friends again for a while."

Robert clenched his fists and dug his nails into his palms, trying to swallow down the knot of anxiety as he listened to Malkin, Lily, and Madame's footsteps echo away down the cargo ramp. Room Thirteen—where was that? What did it mean? And how, by all that ticked, was he going to get them out?

CHAPTER 11

Lily clutched her coat close around her as Madame pushed her and Malkin out of the gondola and marched them along its side through a short stretch of scrubby grass.

Madame, Lily realized, had plans for her and Malkin, but Robert seemed unnecessary. She tried very hard not to worry about what might happen to him left alone in the cargo bay with Slimwood—there was no way she or Malkin could help him right now. All she could do was examine their surroundings—if they wanted to attempt an escape, she needed to recall every landmark.

The men who'd chased them last night were busily erecting the site's high, circular perimeter fence. The kiosk and spike-topped gates set into it were being locked tight. Lily was starting to think that the whole setup was not just to keep gatecrashers and busybodies out, but also to keep the performers in.

They arrived at another door-hatch on the port side of the grounded sky-ship. Madame opened it and shoved them inside, into a stairwell. Malkin bristled with anger and growled through his teeth, but there was little he could do from within the muzzle. Lily put a calming hand on his head and looked about.

What little light there was came from electric lamps that ran along the walls, pulsing in a vague rhythm that matched her stuttering heartbeat.

"This way," Madame said, and they followed her up a set of steps.

The end of Lily's tiger-striped scarf dragged behind her. She thought about tying a loose thread from it to the bannister, like Ariadne, so she could find her way back.

They reached the next landing, and Madame forced them along a narrow, labyrinthine passage filled with numbered, closed cells.

They came to a padlocked, barred gate that spanned the width of the passageway. Beyond it stood a single door. It looked heavier than the others and was studded with rivets. Two large bolts secured a hatch in its center that was stenciled with the number:

13

"*Voilà, salle treize*. Unlucky for some. Or in this case, *you*, Lily." Madame took a ring of keys from a hook on her belt and flicked through them until she found one that fitted the padlock. She opened it and hustled Lily and Malkin through the gate, locking it behind her. "Now empty your pockets. I want everything, including the red notebook."

Lily made a show of searching through her coat and the pockets of her dress. She didn't want to give Madame Mama's notebook. If only there was something else she could hand over instead... Then she found Malkin's birthday present.

"This is all I have," she said, grasping the deceased mouse in her fist and holding it out.

"*Donnez-le moi*. Give it to me."

Madame opened her palm, and Lily dropped the dead rodent into it.

She expected at least a scream, but the woman merely tutted and threw the mouse away.

"The rest, *s'il vous plaît*," Madame commanded.

"There's nothing else," Lily replied.

"Liar, *menteur!*" Madame grasped her arm and pushed her coat aside, patting her down. When she felt the red notebook nestled against Lily's back, she gave a victorious cry of delight. "*Voilà!* Here it is!"

Madame tussled the book free, but Lily was having none of it. She shot out her hand and clasped it by the pages.

"That's mine," she said through gritted teeth. "You may have stolen it from Papa, but you're *not* stealing it from me."

"We shall see."

Madame pulled sharply at the spine, and there was a horrible ripping sound. The clump of pages Lily was clutching tore from the binding and crumpled in her hand.

"Now look," Madame said. "You've ruined a perfectly good book." She flicked through the remainder of it. "I imagine you've read some. How did you find it? I must tell you, I thought your mother's writing rather dull—*très ennuyeux*! Perhaps the loss isn't so great after all."

Lily's eyes narrowed. She clutched the crushed papers in her fist and bit her tongue to stop her tears.

She half expected Madame might try and pry the torn section from her fingers, but the woman was obviously bored of the whole confrontation, for she snapped the book closed and waved Lily away with a flick of her wrist. "Keep those scraps. I shouldn't imagine they contain anything of value. Consider it a consolation prize.

"*Alors…*" She found the key to Room Thirteen and inserted it into the lock. Pushing the door open, she shoved Malkin and Lily inside, and then with a heavy *CLUNK!* the door slammed shut behind them.

Afterward there was just the *click* of the lock, the *clang* of the padlock on the gate, then Madame's footsteps walking away.

Lily sank to the floor, blind with rage, and laid the torn sheaf of papers across her lap, smoothing each leaf flat and trying to calm the ball of anger inside. It was only a book—it shouldn't hurt so badly. But at this moment, it felt like the largest pain there was—as if Madame had ripped Mama from her, pulled the pieces of the past apart, and stood there sneering. Now Lily would never be able to finish reading Mama's story.

"She destroyed it, Malkin," she gasped, tears blurring her vision.

Malkin gave a soft wheezy yap in reply.

Lily glanced down to see he was still wearing the muzzle. "I'm sorry," she said. "I forgot."

She pulled him to her chest and released the buckle from the back of his head. "How are you feeling anyway?"

The fox licked the teardrops from her face with a dry tongue. "Oh, just tickety-boo! That was some welcome from your old friend."

"She's no friend of mine." Lily gave a loud, sorrowful sniff. "Malkin, we have to get out of here! You need to help me make a plan."

She brushed the tears from her face with shaking fingers and took in Room Thirteen.

It was a windowless, four-berth cabin with thick metal walls. What little light there was came from a blinking electric bulb set into the ceiling. A small table stood at the center of the room, a rickety-looking chair pushed underneath it. In the corner was an old tin bucket and a vanity screen, painted with stars, against which leaned a walking stick.

"What is all this stuff?" Lily asked. She half expected another sarcastic reply, but Malkin had gone quiet.

"Don't look now," he whispered at last, "but I think we're surrounded."

And, with a curdling sense of unease, Lily realized he was right.

"Take off that coat and penguin suit!" Slimwood commanded, jamming Robert's arm even higher up behind his back, until his nerves jangled with pain. "You look like you're about to go on in a magic show."

"What should I wear then?" Robert replied, grinding

his jaw with a low whimper.

Slimwood let go of his arm and tossed him the laundry sack he'd been carrying. "There's clothes in there."

"You want me to change in front of all these folk?" Robert asked, for by now the cargo bay was swarming with people, flooding up and down the loading ramp like ants.

"Yes." Slimwood gave him a stinging swipe round the ear that knocked his cap off his head. "We've rules around here, and the first is don't talk back." He folded his arms and turned away.

Robert emptied the contents of the laundry bag onto the floor and started to undress. His heart wrenched as he took off his da's coat—it was the only thing he had of his, but he hadn't lost it yet and whatever happened he would get it back. This he vowed.

He folded the coat carefully and put it in the bag then he started to remove his shoes and socks. He could've sworn Slimwood had said that there were no rules in the circus, but that had been the jovial ringmaster in the show. This Slimwood was different—far more unpleasant. It seemed as if his charm was something he could turn on and off at will, like a water tap.

As Robert unbuttoned his shirt cold air drifted in from outside the cargo bay, pinching at his skin, but his ears burned, and he felt only hot with embarrassment.

Beneath his vest, the Moonlocket glinted against his breastbone. He turned away to hide it from view, but it was too late—Slimwood had seen it.

"I'll take that, if you don't mind," he said grabbing it. "It looks rather valuable." Robert felt a spike of anguish as Slimwood yanked the locket away from his neck. *Careful!* he wanted to shout, but the clasp on the chain had snapped.

The locket came loose in Slimwood's hand, and the ringmaster examined it before putting it in his pocket. "The second rule is no jewelry. And the third rule is anything contraband you thought belonged to you, now belongs to me."

Robert felt sick. It was the only thing he had of his ma's. A handful of men and women in linen shirts and thick woolen breeches spattered with mud bustled behind him, ignoring this injustice. Together they worked to remove the wheel-blocks from beneath the carnivores' cage and wheel it out.

Robert took off his trousers and stood there in his cotton vest and woolen drawers. More people arrived. They pulled heavy bags and boxes from the shelves and carried them down the ramp on their shoulders. None of them looked him in the eye.

In the far corner of the horse stall, a boy and a girl

were tending to the two stallions. Robert recognized them from the show as Silva Buttons, the gymnast, and Dimitri, the youngest horseman of the apocalypse.

Silva wore a red, spotted neckerchief, and Dimitri sported leather riding boots. He didn't look apocalyptic today, more run-down and tired, which was how Robert felt too. Dimitri stroked the horses' manes and whispered to them softly, while Silva brought them water in a bucket, all the while glancing sidelong at Robert. When she noticed Slimwood, she tried to look twice as busy as she already was.

"Don't dawdle, boy!" Slimwood snapped at Robert. "Get on with it!"

Robert picked up the clothes from the bag. They looked like the same brown and gray colors as everybody else's and smelled of dirt and damp. When he climbed into the trousers, their coarse material itched against his skin.

He buttoned up his rough shirt. He missed the cold feel of the Moonlocket against his skin. He folded the last of his clothes neatly and put them in the laundry bag.

"And the cap," Slimwood said. "You won't be needing that again where you're going. It's a smart cap for a smart boy, and stupid's more your style." Slimwood laughed at his own joke, his gold teeth flashing once more.

With a heavy heart, Robert did as he was told. His cap

was like an extra limb to him.

When he was done, Slimwood seized the bag from him and threw it into a basket in the corner, piled high with identical sacks. Then he took Robert by the elbow and steered him down the cargo ramp.

Outside, the morning sun was warming the last of the dew from the grass of a scrubby clearing surrounded by a spiked fence. It didn't look anything like Robert had imagined Paris.

Some of the circus folk—the bigger, burlier men who'd chased them last night—were busy with sledgehammers, driving stakes into the ground in a big circle. Others—people from the show—were sorting through the bags and trunks, bringing out rolls of canvas. Slimwood watched their progress proprietorially. Anyone slow in their work got a lash from his whip.

"You'll help set the site today," he told Robert as they skirted a figure struggling to unwind a big ball of guy rope. "Mostly you'll assist in putting up the Big Top. It needs to be erected by evening so we can start rehearsals for the new show tomorrow. Understand?"

"I—" Robert said.

"Good." Slimwood dug his fingers into Robert's elbow, and Robert winced in pain. "Everyone here gets three chances." He led Robert away from the busy crew, off round the front of the sky-ship, past the wooden angel figurehead. "For your backchat earlier and your hiding of valuables, you're down two strikes, but work hard, don't ask questions or play games, and we'll get along fine. Run, hide, stir up shady activity or incite trouble in my crew, and I'll have your guts for garters. And I don't mean that metaphorically."

He pointed out a row of items hung from hooks on the gondola's starboard side. "See those? What do you think they are?"

Robert shook his head. He'd no idea. He stared at the things. There was an old battered clown hat with its pom-poms missing, a burned-looking spangled leotard, a set of stirrups, five juggling clubs on a rope, which jangled together in the wind, and what seemed to be a human thigh bone and a wrinkled elephant's foot.

Slimwood slapped this last item with a palm. "They're mementos," he explained. "Relics and trophies of troublemakers past. Circus acts who mysteriously disappeared." He sniggered to himself. "I keep them to remind my crew who's boss and what happens to any blackguard who crosses me."

Robert felt sick. He stared fearfully up at the line of grim remains. Whatever happened, he didn't want to end up like those poor souls. He had to find Lily and

Malkin as soon as he could, and escape.

"Remember," Slimwood said, escorting him back round to the busy side of the gondola, "you've only one strike left. I'm a fair master, in the ring and out. Too fair, Madame says—but that's my way. You know the rules, so if—and when—the crunch comes, you can't say you weren't warned."

He paused and let Robert digest that last bit of information. Robert imagined he'd made this vile speech a thousand times before.

"The Lunk'll be along in a minute to assign you your chores. I suggest you do as he says." Then Slimwood stalked off to shout at someone who wasn't banging stakes in to his liking.

Robert remained in the shadow of the Skycircus gondola. He was hollow inside, and his skin felt as thin as eggshell, as if, any second now, it might crack open and an overwhelming feeling of fear would come flooding out.

He wished he hadn't lost his ma's locket. At least he had the rest of his things. He shoved his hands in his pockets and realized with horror that his penknife and pencil and the lockpicks were all missing. How could he be so stupid? He'd left them in his da's jacket, in a laundry bag along with a dozen or more identical others, somewhere in the hold. How could he possibly find Lily and Malkin and get them out now?

Lily's legs shook beneath her as she stared into the dark recesses of Room Thirteen. "I can't see anyone," she whispered nervously.

"They're in here somewhere," Malkin replied.

She took a few steps forward, peering into each of the four berths in turn.

Malkin was right. Though the first bunk was unoccupied, save for some folded bedding, the other three were most definitely not!

A set of worried eyes shone out from each of them, three figures staring from beneath their blankets—they must've hidden when they'd heard Madame bringing her and Malkin along the passage. What were they so frightened of that they had to conceal themselves in their beds?

Lily and Malkin waited in silence, not knowing what to say, until finally a soft girlish voice from the top left-hand bunk spoke.

"Who's that girl in the tiger-striped scarf, Luca? She's not one of us."

"No," came the gruff answer from the bunk beneath. "She's most certainly not. And neither is her scruffy orange dog."

Then Luca the Lobster Boy threw off his blanket and jumped to the floor, clacking his metal claws together.

"Had a good look, have you?" he jeered, lurching toward her. "Come to stare at the freaks?"

CHAPTER 12

M alkin growled and stood before her, but Lily couldn't tear her eyes from Luca's great claws. She recalled what the ringmaster had said about them: *"His gruesome appendages can cut through steel like paper. Don't get too close or anger him, ladies and gents, for he can tear off your nose with a single snap!"*

Malkin bared his teeth at the boy, and Lily felt a sudden flash of panic.

She grabbed the fox's scruff to stop him from attacking.

"Why are you here?" Luca demanded, stepping closer with a face like thunder.

Lily shuffled back toward the door, the end of her

scarf dragging in the dust. She felt lost for words. The sight of Luca, with his clattering claws and his deep blue angry eyes, didn't fill her with dread—it only made her confused. They were so alike, her and him, but she wasn't sure how to explain it.

"We're here because Madame took us..." she said haltingly. "Kidnapped us...last night...after the show."

"Fox-napped, in my case," Malkin added through his teeth.

"Her and Slimwood's ruffians...I mean, the circus men," Lily continued, "they trapped us in the hold then spirited us away."

"I tried to warn you," Malkin groused. "But you wouldn't listen."

"We couldn't understand you, Malkin, you had a muzzle on."

"This is your fox?" Luca pointed a claw at Malkin. "And I assume you're an orphan?" He gestured at Lily, his face softening on that last word.

"I think you mean she's my human," Malkin said. "Tell me, how *do* you live in a place like this? It stinks to high heaven."

"Shush!" Lily gripped him tighter by the scruff of the neck. If she wanted to persuade what she guessed were the other two hybrids to come down and convince all

170

three of them to help her escape, she'd need to stop Malkin causing any trouble.

"Yes," she said to Luca. "He's my fox. Papa gave him to me as a present. He's a mechanimal. His name's Malkin, and mine's Lily… We're awfully pleased to meet you," she added, for she'd been taught to be polite, and though she wasn't always, in this case she felt like she should try to make friends.

Malkin didn't seem to agree. "I've yet to decide if I feel the same way," he said with a low growl, raising his hackles and pulling back his lips to reveal his yellow teeth.

Luca laughed. "Very sensible. And what home are you from?"

"Brackenbridge Manor. It's in the town you visited yesterday."

He looked confused. "I've never heard of that one."

"Weren't you listening, Luca?" said the high-pitched voice from above. "She said she had a papa. She's not from an orphanage. She's from a *real* home."

The girl who'd spoken peered over the side of her bunk. Her face was round and friendly, with doughy cheeks and a warm smile. She shifted awkwardly and began to climb down, and Lily saw her mechanical legs. It was Deedee—the wire-walking hybrid from the show.

Surely that meant the third figure, up in the top

corner bunk, had to be Angelique? Lily darted her a glance, but she was still huddled beneath her blanket.

Deedee jumped to the floor. "Do you have a mother and father?" she asked, hiding nervously behind Luca. Her mechanical legs whirred beneath her when she moved. They were a little too long in proportion to her body, and made her look delicate and stork-like, as if she was perched on miniature stilts.

Lily shook her head. "Only a father. I never knew my mama well," she added hesitantly. "She died when I was quite young... Although lately you might say we've started talking again." She felt for the torn pages in her pocket.

Luca looked at her as if she was mad, but Deedee didn't seem to have noticed her odd comment.

"We three are from different orphanages," she explained to Lily. "We were taken years ago. Not by this circus, although this is where we've ended up." She had a habit of holding her arms away from her body when she talked, as if she was thinking about balancing all the time.

"We weren't always hybrids," Luca added. "We were human once too, like you. An evil doctor called Droz plucked us from our orphanages, changed us in a lab, and sold us on to the circus."

"That's terrible!" Lily felt sick. In her notebook Mama had mentioned being taught by Dr. Droz. Lily hated to think that her mama had had a connection to such an awful man.

Then, for the first time, Angelique spoke. "Droz only takes children no one will miss," she explained quietly. "Children like us." She had shifted to the edge of her berth and was peering down at them.

Her hair was pinned in two thick dark bunches, and her brown eyes were set wide apart under wispy eyebrows, the left one marked by a cut.

"You were at the show last night," Angelique said. "Sitting next to a boy I recognized. Bartholomew, his name was."

"Tolly, you mean?" Lily asked.

"Is that what he's called now?" Angelique's eyes brightened. "I remembered his face. There was something familiar about it."

Lily recalled what Tolly had said last night at the show. "He told me you were at an orphanage together, in London," she said to Angelique.

"Yes, the Camden Workhouse for the Infirm and Physically Incurable. I was taken. He wasn't."

Angelique jumped from her bunk, flapping her wings. Her feathers scraped the metal walls of the cell as she wafted down to float a few inches from the floor. Finally she seized her stick from where it leaned against the edge of the screen and came to rest fully on the ground. She moved with concentration, like the slightest misstep or loss of control might bowl her over. As if gravity might sneak up on her from behind and tip her off her feet. Lily thought it a strange ballet, but rather beautiful.

"I never spoke back then," Angelique said. "Fear made my words dry up inside me. Tolly changed that. He was the only one who ever showed me any kindness." She smiled at the thought of him.

On the ground, she looked slighter than the other two, though her wings made her seem grander. And her demeanor toward the pair, like an older sister, made Lily sure she was the eldest of the three—older than she'd looked on the ticket—perhaps sixteen or seventeen?

"He would send up my lunch in the basket every day, and when I returned my plate to him, I would send him little gifts and notes, and he would do the same. Is he with you? I would dearly love to see him again. I heard there was a new boy brought aboard too. Is that him?"

Lily shook her head. "No, that's my friend Robert. Tolly managed to escape. He's back in Brackenbridge. He'll tell Papa what's going on, and they'll come and rescue us." She didn't know if this was true or not, but it sounded reassuring.

"They'll have to find us first," Deedee said. "We've traveled a long way since last night."

"Did you hear where we've landed?" Luca asked.

"Madame told us Paris," Lily said. "Only it didn't look much like it when she took us out of the cargo bay. More of a wood really, with some buildings behind it on the horizon."

"Paris again?" Deedee whispered, and the three of them shuddered.

"That's a long way from home," Luca said.

"Yes, it is," Lily replied, although she wasn't sure if they were talking about her home or theirs. "But Tolly will get a message to my father," she added again, more to reassure herself than them.

Malkin nodded wisely. "He's a good pup."

"If he's a friend of yours," Angelique said, "then I think we can trust you."

"I've another question," Deedee interjected. "If you weren't kidnapped from an orphanage or sent by Dr. Droz, then why's Madame put you in here with us?"

"I can't answer that," Lily said. The secret of her Coghcart had already led her into this danger, and the thought of more people knowing about it filled her with an itching anxiety.

"Can't or won't?" Luca said, peering at her. "You're a

175

strange one, Lily. Neither fish nor fowl. You look human, but Madame put you in Room Thirteen with us, so I'm guessing you might be a hybrid."

"If she doesn't want to tell us, she doesn't have to," Angelique admonished Luca softly.

"That's right," Deedee agreed. "She's scared, poor dear, and she's no idea what's what. One moment she's in the audience, enjoying a show, the next she's imprisoned here." She put out a hand and touched Lily's shoulder.

Lily realized the hybrids had no inkling of Madame's plans for her or who she really was. To stand any chance of breaking out of this place, she would have to gain their trust. Yet the thought of speaking to them about the Cogheart sat heavy inside her, like a giant immoveable boulder that was not ready to be rolled aside. She glanced at Malkin.

He said nothing.

Should she tell her secret? Was it safe? In the past Papa had used silence to keep the truth hidden, even from her. It hadn't worked. She'd found out about the Cogheart. And so had others: three evil hybrid men, named Roach, Mould, and Silverfish, who'd tried to kill her for it. Since then it always took her a long time to trust people.

But these hybrid children were different. More like

her. Last night at the show they'd looked sad and downtrodden—as frightened of the rest of the circus folk as everyone in the audience had been of them. But here in this room, they were friendly and attentive. Deedee's expression was placid and neutral, while Luca wore a concerned frown. Angelique's eyes were wide with anticipation and intrigue.

There was something about her that made Lily believe she could be trusted. Perhaps she would understand? Perhaps they all would. If Lily opened up to them, told them the story of her heart, maybe they would open up to her in return? Because truth mattered. And so did what you really were. Mama had said so, hadn't she? Whereas Papa's lies had only caused their family trouble.

No, to survive here, Lily realized she would have to be like Mama. Suddenly she remembered Mama's exact words, written in the red notebook: *What would you do if you weren't afraid?* She looked round at the hybrids, all watching her expectantly, and just like that, she knew she would tell them her truth.

Robert stood alone in the freezing clearing, waiting for the Lunk. He rubbed his hands together, feeling rather sorry for himself as he watched the progress of the circus folk who were busily attaching lengths of rope to two large tent poles the size of tree trunks.

The clothes Slimwood had given him were threadbare and covered in big splatters of mud. If Mrs. Rust or Miss Tock could see how scruffy he looked, they'd probably blow a gasket each. He did miss them. Brackenbridge Manor too. He would so dearly love to be there now, with John and all the mechanicals jittering round the house. Even Rusty telling them off for sneaking out would be better than this. *Anything* would be better than this!

He wished he still had the Moonlocket. It reminded him of his ma and gave him hope—that was, before Slimwood took it. It seemed to Robert that Slimwood and Madame had similarly stolen everyone's hope in this place, and he'd need to keep a hold of his if he wanted to get his locket and the rest of his things back and find Lily and Malkin.

"HEADS UP! COMING THROUGH!" came a shout from behind.

Robert turned to see the two horses trot round the stern of the sky-ship. Dimitri was riding the black horse bareback and ducked under the engine prop. Silva followed, riding the white horse.

Dimitri and Silva circled the horses about. Then Dimitri jumped down from his mount and handed its reins over to Silva. Someone threw him a length of rope that was attached to one of the poles, and he tied it to a harness hanging over his horse's back.

"Oi, you…flattie!" Silva called down at Robert from where she sat. "Don't just stand there goggling at everyone like an owl in an ivy bush, lend a hand!"

"You talking to me?" Robert asked.

"Who else would I be talking to?" Silva replied. "Flattie—means landlubber. Get over here, would you?"

"I can't." He shook his head. "I'm supposed to wait for the Lunk to give me my chores."

"That creaking calamity!" Silva spat. "I wouldn't do that if I were you. Come with us instead. We'll give you a job, make sure you look busy."

"Thank you." Robert advanced anxiously toward them, unsure about the shifting horses. "Have you seen my friends? They were taken to Room Thirteen. I need to get a message to them. Oh, and I need to get my clothes back from the laundry."

Silva jumped down from the back of her horse and took its reins. "No, I haven't seen your friends. As for your clothes, it's wash day tomorrow—if you sign up for tub duty you might be able to find them then. Otherwise you'll discover they get absorbed into the outfits for the show."

"But they belong to me," Robert exclaimed. "They have my things in!"

"Valuable things?" Silva asked.

Robert nodded.

"Then the best you can hope for is that Slimwood doesn't find them." She gestured to Dimitri, who was busily harnessing a rope to the back of her horse now. "I'm Silva, by the way, and this is Dimitri."

"My name's Robert." He nodded at Dimitri, who had the same coal-black hair and brown eyes as Silva. "Is he your brother?"

Silva laughed. "No. I suppose we do look alike, but he's nobody's brother. He's got no folks."

"I may be nobody's brother..." Dimitri replied with a soft Russian accent, "but I'm everyone's son. I belong to the whole Skycircus."

"What's that mean?" Robert asked, intrigued despite himself.

"Fourteen years ago," Dimitri explained, "when old Slimwood senior—Slimwood's father—was navigating the circus through the steppes of Russia, he found me hidden behind a hay bale in the horse stalls. I'd snuck aboard when they'd stopped at their last atchings—"

"That's polari," Silva interrupted. "Traveler speak for—"

"I know," Robert said. "Place to land, make camp."

"Very good, flattie." Silva looked impressed. She led both horses forward until the ropes behind them stretched and grew taut. The tent poles gradually began to rise, pivoting from the base as the horses strained to pull them upright.

Dimitri lent a hand, pulling on the rope along with the horses, trying to make it easier for them. "One of the old rousties, Ted," he explained, "was a horseman in the show—"

"Roustie means roustabout," Silva said, interrupting Dimitri again. "Which is to say, people who put-up and take-down the circus, but who aren't your actual acts. There are quite a few rousties on this crew." She nodded at the men who were pinning out guy ropes now to hold the poles in place. "They work for Slimwood and Madame and aren't to be trusted."

"Can I continue?" Dimitri asked, amused. "Ted took care of the horses and me, and the circus became my family. Then, when I was big enough, I looked after the horses too—they were always my favorites—and when I wasn't in the stables, everyone took turns caring for me. But that was before…" He paused.

"Before what?" Robert asked. "What happened?"

"Old Mr. Slimwood died—just eight months ago."

Dimitri nodded at the juggling clubs that hung from the side of the sky-ship's gondola. "Those are his clubs right there, and those are Ted's stirrups. Now Slimwood's son's in charge, along with that awful Madame. Circus doesn't mean family to them—only money."

More circus folk were laying out strips of canvas beneath the newly erected poles and lacing them together. Slimwood paraded among them, wielding his whip on anyone who wasn't working fast enough. He was a horror show. Robert couldn't believe that this was his family circus, his father's, and he'd turned it into such a miserable place.

"Grab hold of that horse, will you, flattie?" Dimitri called, bringing him back to the present. "Silva can't manage them both on her own."

Dimitri began untying the hauling ropes and harnesses from the white stallion. Robert did as he was told. He stood behind Silva and took up the reins of the black horse, stroking its steaming flank to try and calm it down.

He could feel the animal's ribs beneath its fur as it breathed in and out.

"Why's he so thin?" he asked Silva.

"Slimwood doesn't feed them properly," she explained. "And they're made to do all this heavy lifting, just like us."

"Did he really kill all those people?" Robert stared at the line of trinkets hanging from the ship.

"He got rid of them somehow," Silva said, stroking the muzzle of the white horse. "Him and Madame. Acts that'd been here years. They said they were leaving. Promised to write. But we never heard from them again. So, yeah, for all we know they could be dead."

"After Slimwood Senior was gone," Dimitri continued, "Madame and Slimwood took over his quarters and the office and the comms room on the top floor." He nodded at the highest row of windows in the gondola. "They stopped anyone going up there. Pretty soon that part of the Skycircus ship was totally out of bounds. Private, for their use only. Then they hired new roustabouts to guard everyone, put up fences, and locked us all in our berths."

Silva gestured at the high wall around the site. "Before we knew it, the place became a prison."

The black horse whinnied and pulled away from Robert.

"Hush, Zampano," Dimitri said softly to it as he finished unyoking the white horse and started in on the black.

"Don't let him go," Silva whispered. "If you do it'll be bad news for him and for us."

Robert could feel his feet slipping. The rope chafed

183

against his palms, coarse against his skin. He gritted his teeth, locked his fingers together and stood firm, until his shoulders ached from grasping the rope.

"Thanks for your help, flattie." Dimitri took the reins of the black horse from Robert and tied him up to a ring on the gondola.

Silva tied up the white horse herself next to him. It appeared to be called Mr. Kite.

As Robert watched them talking to the animals, he realized things might not be quite as bad as they'd seemed. He'd made new friends.

PRIIIPP! PRIIIPP! PRIIIPP!

Three short blasts sounded on a whistle.

"Scran's up!" Dimitri said.

"That's lunch, flattie," Silva explained.

Everyone abandoned the half-constructed tent, downing tools and heading for the main hatch door on the port side of the Skycircus gondola. The Lunk stood in the doorway, his metal jaw grinding up and down, silently counting them all in.

As Robert, Dimitri, and Silva joined the line on the ramp, Robert spotted something over the treetops: a gigantic spiked tower of iron. Zeps bobbed around it like bees on a flower. A few were even moored to it by anchor ropes.

"What's that?" he asked the other two, pointing the tower out to them.

"The Eiffel Tower Airstation," Silva whispered. "Flights arriving into Paris take off and land there."

"How far away is it?" Robert said quietly.

"Miles," Silva replied under her breath. "This is the Bois de Boulogne, which is a wood on the outskirts of the city."

"We're prisoners anyway," Dimitri muttered. "We're not allowed near places like that, so you won't get to see it."

"I will if we get out," said Robert softly to himself.

As their part of the line reached the gondola and they trooped inside, a thousand and one plans flitted through his mind. First he had to save Lily and Malkin from Room Thirteen, then get a message to John in England, then get his locket back, and finally get them away from here in one piece. And he would start as soon as he'd recovered the laundry bag.

CHAPTER 13

*S*PLAT!

A gray scoop of slop hit Robert's plate. Lardy porridge peppered with onions. He peered grimly at it. A rancid, unappetizing steam rose from its depths. It seemed there was to be no more cotton candy or popcorn or peanuts.

"Enjoy your lunch," said the fellow ladling the stuff out from a large tureen. "Don't eat it all at once, you useless bunch." He spoke in rhyme, Robert realized—it was Joey the clown. Though he wasn't wearing his makeup, he had the teardrop tattooed on his face—the one Robert had thought was only drawn on yesterday.

"We call this sloup," Silva whispered as she and

Dimitri led him away from the long queue of circus folk that meandered down the length of the mess hall. People in tired muddy work uniforms with tired muddy faces. "Mainly because it's a cross between slop and soup. Want some extra? You look like you need it."

Robert shook his head, but it was too late—she poured half her sloup onto his plate anyway. He tried not   to spill it as she and Dimitri took him to a second table, where they each grabbed some cutlery and a tin cup from a box.

"Keep your spowl and boon safe," said the toady fellow with bright orange hair in charge of the water jug. He wasn't wearing his makeup either, but Robert recognized him as Auggie the clown—with his habit of putting the wrong letters on the front of the wrong words.

"Anyone who sposes his loon or can gets fed to the tions, liger, and bear," Auggie informed him, filling his tin can with greasy water.

"He means if you lose a spoon or can, you get fed to the lions, tiger, and bear," Silva whispered.

"Don't be fraternizing with those clowns," Dimitri admonished as they joined the line for seats. "They're spies for Madame and Slimwood."

"I won't," Robert said. He felt glad to have Silva and

Dimitri looking out for him. He hoped Lily and Malkin had made some friends too and glanced worriedly around the mess hall, searching for them.

A few of the roustabouts who'd chased them last night were sitting at one long table, and the four-piece band at another. The rest of the benches were filled with jugglers, tumblers, plate-spinners, and even the wizened old man, who looked to be enjoying his sloup far less than the crockery he'd eaten in last night's show. But there was no sign of Lily or Malkin, nor of the other hybrids. What the clank had Madame and Slimwood done with them?

"Each family or group sits at the table corresponding to their room number," Silva explained when she saw him staring worriedly about. "Me and Dimitri and my folks, we're in Room Six, so we sit at table six. There's a space there, if you want to come with us."

Dimitri and Silva led him between the rows of gray people to the table nearest the door, which was indeed marked with a six.

"Papi, Mami, this is Robert." Silva said. Robert recognized the two older acrobats from the Bouncing Buttons act.

A few feet behind them, the Lunk loomed, his swivel-eyes lurching from side to side as he took in everything and everyone in the room. Nothing escaped his beady gaze. Robert cowered away from him. "Good afternoon, Mr. and Mrs. Buttons," he whispered, perching on the end of a bench opposite Silva and Dimitri.

"Please, call me Gilda," Mrs. Buttons said. She was so petite that, except for the lines on her face, she might've been mistaken for a young girl.

"And Bruno," Mr. Buttons added, shaking Robert's hand. His grip was sure and strong, his arm as slender and solid as a tree branch, his shoulders broad, and his head flat on top, as if he might have balanced on it too many times—which, possibly, he had.

"How are your horses, Dimitri?" Mr. Buttons asked.

"Fine, thanks, Bruno," Dimitri replied. "If there's time after the tent's up this afternoon, and Slimwood allows it, I'll give them a quick trot around the ring."

Robert tried a mouthful of the sloup. It tasted disgusting, like dirty gravel in lukewarm water. He ate what little he could manage, enough to quell the groans of his stomach, then pushed the rest aside and looked around the room again, searching for his missing friends, but he still couldn't see them anywhere. "Please," he asked the others, "my friends were taken to Room Thirteen, but I can't see them. Where's table thirteen?"

"There's no table thirteen," Gilda Buttons said. "So your friends are in there, with *them*? The freaks?"

"You mean the hybrids?" Robert said.

"Everyone eats in the canteen except those half-and-halfs," Bruno Buttons explained, ignoring Robert's correction. "You've seen them in the show—they're different. The skills they have are built into them, not learned, like with us."

"Yeah." Silva nodded. "They could get away easily with their freakish abilities. That's why Madame and Slimwood keep them under lock and key at all times."

It was disturbing the way the Buttons spoke about the hybrids, almost as if they'd been brainwashed by Slimwood into thinking they weren't truly human. Robert wondered if he should defend the hybrids, but then thought it best not to rock the boat. He needed their help after all. Nevertheless, he wondered if there was anything he could say to get them to change their minds…

"Usually, they avoid snatching people during the show," Gilda was saying, "because it draws attention to them and can be traced back easily, but in the case of your friend they seem to have broken their own rules." She glanced at Madame and Slimwood, sitting at the head table at the end of the room. They were eating green beans and roast beef and looked like they were enjoying themselves far more than everyone else with their sloup. "She must be some sort of special freak for them to do something as risky as that."

Robert felt queasy. Gilda was right—Lily was special—but so were the other hybrids, and being different wasn't bad.

"I have to get her out of here," he told them. "Malkin too. And I'll need your help to do it."

Silva laughed. "Not a chance. There's no escaping Slimwood's, believe me. We tried. Twice."

"Once on horseback," Dimitri added. "But the Lunk beat my horses at full pelt. He watches everything. Reports back to Slimwood and Madame. They'll know if you try to do a bunk."

"And now we need to be careful," Bruno Buttons advised. "A third failed attempt could see us end up nailed to their wall."

"Surely they can't be watching constantly?" Robert asked. "What about at night?"

"At night, Slimwood and Madame lock us in our bunks," Silva said, "then the Lunk patrols the corridors to make sure nothing's going on."

"The only good thing," Dimitri said, "is he creaks so loud you hear him coming."

"Why does he creak so?" Robert asked.

Silva shrugged. "Too much metal. He's so big he can't oil his whole body in one go, like human strongmen. So his parts go rusty, and every move he makes sounds like fingers being scraped down a blackboard."

"Don't speak so loud," Gilda Buttons admonished quietly. "He'll hear us. Even when we're permitted outside the gondola for work or a show, he's always watching. And we're *never* let out of the compound itself. Try to skip away if you like, flattie, but you don't stand a chance."

Robert wasn't so sure about the Buttons' and Dimitri's pessimism. After all, he was the grandson of the world-famous escapologist, Jack Door. A man who, though thoroughly unpleasant, had broken out of Pentonville Prison—England's toughest jail. Robert had seen a few of Jack's tricks up close and learned from them. And he reckoned if anyone could pull off a great escape from the Skycircus then he, Robert Townsend, would be the one to do it. And he had to. For Lily.

"What if everyone worked together?" he suggested. "Circus folk and the frea— I mean, hybrids? Couldn't you escape then? Surely with their talents…"

Bruno Buttons shook his head. "We don't talk with them. They don't talk with us."

"Why not?"

"Well, for one thing, Madame and Slimwood don't allow it. And for another…How can I put this…?" He leaned in closer, until Robert could see every hair in

192

his neatly trimmed moustache. "They're *odd*. More like mechanicals than humans. No, I think you'll find it's every man for himself in here, flattie, and that's the way it has to be."

Robert was certain he was wrong. Maybe if he spoke to the hybrids, or to Lily, he could find a way to get everyone working together, then perhaps, somehow, they'd stand a chance...

It felt like the beginnings of a plan, but he needed to give it more thought and concentrate on making it happen. And if that didn't work, he hoped John would be here soon to rescue them.

His stomach rumbled, but he quelled it with thoughts of Lily. Hopefully she was getting something to eat in Room Thirteen that was more appetizing than his sloup.

Lunch had been some sort of disgusting gruel on tin plates handed through the hatch in the door. The others had polished off their portions pretty quickly; only Lily's lingered on her plate. She'd refused to finish it after Malkin had said it looked like cold cat sick. Now she slumped back in the rickety chair and hugged him for support, balancing him on her lap. His brush tickled her face, and she folded the tiger-striped scarf around them both. "I've something to tell you all," she said at last.

Deedee, Luca, and Angelique gathered expectantly on the far side of the table. Luca rested his hands on its surface. Deedee fidgeted from side to side, stretching out her long legs. Angelique leaned on her cane, her wings open and draped behind her like a feather overcoat. All three waited for Lily to speak.

Lily pursed her lips together. "There's something different about me," she said. "Different from people outside this room." The words felt sharp and scary, but she wasn't stopping, she knew what came next.

"I'm a hybrid. I have a Cogheart—a heart made of clockwork."

She paused and looked at the others for their reactions.

It was a relief to find that the news didn't seem to surprise them. In fact, their faces had become more friendly.

And so, feeling a little easier in herself, Lily decided to tell the rest of her tale. She told them how Papa had given her the Cogheart to save her life when she'd almost died. That the heart was a perpetual motion machine which meant she might live forever. That an evil man called Professor Silverfish had tried to steal it, even enlisting the help of Madame when she'd been Papa's housekeeper, and how, when Lily had met Robert under those terrible circumstances, he'd saved her life, and she his.

"I, of course, have saved both of them many times during their adventures," Malkin added, poking his snout from beneath the end of the scarf, not to be left out.

"So now Madame has come back for me," Lily said finally. "Partly for revenge, and partly…" She shrugged her shoulders. "Well, the thing is, I'd rather not wait to find out what the other part is. Me, Robert, and Malkin need to break out of here as soon as possible, and we'll need your help to make it happen."

"We'll try our best," Luca said. "But an escape won't be easy—this place is on permanent lockdown. Most people only leave in a wooden box."

"Do you think the other circus performers would help?" Lily asked.

"No," Deedee said.

"They don't care for hybrids," Angelique explained. "They'd betray us, like all humans. To them we're nothing but freaks. But that's all right. We don't accept them; they don't accept us. That's the way it's always been, and that's the way it always will be. You don't need their lies, Lily. If we help get you out, it will have to be us and only us who go."

"And Robert," Lily said. "We can't leave him behind. He might be in terrible trouble."

That thought made her feel queasy. But now that she had persuaded the hybrids to help her, she felt better about their chance of escape. It was time to take a proper look around.

She stood and checked the room for any weak points, knocking on the walls and panels. They each sounded disconcertingly solid. She glanced over at the door.

"It's six inches of steel," Angelique said, as if she could predict exactly what Lily was thinking. "Kept locked at all times. They open this hatch to bring us food, but otherwise it's bolted shut from the outside."

"You must be let out sometimes," Malkin said.

"Only to wash in the bathroom and empty the bedpan," Deedee said, pointing at the tin bucket in the corner.

"Eww," Malkin said.

"Rehearsals too," Luca added. "But we're watched by Madame and Slimwood during those. And the Lunk guards us during the evening performance on show days."

"Then we're locked back in here afterward," Angelique explained. "And it starts all over again the next morning."

"Unless it's a move-and-set-up day, like today," Luca added. "In which case we're banged up for twenty-four hours."

"They treat you worse than animals," Lily said. She approached the thick metal door. Something about it had caught her eye and given her the tiniest glimmer of hope.

It was the hinges for the hatch. They were on the inside. She peered at them closer. The two halves of each hinge were set wider apart than usual, so that between the knuckles, you could see the pin that held them together. The pin was made of wire, and she guessed it was no thicker than a nail.

She tapped it with a finger. "Do you think you could cut through this, Luca?"

Luca came over. "Clanking clockwork! I've never noticed that before!" He peered closely at the hinges. "Sometimes the solution's right under your nose."

"You still won't be able to open the hatch," Deedee said. "It's locked with bolts on the other side of the door."

"When you cut the hinges it'll pivot from the bolts in the middle," Lily explained. "Then I can stick my hand through, undo them, and pull the whole hatch away, so I can get at the lock outside."

"Genius!" Luca smiled. "Why did we never see it?"

"Perhaps you haven't read enough penny dreadfuls?" Malkin suggested as Luca carefully used his claws to snip the pins in the hinges of the hatch.

The flap opened, pivoting around the bolts as Lily had said it would.

Lily put her hand through the gap, undoing each bolt before the entire hatch came away. She pulled it into the cell, leaving a hole in the center of the door about twice the size of a letter box. Then she took one of the hairpins from her head, straightened it between her teeth, and thrust her hand through the gap.

She turned her wrists until her fingers found the keyhole and thrust the hairpin into it, jiggling it about. The lock didn't shift. There was no give in it. She tried again, but she could feel the hairpin bending. It was about to snap.

She couldn't let that happen, or someone would know what they were up to. She pulled the hairpin out and drew her hand back through the gap.

"It's no use," she said. "I can't open it without the lockpicks."

"Do you want me to go get them from Robert?" Malkin suggested, nodding at the hole in the door. "I can probably fit through there."

Lily smiled. "Now why didn't I think of that?"

"Because you always want to do everything yourself," Malkin replied.

"We'll have to put the hatch back when he's gone," Luca said. "In case someone comes to check on us while we're waiting."

"I'll scratch the bottom of the door with my claws," Malkin said, "so you know to open it and let me back in."

Lily nodded. Then she picked up Malkin and kissed him on the top of the head. "Be safe," she said, and she stuffed him through the gap.

"Don't push so hard! " he cried softly as his fur rucked up against its sides. "I'm not the Royal Mail!" But he just about fit through, and he landed on all fours on the outside, light as a cat.

Lily watched him through the gap. She caught one last glimpse of his red brush as he squeezed through the bars of the padlocked gate and slipped into the shadows along the far side of the corridor.

When he was gone, she slotted the hatch back into place and threw the bolts back across, thcn shc and Luca closed it and replaced the snipped hinges as best they could so no one would be able to tell it had been tampered with.

Lily took a deep breath and tried to relax. It might be a long wait. She hoped Malkin would be all right sneaking around the sky-ship on his own. He'd have to keep as quite as a mouse—quieter than the dead one he'd brought her—if he didn't want to get caught. She crossed her fingers and silently wished him luck.

CHAPTER 14

That afternoon, Robert and the rest of the circus crew returned to the hard work of raising the Big Top. A crisp wind blew across the site. Over the top of the spiked fence and gate, Robert could make out the crowns of the trees in the Bois de Boulogne. The glimpse of their crinkled leaves shaking somehow gave him hope as he fell into line with Silva and Dimitri and the rest of the crew, who were hauling on pulleys to raise the canvas roof.

The red-and-white striped canvas undulated in the breeze, pulling him and everyone else from side to side as if it were engaged in a monstrous tug-of-war against them.

"Keep the line taut," Silva warned Robert, leaning into him as the rope ran through his fingers. The roustabouts to each side of him kept giving him horrible disapproving glances. "If our side doesn't raise straight, there'll be trouble."

Robert gripped the rope tighter, yanking it length by length along with Silva, until his knuckles whitened and the fibers burned sharp against his fingers, and it felt as if all the energy had been sucked from his body.

Finally the roof was raised.

"TIE HER OFF!" Slimwood shouted from the far side of the tent, and everyone rushed to knot their length of guy rope onto the nearest stake.

After that there were side poles to add beneath the floating roof, more guy ropes to tighten, and the long strips of walling that had to be sewn together and wrapped around the sides of the tent. Robert looked for the section of canvas he'd cut through yesterday with his knife, but he couldn't see it. Someone had repaired it already.

As he followed Dimitri and Silva around learning each job, he made sure to glance about for Lily and Malkin. But there was no sign of them or any of the other hybrids from Room Thirteen. Other times, he checked to see if the cargo-bay door was open, so he could find his clothes and things. It never was. And he was unsure what he could do about either of those problems without using up his last chance and bringing more trouble down on himself.

The final job of the day, once the tent was up, was adding the banners and bunting to decorate it. While everyone was busy with this, the gates in the fence opened and a long black steam-wagon pulled through and parked just a few feet from the edge of the tent where Robert was standing.

Joey, in a scruffy suit, jumped down from the steering compartment and closed and locked the gates behind him as Auggie ran around the edge of the tent to meet him.

"Where d'you get that weam-stagon?" Auggie called.

Joey said something indistinguishable in reply. Robert stopped what he was doing, looked around to check he wasn't being watched, and stole a little closer to them so he could overhear the rest of what they were saying. While he listened, he kept behind the curve of the tent wall, out of their sight line.

Auggie was pointing at the steam-wagon. "It looks like a hearse."

"It is," Joey said. "Madame's bought some new device for the evening show on Sunday. To put Miss Hartman in—or Miss Valentine, I should say! They've added her to the posters. Made her look quite pretty. They're arriving later, and we're to go into Paris to plaster 'em around the city."

"Pore mointless errands!" Auggie complained. "And what's dis thevice?" he asked. "I mean, what's this device?"

"I'm not a boffin," Joey said. "But I think it's some kind of electric coffin."

Robert tensed, his pulse throbbing in his chest. He had to keep his head. He tried hard not to let this news fester and listened instead to the rest of what was being discussed.

"The doctor who's making it is not quite done." Joey slapped the roof of the parked steam-hearse. "But we're to collect it tomorrow in this, and Madame will come."

So that was their scheme! They were going to put Lily in some coffin-machine and display her in their show. On Sunday night—which was only two days away! He needed to tell her as soon as possible. Their escape plan had to be ready to go before those two days were out. Otherwise, whatever terrible fate Slimwood and Verdigris had lined up for Lily might come to pass, and that didn't bear thinking about.

Robert crept back to Dimitri and Silva, who were hooking up the last roll of bunting.

"There," Dimitri said, tying it off. "Done and dusted."

The light was fading fast. The whistle blew for dinner.

As they lined up with the rest of the crew to go in for the night, Robert told Silva and Dimitri what he'd overheard the clowns saying.

"It doesn't sound good for your friend!" Silva said softly.

"We have to get a message to her right now!" Robert wiped his clammy hands on his work clothes. The line had started to shuffle in through the side door of the sky-ship. "We can sneak off when we go inside."

Silva shook her head. "They'll see us, and you've only one strike left. Besides you won't be able to get to their door—there's a padlocked gate in the way."

The first of the circus folk had reached the door hatch and were being counted into the gondola by Slimwood, who ticked them off on a numbered list.

Soon they were at the front of the line and bundled inside along with everyone else, up the stairs to the mess hall, and it was too late to come up with any kind of plan.

At dinner, Robert sat at table six with Dimitri and the Buttons once again. The meal was more gruel. He could barely keep it down. He kept coming back to the mysterious fate that awaited Lily in the show in two days' time. He needed to get a message to her about it as soon as possible, and he'd no idea how.

Just as Robert was thinking this, a red shape streaked from the shadows of the doorway to under their table, and a moment later a snouty face appeared between his legs. "Malkin!" Robert whispered in delight, his heart soaring with relief at the sight of his old friend. He tried not to make it obvious to those around him that he was looking down. He threw a quick glance at them, but they were too busy chatting amongst themselves.

Only Silva noticed. "Who are you talking to?" she asked.

"No one," Robert blustered, but she had felt the fox brush against her leg under the table, and when she peered down, she saw him. If she was shocked to spy a talking fox under the dinner table it didn't show in her poker face. "Don't worry," she said, "I'll keep your secret, just raise your head like you're talking to me, then no one will notice."

Robert nodded. With his eyes on Silva, he tried to converse with Malkin under the table, aiming his words down. It was more difficult than it looked.

"How did you get out?" he asked the fox softly.

"Lily managed to open a hatch in the door of Room

Thirteen," Malkin explained.

"How is Lily?" Robert asked through the side of his mouth.

"Moaning about everything, as usual."

Robert was relieved to hear one of the fox's barbed comments for once. He couldn't resist a peek at him. Malkin's toothy smile widened into a lopsided grin.

"Look at me," Silva told him again. "You need to be quick now."

She was right. The Lunk was patrolling the room, and at any moment he might register what was going on. In whispered murmurs, Robert told Malkin about the conversation he'd overheard between Auggie and Joey, and how Madame was planning to put Lily into some sort of coffin-like machine that had been made by a doctor and was being delivered tomorrow night.

"That doesn't give us much time," Malkin said in a hushed voice. "We have to try and get out tonight. Lily needs the lockpicks. You'll have to give them to me."

Robert gave a dry gulp at the back of his throat. "I can't. They're lost."

"What?" That one word was shaded with disappointment. "Did Slimwood take them?" Malkin asked.

"No." Robert bit his lip. "They're in my other clothes

in a laundry bag in the cargo bay."

"Then I can get them," Malkin said.

Robert shook his head. "You won't be able to. They locked all the doors for the night when they brought everyone in from putting up the tent."

"Oh." Malkin's whiskers drooped in despair.

"But don't worry," Robert added. "I'll get the picks back tomorrow. Silva and Dimitri will help me."

Silva nodded. "Tell Lily we'll find them for her," she said.

"When? How?" Malkin asked.

"We don't know yet," Robert said. "But we'll think of something."

Everyone had finished eating by this time, and a whistle rang out.

"You'd better run," Silva whispered to the fox, "before the Lunk starts taking people to the cell corridor and you won't be able to get back."

"Good luck," Robert muttered. He watched as Malkin disappeared under the table and sneaked out of the mess hall while no one was looking. He hoped the mech-fox would get back to Room Thirteen okay. He imagined Lily would be disappointed when she got his message and no lockpicks. He'd need to get them for her tomorrow, because time was running out. He wondered if Tolly had got back home to John and explained what had happened to them. But there wouldn't be time to wait for rescue now—not since things had begun to move so fast. No, he, Lily, and Malkin would have to escape from this place by tomorrow night, and that wasn't going to be easy, even if he managed to recover the lockpicks.

When he looked up again, he saw that theirs was the last table of circus folk left in the room. There were solely roustabouts in the canteen now. They all leered at him. And it was only then that he realized he'd no idea where he was going to sleep.

"Don't let them put me in with anyone bad," he mumbled to Silva and Dimitri.

"That's all right," Silva said. "You can come with us; we have space in cabin six. When the Lunk comes to get us, just follow along."

Robert felt relieved to have found a friendly family in this horrible place. It made him remember his ma and sister, who'd given him the Moonlocket that Slimwood had taken. They were show people too, and just like the Buttons, they were kind folk who had become lost in a bad place for a while.

The Lunk had returned to collect them. Robert did as Silva suggested, standing up with the Button family and Dimitri, and losing himself in the middle of the group as they were marched from the mess hall.

Robert tried hard to remember the way as the Lunk led the family down the stairwell and along a passage of cabins to somewhere deep within the sky-ship.

Finally the mechanical man opened Room Six, and the Buttons and Dimitri stepped inside. Robert was the last in and with a *CLUUUNNnnkk!* the Lunk slammed the door behind him and locked it.

As soon as he was gone, the Buttons busied themselves getting ready for bed.

There were only four berths in the room, and each one was taken already, but Dimitri went to a trunk in the corner and pulled out a hammock for Robert, and the rest of the family helped him string it across the center of the cabin.

When they were finished, he climbed up into the hammock and settled himself on his back. Its dusty sides gathered in around him, holding him tight in its grip. Every time he shifted, it would rock back and forth ever so slightly. It felt strange, but not uncomfortable, like being the pendulum of a clock or lying in a cradle floating on the ocean.

He listened to the sleep sounds the Buttons made— Bruno Buttons's snores and Gilda Buttons's wheezing— and wondered if Lily had found a proper bed with a proper pillow. Most of all he hoped Malkin would get his message to her. Tomorrow, he, Robert, would find the lockpicks and the three of them would make a plan to get out of this terrible place before it was too late. He'd need his wits about him for that, so he should probably try to get some rest. He closed his eyes, and his breathing softened as he gradually drifted off into strange and troubled dreams.

CHAPTER 15

In the dark narrow confines of her bunk in Room Thirteen, Lily had spent an uncomfortable night wide awake. Her scarf was wound round her neck, and Malkin was wound down around her feet. But her thoughts itched and so did her scars as she thought of all she'd learned that evening while she and the hybrids had waited anxiously for the fox's return.

It had been an uncomfortable few hours, hoping upon hope that Malkin would not get caught and would eventually make it back. So, partly to pass the time, partly to assuage their nerves, and mostly because Lily had given them her story, each of the hybrids had told Lily the terrible tale of their past.

Luca had gone first. His parents had died when he was thirteen, and he'd lost his hands in an accident working in a factory. After that he was sent to a children's home in Manchester where he never went out or spoke to anyone. Then, one day, a doctor came and spirited him away, brought him to Paris, and made his iron claws… That doctor had turned out to be Droz. Lily had shuddered to hear the name again, and Luca had trailed off after that, as if he didn't want to relive the rest of what had happened to him. Finally he'd finished with, "After it was all over I was sold to the circus."

Deedee spoke next, telling of how she was born in a painted wagon to a family of wire-walking show people. She had no legs from birth, and when her folks realized that she mightn't be able to carry on their profession, they were distraught. "They didn't want me to end up in a freakshow in some down-at-heel carnival, gawked at by penny punters," she explained. "But the midwife who delivered me had heard tell of a place in Paris where I might be able to walk with the aid of mechanical prosthetics. The doctor there would pay to use me in experiments. They said it would make me 'better.'" The rest, she didn't want to talk about. Except to say that her parents had died in a circus accident and she'd never gotten to go home. "Eventually," she said, "I too was sold to the Skycircus." Then she had put her head in her hands and sobbed.

Lily shuddered at the thought of the terrible things that had happened to her.

Finally it had been Angelique's turn. She'd leaned back on her bunk and slowly folded her arms around her knees, wrapping her wings around her body to block herself off from the others.

She'd told how her father had been an airman from Freetown in Sierra Leone on the coast of West Africa. "He always wanted to travel," she explained, "and one day he got a job as a cabin boy on a zep that was heading to England."

In London he had met Angelique's ma, who was a chambermaid in a fancy hotel, and they'd fallen in love and gotten married. They were overjoyed when Angelique's ma had fallen pregnant, but they didn't have much money, so her father had found a commission on another airship where he could earn enough for his growing family. He was a crewman on the Atlantic zep *Hawksmoth*, flying from London to Alaska, but on the maiden voyage they were lost in a storm, and he never returned. Angelique's mother had died in the Camden Workhouse years later, when Angelique was nine. She survived them both, but her bones were brittle. Hollow in the middle, lighter than air. She'd broken her leg twice while she lived in the workhouse, and when she was sixteen, Droz had found her in the attic there and brought her to Paris. Then the experiments lasted a year before Angelique got her wings and was sold to the circus.

"It took me many months in rehearsals to learn how to use these extra limbs," Angelique continued, picking at her feathers with frustration. Lily could see she found speaking about it uncomfortable. "It wasn't a natural process, becoming a bird—it wasn't engrained in my being, like with fledglings. I had to practice every day before I learned to glide and swoop. To fly strains every muscle in a body."

She shook her plumage angrily. "People were not meant to live like this, Lily. Airships and zeppelins are one thing, but flying humans should never have made their way into the world. To fly is a dream, but sometimes, when you achieve your dreams, you discover nothing can stop you from falling."

"I wish I'd never met Droz," Deedee said sadly when Angelique had finished.

"Me too," Angelique answered.

Lily had been about to say something then. To tell them of her mama's connection with Droz, when, at that moment Malkin had scrabbled at the base of the door.

They hurried to let him back in through the hatch, and he revealed the bad news. How Robert had lost the lockpicks and how the clowns were bringing Madame's coffin-machine tomorrow evening—whatever it was— and Lily was to be put into it for the show.

Thinking back on it now, Lily felt nauseous, not just for her own fate but because before she'd met Angelique, she'd never once considered that to have wings, or any of their adjustments, might be an unpleasant affliction. Yet the way Angelique spoke about them made them sound like a curse.

It was, Lily reflected, how she felt about her heart. Some days her scars ached and the heart felt so heavy it seemed as if it might fall through her ribcage. She had to will herself through those times and know that her heart was what kept her alive and brought her moments of joy too. Maybe Angelique had lost that sense of her wings. It had become tangled up in the terrible things that had happened to her.

She was glad, in that moment, that she hadn't told the whole truth. She'd left out the small fact that her mama had known Droz and that the doctor's interest was something to do with why Madame had taken her in the first place.

How would Angelique feel if she knew Lily's own

mother could have provided part of the research that helped make the wings that caused her so much pain? Would she still want to help Lily escape then? That question made Lily's chest tighten.

Angelique, Luca, and Deedee had lost so much; they'd been prisoners nearly all their lives. But now she had earned their trust, and she needed to honor it. Lily glanced at Malkin, who'd wound down at her feet, and thought of Robert locked up somewhere on the ship too. And she decided, no matter what, she was going to get them all out. She had no idea exactly what terrible fate Madame had planned for her with her machine, but Lily really couldn't afford to wait around and find out. She hoped that Robert could get the picks to her tomorrow. Even with them, escaping was still going to be tough, and she'd need the hybrids' help to get out.

She sat up and took the ripped pages of Mama's notebook from her pocket and flicked through them, squinting in the low electric light of the room in an attempt to read. She hoped she would find something to set her mind at rest and feel better, or that at least might aid her plans.

Saturday, 8th November 1884,
Riverside Walk, Chelsea

John's partner, Professor Simon Silverfish, has visited us a number of times in the last month to discuss business. I have been telling him about my studies into hybrids when I was at college, brought about by my interest in Lovelace's Flyology and the idea of creating someone with wings. He seems remarkably interested. He says it's something he would like the company to work on. A second division, separate to the building of mechanicals, that would create hybrid machines that could be implanted or attached to people.

John disapproves of this work, I can tell, but says nothing.

I suggested to the professor that he might contact my old college tutor, Dr. Droz, who is an expert in such matters.

Droz again. With a heavy heart, Lily read on. On the second of the ripped pages she had grabbed, almost five years had passed. She would've been nearly six years old at the time it was written, and soon after she'd turned six, Mama had died.

Saturday, 1st June 1889,
Riverside Walk, Chelsea

It was a beautiful afternoon. Lily and I spent the best

part of it outdoors on the terrace, at the far end of the garden.

There is a good deal of shade there beneath the topiary hedges and also a darling folly—a summer house, with a secret passage running beneath it that leads back up to the main house. At the far end of the terrace, a weeping willow masks an iron gate that opens out onto a pier on the River Thames.

Lily and I were sitting in deck chairs on the terrace around midafternoon when Professor Silverfish and Dr. Droz paid an unannounced visit.

Lily's heart stopped in her mouth. She hadn't realized she'd met Droz herself. She tried hard to picture his face in her mind's eye, but could not. The most she could come up with was a gray cloud of hair. Then again, she had, she supposed, only been five. She searched the rest of Mama's entry for more information, but there was nothing else about him…

Mrs. Rust—one of the new mechanical servants John has been constructing—brought us tea on the lawn. She was about to pour the tea when she started shaking awfully, as if she was having a terrible fit. It seems it was some kind of malfunction of the cogs in her primary motor cortex, but Dr. Droz showed me how to turn her off with her winding key by setting it in her keyhole and turning it sharply anticlockwise, then opened her head and adjusted the cogs. When we subsequently rewound her and started her up again, she was perfectly fine.

I told the professor and Droz that perhaps theirs and John's mechanicals needed some additional work before the Hartman-Silverfish Company attempts to market them commercially, and this caused much amusement.

Lily seems to love Mrs. Rust as much as she does me and John. She's a remarkable child and treats these new mechanicals quite as if they were human.

Lily finished reading and squeezed her eyes shut. Tears flooded out, and she brushed them away with the end of her scarf. She'd missed Rusty since she'd been here.

And there was so much else to consider. It wasn't true what the hybrids said about regular people—they weren't all nasty, and they wouldn't all betray you. Mama had wanted to make hybrids because she thought it was a good thing. It was Droz and Silverfish who'd had bad motives that benefited themselves.

Lily knew she'd have to prove that to the hybrids if she was to persuade them to go through with her plan tomorrow night and come with her when they escaped.

She tried to settle herself, but she couldn't quite keep

still. Her mind was still whirring with the new things she'd learned. She took out the next ripped page from Mama and read on:

This morning we went fossil-hunting on the beach at Church Cliffs. It was quite windy. John had his walking cane with him and used it to point out some landmarks at sea. Rows of iron prison ships and a tall spider platform where they are drilling for oil and gas.

Along the tideline of the bay I discovered a promising-looking stone submerged in the sand. I managed to break it open with my rock hammer and wash the two halves in the sea. Lily had been playing in the breakers nearby, but she ran up to me and asked what I had found.

"A fossil," I said, giving her the stone.

Lily took the two halves from me and pulled them apart. When she saw the golden petrified ammonite within the stone, her eyes widened and she smiled.

"The secret's at the heart of it," she said.

At nearly six years old she already has the most amazing mind—sharp as a fox and flighty as a raven. She wants—no, needs—to discover the truth behind everything. It compels her.

She takes that stone everywhere with her and will not put it down. She's continually asking me about it, probing for answers. I hope she remains as inquisitive always—one can achieve so much with attention, go so far.

One day I intend to tell her about the Flyology project.

Lily could remember that afternoon at the beach vividly. In the past, she'd dreamed about it often, and she still had Mama's stone on her bedside table. She hoped she was still asking all the questions of others that she had asked of Mama back then. Mama had always told her the truth. At least, when she could. And she too wanted to be honest, but would the other hybrids trust her once they knew her mama had been involved with their hated creator? And would they still want to come with her once she and Robert got the lockpicks back?

It was all too much to think about. For now, there was only one thing left to do: sleep.

CHAPTER 16

Robert opened his eyes. He felt disheveled and groggy from sleeping in his work clothes. Every muscle in his body ached from helping to set the site yesterday. His stomach rumbled loudly from lack of proper food, but he chose to ignore it and thought of Lily and Malkin instead. He needed to get the lockpicks to them as soon as possible. Otherwise there was no chance of a breakout tonight.

Morning light tumbled in through the small porthole window. He sat up in his hammock and stared out through the streaked glass. From the height of the sun in the sky he guessed the hour to be around six in the morning.

He still had a whole day to set things right.

PRRIIIPP! PRRIIIPP! PRRIIIPP!

Three short blasts of the whistle sounded in the hallway outside.

Then there was a clank of bolts being pulled back, and the door swung outward. The Lunk loomed in the passageway, his big mechanical body filling the entire opening. He stood there silent and watching, his face expressionless, his headlamp eyes dead. His head turned from side to side, taking in Robert and the Buttons as if they were a puzzling new species of ant he'd just come across.

Eventually the iron man raised his arm, beckoned them out of the cell, and escorted them to the washroom, where they scrubbed themselves at long water troughs, and then on to the mess hall, where they each took a metal plate, cutlery, and a tin can and lined up with the rest of the performers and roustabouts.

Breakfast turned out to be an anemic-looking roll and a cup of gray cocoa. The only thing that broke the silence was the horrible sound of multiple jaws crunching on stale bread and multiple lips slurping the watery granules.

Afterward, the rest of the circus crew were given buckets and mops from the equipment store in the hull and set to work by the roustabouts, cleaning the ship. Silva and Dimitri managed to wangle Robert onto the laundry detail outside instead.

The weather was finer than yesterday. Under the watchful eyes of Auggie and Joey, they took a laundry basket from the cargo bay and set it up on the grass. Then they rolled out three large wooden tubs, a washboard, and a wooden dolly for agitating the clothes, plus an enormous copper pot for boiling up water. Every trip to the cargo bay wasted a little more time, and the hours of the morning were quickly ticking away.

The Lunk, who seemed to be the only one allowed outside the fence, brought wood for the fire.

Silva showed Robert how to fill the tubs with buckets of cold water, which they drew from the hand pump in the center of the site. When the fire was lit they set the copper on it and filled that with more water and soap, soda, and lye. As they tipped out all the laundry onto the ground and emptied each bag in turn, Robert's guts twisted with hope that the next one might contain his things.

But none did.

"Where are my clothes?" he whispered to the others.

"They might be in another basket," Silva said. "Some of them aren't due for washing today."

"Don't worry," Dimitri said quietly. "When they're not watching, I'll sneak into the cargo bay and check."

But the Lunk and the clowns were never not watching.

To pass the time and avoid suspicion, Robert, Silva, and Dimitri chatted casually as they worked.

"How did Madame come to be here?" Robert asked, picking out a bright-red uniform with shiny brass buttons from the pile of clothes.

"Nobody quite knows," Silva replied, shaking out a checked suit that looked like it belonged to a giant. "I think she met Slimwood Junior nine months ago—the last time the Skycircus was in Paris."

"At the time they were looking for acts for the new season," Dimitri explained as he sorted through a big pile of handkerchiefs, throwing the spotted ones into a pile of colorful clothes and the white ones in with the shirts. "Madame must've bought a fake beard and made up that stupid stage name and somehow landed a part in the show."

"Then old Mr. Slimwood upped and died." Silva glanced up at his juggling clubs hanging with the other mementos on the wall of the sky-ship and dumped a pile of clothes in Robert's arms. Robert found himself holding a handful of stockings, ladies' bloomers, and frilly drawers. The wrinkled, pleated, frilly, and ruched shapes made him blush.

"Some of us reckon the pair of them might've poisoned him." Dimitri stuffed a handful of soiled clothes in the big copper pot to boil-wash them and picked up a bar of lye soap and began lathering it up in the hot water. Silva did the same. Robert copied them, then they took turns dragging items up and down the washboard. Sequins flew off everywhere, popping in all directions. Robert thought of Mrs. Rust, who had to do this every day. No wonder her arms were so rusty—though at least she wouldn't have rubbed-raw skin like his.

Eventually, after they had been talking and washing clothes for one whole drudge-filled hour, the clowns and the Lunk had stopped paying them much attention.

Silva tapped Dimitri on the shoulder, and he slipped off and snuck into the hold, returning moments later with one extra bag.

Robert pulled it open and saw with relief that all his clothes were still inside, along with his cap and Da's coat, its pockets filled with the leather pouch of lockpicks, his penknife, the stub of a pencil, and the chocolate wrappers. Robert transferred everything quickly to the pockets of his new clothes, then stuffed the coat and cap back into the bag and hid it under a pile of dirty laundry for the time being.

"I have to get these picks to Lily," he said.

"She'll probably be in the Big Top with the other hybrids later," Silva replied. "You can try and hand them over to her during the crossover between the hybrids' and humans' rehearsals. We have to go anyway, so we'll help you if we can."

They finished scrubbing the washing and rinsed it out. There was no mangle, so they just wrung each piece out by hand and pinned it wet to the washing line that stretched across the site. The clothes flopped heavily like dead bodies, drying slowly in the sun.

While Dimitri turned the buckets and copper over to dry out, Robert and Silva gathered up the empty laundry bags. Robert hid his bag of clothes among them and hoped that no one would notice before he found somewhere else to conceal it. He didn't like to think what would happen to him if anyone discovered that he'd stolen it back, let alone that he was plotting an escape—something terrible, probably. It would be strike number three, and no one survived three strikes.

"INSPECTION TIME!" a voice shouted outside Room Thirteen.

Lily sat upright in bed. She felt woozy and disoriented.

She shouldn't have stayed awake so late reading and thinking.

Luca, Deedee, and Angelique were already up, their clockwork limbs jittering and Angelique's wings aflutter as they busily folded their covers into neat squares to make their bunk beds.

"Get up quick!" Angelique hissed at Lily.

Lily slipped on her red dress over her petticoat. With no time even to make her bed or to wind Malkin, she scrambled from her bunk.

There was a clank of bolts being pulled back, and the door swung inward, hammering on the wall. Lily waited with bated breath as the hatch on the door shook. She hoped their temporary fix wouldn't give and reveal what they'd been up to. If the hatch fell out now, her escape plan would be discovered.

Her heart pounded fearfully against her ribs.

Luckily, though it rattled a little, the hatch stayed in place.

Slimwood paraded in, carrying his whip. "SURPRISE INSPECTION!" he shouted. "Nobody eats until I've checked this room."

Auggie waited in the doorway, carrying a tray with a metal tureen of gruel and four plates.

"What do we do now?" Lily whispered to Luca.

"QUIET!" Slimwood shouted at her. "No speaking unless you're spoken to! That's one strike on your copybook."

He brought the handle end of his whip down with a crash on Lily's back; it smarted as hard as a balled, metal fist and made Lily cower like a frightened animal.

Slimwood strolled slowly around the room, poking at each mattress with it.

Finally he searched under the pillows and found the pages from the red notebook. "Ah," he cried snatching them up, "what are these?"

"Please," Lily said. "They're my mama's pages. Madame said I could keep them."

Slimwood glanced at the rumpled papers and shrugged. "Fair enough, but it's another strike on your record." He let them drop to the floor and stepped over them as they scattered at everyone's feet. "You're clean, freaks. Inspection passed. Bring 'em their bucket of breakfast, but dock one portion for the new girl's infractions."

Auggie placed the tray on the table, and as the pair of them left, slamming the door behind them, Lily rushed over and put her hand over the hatch, just in case it might fall.

When she turned back into the room, she saw that Angelique and the others were busy picking up her papers.

"You didn't mention these yesterday," Angelique said angrily.

"That's because they're private." Lily's brain was still woozy, but the look of betrayal on Angelique's face made a sudden flush of guilt pulse through her.

"Droz," Angelique said, gathering the papers up from the other two, her fists scrunching around their edges. "I can see that evil doctor's name on every page." She took a deep breath, but it did nothing to quench the anger in her eyes, and Lily felt instantly afraid, more afraid than she had been of Slimwood. At least she'd faced him with the others on her side—now she was suddenly on her own. She didn't even have Malkin because there had been no time to wind him.

Angelique was reading from one of the pages, her voice rising and falling with agitation as she narrated the entry at the front of the pile.

Tuesday, 3rd September 1889,
Riverside Walk, Chelsea

Today I visited John at his new offices. I brought my daughter, Lily, with me, and we dropped in on Professor Silverfish and Dr. Droz in their laboratory.

I'm so overjoyed with what they said that I will record it directly.

"My dear Grace," the professor told me, "we miss you at the factory."

"We need your insight and incisiveness," Dr. Droz added. "I cannot do my work without you. We want to develop the Flyology project further and begin work on our other hybrid ideas."

"What progress have you made?" I asked them.

"We're finally able to get human bodies to accept our designs on a cellular level," the good doctor replied.

"And what has the guild to say about that?" I asked. "Is it a worthy idea?"

"Why, what do you mean?" Dr. Droz said. "What have you heard?"

"John has told me the Mechanists' Guild don't approve of hybrid experiments. He warned me that they'd disbar anyone involved in them."

"But, Grace," Droz said, "these developments are a good thing. They'll help us cure illness and disease."

"Agreed," Simon said. "All of us, at some time or another, may be in need of hybrid technology." He winced and momentarily clutched his chest as if something was amiss, but then was all smiles once more.

Considering it now, I can't help but feel that both their sentiments about these new hybrid devices are right.

Angelique stopped reading. "That doctor destroyed my life. Deedee's and Luca's too." She paced back and forth across the floor of the cell, her knuckles white as she clasped her stick tightly, her wings twitching anxiously behind her. "And it seems your mama was a part of it."

"You lied to us!" Luca shouted angrily, snapping his claws together. His face had turned lobster red, and his eyes blazed venomously, so that he looked even more fearsome than he had in the show.

"We trusted you," Deedee said, her voice choked with emotion. "And you betrayed us. Even after we told you our stories, even then you wouldn't tell us the whole truth."

"Please," Lily begged, "I couldn't. I thought…" She paused, lost for words. "But that page, it means nothing. Mama wasn't like that; she was a good person. She never experimented on anyone. I didn't want to tell you because I knew you'd be upset. But that doesn't mean we can't be friends. Please," Lily pleaded, her eyes sharp with tears, her guts twisted up with guilt. "We have so much in common. I told you everything about myself—the truth of who I was—and I thought you three would understand."

Angelique shook her head. "You said you'd given us your whole story, Lily. But you lied—you'd left a part out. You're just another person who's betrayed and deceived us."

Lily's heart beat loudly against her ribs. She realized with horror that Angelique was right. Now she'd have to earn the winged girl's trust, and Luca and Deedee's, all over again. In the meantime, the escape was still supposed to happen tonight, but without their help, Lily didn't know if she would be able to manage it alone.

CHAPTER 17

The rest of the morning passed with the hybrids stewing in silent anger. Lily had wound Malkin and explained to him quietly what was going on, but he'd said little. He was tired from his previous night's excursion, and anyway, he counseled Lily, it was best to give the other children some time and space to calm down.

The fox had wanted to go out again on reconnaissance, but the hybrids had angrily insisted it was too dangerous. The Lunk was coming to fetch them for rehearsals later, and if he found Malkin missing, or if there was another snap inspection and the fox wasn't there, then there would be hell to pay.

The Lunk did indeed arrive that afternoon to fetch

Lily and the others from the cell. Malkin tried to go with them, but the mechanical man shoved him back violently and slammed the door on his scritching claws. And so Lily found herself alone in the company of three people who were not talking to her as the Lunk unlocked the gate outside Room Thirteen and escorted them along the labyrinthine passageways of the gondola.

When they descended the stairs and stepped through the exit hatch, Lily made sure to note what type of lock it was, knowing she would probably need to pick it later. She hoped Robert had managed to find her lockpicks.

It was cold outside in the field. Lily wound her scarf tightly around her. The other hybrids had changed from their gray prison clothes into show outfits from their trunk in the corner of the room, but she was still wearing her ragged and rumpled red dress. As the Lunk led them toward the Big Top, Lily tried to join Angelique at the back of the line, but the winged girl turned away and put her stick between them, so that Lily could come no closer.

The only time she smiled was at a flock of sparrows twittering around a puddle. Angelique pulled handfuls of breadcrumbs from her pocket and held them out to the birds, whistling softly to imitate their calls. Some of the sparrows flitted over to her and sat in her palm, pecking at the stale bread that Lily realized she must've saved from the breakfast tray.

Lily and the rest of the group skirted round the edge of the Big Top, passing a stitched scar. It was the hole Robert had cut in the tent the other evening, already sewn up.

The Lunk peeled back the flap of the artists' entrance and ushered everyone through.

Inside the tent, sunlight filtered through the striped canvas, throwing blocks of red and white across two makeup tables, a rail of costumes, stacks of props, and the big red curtains that separated "backstage" from the performance arena out front.

Lily followed the hybrids as they crossed the cluttered area and pushed aside the velvet curtains. The seats were already set up around the ring, and as she glimpsed the VIP area in the center of the front row, a horrible feeling came over Lily.

Little more than a day ago she'd sat there watching the show with Robert, Tolly, and Malkin. And tomorrow night she was destined to be a part of it, to be put in some terrible machine of Madame and Droz's devising. Unless she could escape…and she would need not only Robert's help for that—who she still hadn't seen today—but also the hybrids', and they weren't speaking to her.

She felt sick. How could this be happening? And she missed Papa. Why had he not come to rescue her? She wished she'd listened to Mrs. Rust and never left the house.

"You're all here, good." Slimwood stepped from behind one of the stands out into the center of the arena. "We'll start with five minutes' warm-up," he said to the hybrids. "Then you practice your routines. I want to see PERFECTION today! Tomorrow's show is Lily's debut." He gave her a gold-toothed leer. "And I want the rest of you to be at your VERY BEST to help make this new extravaganza our CROWNING GLORY!"

The hybrids spread out around the sawdust ring and began their warm-up exercises, Angelique opening out her wings and checking each feather, Deedee stretching her legs until the wires in them whirred, and Luca clacking his claws and shrugging his shoulders to try and ease his arms into movement. The Lunk stomped squeakily around the ring, observing them.

Lily didn't know what she ought to be doing, so she stood and watched the others, while also keeping her eye out for Robert in case he was nearby. A handful of roustabouts were wandering around the tent, and Lily looked for him amongst them. But he wasn't there.

Staring at the empty stands, she suddenly imagined what it might be like when they were full and all eyes were on her. She wondered what Slimwood and Madame had planned with their machine. What were they going to make her do? And how could she avoid it and get out of here, now that Angelique, Deedee, and Luca were no longer on her side?

Eventually, she looked up to see Madame had arrived. She and Slimwood were huddled in the middle of the ring, whispering to each other and throwing occasional glances her way.

Lily shuffled closer to them to try and hear what they were saying.

"*Zut alors!*" Madame muttered angrily. "Those clowns are so late with my machine. I wanted to try it out this morning."

Slimwood stroked her arm. "You'll just have to leave it for now, my dear."

"Never mind." Madame sighed and pushed his hand away. She strode over to Lily and grabbed her by the arm. "Enough of your eavesdropping," she said. "It's time we practiced your curtsy and found something for you to wear for your routine tomorrow night."

Madame dragged Lily across the ring; Lily's palms itched and her stomach flipped while she wondered what horrors they had in store for her. Time was running out, and Robert still hadn't arrived with her lockpicks.

A twinge of terror tore through Robert as he, Silva, and Dimitri stepped through the flap into the backstage area of the Big Top. Beneath the pile of freshly washed things they were bringing to hang up on the costume rail for the performers, Robert was smuggling in his own bag of clothes. His plan was to hide them among the outfits, where they might not be noticed, then he would collect them later during their escape attempt.

The makeup tables, costume rail, and a rack of props were set up in the center of the tent. While Dimitri and Silva hung up the clean washing, Robert pulled his clothes from the bag, found a free hanger, and hung them on it. He placed his da's coat over the suit and was just stuffing his cap in its coat pocket so that everything was in place to collect later during their escape, when he heard a noise coming from the arena.

Robert stuffed the laundry bag into a large polka-dot clown suit and sneaked over to peer through the velvet curtains.

In the ring, the hybrids were rehearsing. Slimwood was sitting in the front row of seats, barking orders.

"Look at that lot," Dimitri said. "They have it so bad. Worse than us. I know I'm not supposed to, but I do feel sorry for them."

Robert was relieved to hear it. Surely, he thought, if Dimitri and the others did have empathy for the plight of the hybrids, then there was some chance, however slim, that he could persuade them to work together and help each other get out.

His heart leaped to his throat as he caught sight of Lily. She was with Madame, and they were walking from the edge of the ring to its center. Robert couldn't help but think of that cold winter's day when they'd first met. Lily had been trapped by Madame back then too, in Brackenbridge Manor, and she had climbed out of her window to come and speak with him.

He'd missed her so much in the day they'd been apart, and now the anxiety that had scrunched up inside him in a tight ball since they'd parted began to loosen ever so slightly. Because here she was, right as rain, and looking much the same as she always did. And while he was in his new threadbare uniform, with mud around the edges, she was still wearing her bright birthday dress.

Madame seemed to be explaining how to bow and curtsy to the crowds. Robert wondered again what the woman had planned for Lily and what she'd done with Malkin, for he was nowhere to be seen. He felt for the wallet of lockpicks in his pocket. How was he to get them to Lily if Madame was training her one-on-one like this?

Robert was deciding whether to try and sneak a little closer to hear what Madame was saying, when Silva put a hand out to signal he should keep still.

Across the ring, Luca had fallen to the floor.

Slimwood strode over to him. "Get up!" he shouted, hitting Luca around the hips with his whip.

Luca shook his head and clacked his claws. Then, with a clenched jaw, he rose and continued with his rehearsal.

"See?" Silva sucked her teeth. "They'll beat you, but not on the arms or legs. They take care to do it where it won't be seen in the show."

It seemed that the hybrids' rehearsal time was over. Strange, because Lily hadn't actually rehearsed her act, and the machine the clowns had mentioned last night was nowhere to be seen. But before he could think more about this, the rest of the circus families began arriving in the Big Top, escorted in by the roustabouts. As Robert watched each performer find a free space in the arena and begin warming up, Madame and Lily left the ring.

"We have to join everyone else for rehearsals," Silva whispered. "If we're missing, there'll be trouble. But if you want to talk to Lily, you should hide in here and give her the lockpicks as she goes past."

Robert nodded. As Silva and Dimitri disappeared off into the arena, he concealed himself behind a costume rail and ducked down, crouching against the floor. His pulse echoed in his ears, and he wrapped his arms around his knees to stop his hands from shaking. This might be his one chance to get the picks to Lily.

Madame brought Lily backstage through the velvet curtains. Lily looked tense, her fists clenched at her sides and her shoulders stiff. Her face was pale, her eyes red and tired as if she'd been crying.

Madame took her over to the rack of costumes and began searching through them. Robert balled himself up tighter beneath the rail as she flicked through the clothes above him. Her black lace boots paced to and fro. Lily, still clad in her party shoes, stood stock still.

"*Bien*, we shall find something to fit you," Madame was saying as she perused the rail of spangly outfits.

She pulled out a green dress and held it up.

"*Non*, too big."

A frilly blue tutu.

"Too small."

A black sequined leotard.

"Too spangly."

Madame swished through costumes on the rail, getting closer to him. Robert's pulse was so loud in his ears he was surprised she couldn't hear it. Her perfume was making the back of his throat itch, and he sensed a sneeze coming. He pursed his lips together, trying to stifle it. Madame was only a few feet from him now. Lily trailed a step behind. This might be his only chance. He was determined to get the picks to her. He pulled the pouch from his pocket, then thought for a moment before taking out his pencil stub and a chocolate wrapper, which he wrote on:

Meet me at midnight. I'm with the Buttons in Room...

He turned the wrapper over and scrawled on the other side:

6

He folded the message and stuffed it behind the lockpicks. Then he closed the wallet and threw it gently across the floor so it landed at Lily's feet.

Lily saw the wallet and was about to bend down and pick it up when Madame pulled something off the rail.

"How about this?" Madame said. She had chosen a sparkly white dress. "We will sew a heart on the front." She held it up against Lily. "Yes, perfect. You must try it on."

"Now?" Lily kicked the wallet behind her back foot.

"*Oui, maintenant*. And don't talk back. Go behind the screen over there." She held out the dress. Lily went to take it, but dropped it.

"Oops. Butterfingers."

"You really are the most clumsy *jeune fille*."

"Sorry. I'll get it."

Robert gulped. Surely Madame would see the wallet when Lily picked the dress up?

Lily crouched down and gave him the briefest of smiles through the rack of clothes. A grin like a warm ray of sunshine.

Robert grinned back, relieved that she'd seen him.

When she stood back up, clasping the dress, the wallet was gone. She had it and would get his message.

All he needed to do now was wait for them to leave and then sneak out front, like he'd been with the others all along.

Lily stepped between him and Madame, holding the dress up so he wouldn't be spotted.

He shuffled farther behind the hanging rows of clothes in his hiding place to make sure he was out of view. But, as he did so, the itch in his nose grew, and the sneeze he'd been stifling came suddenly rushing out.

AAATCHOOOOOOOOOOOoooooooooooo!

Madame gave a blood-curdling scream, which was joined by the piercing blast of a whistle from the ring and before Robert even had time to take another breath, the Lunk had burst through the backstage curtains and collared him from behind the rail of clothes.

The Lunk dragged Robert to the center of the ring and threw him down in the dust.

Slimwood gave Robert's legs a swipe with his whip that smarted sharp as a stinging nettle. "What have you done, boy?" He prowled round Robert, crouched on the floor.

There was a laugh as Madame entered the arena, clasping Lily who had now changed into the spangly costume. "He was hiding in the dressing room. I'm sure he's been stealing," the ringmistress snapped.

"Empty your pockets," Slimwood shouted.

Robert tried to turn away, but Slimwood yanked him to his feet and rifled through his pockets. The penknife and pencil stub tumbled out into his palms.

"CONTRABAND!" Slimwood shouted. "That's your third black mark, boy. Now you will be punished."

Madame smirked at Lily, still holding her arm in a viselike grip. "I'm afraid your friend couldn't obey the rules, and we need to make it absolutely clear what happens to *perturbateurs* and troublemakers who don't toe the line."

She nodded to Slimwood, who shouted loudly, "BRING OUT THE BEAST WAGON!"

A shiver rippled through the crowd of circus folk, and

they whispered to one another. They knew exactly what that meant.

Lily glanced queasily at Robert. The color had drained from his face.

In a bevy of loud screeches and growls, the Lunk wheeled the animal cage into the center of the ring. The big cats and the bear inside were going crazy, throwing themselves against the bars as he brought it to a stop beneath the high wire. Slowly, he turned a ratchet on the side to open the top of the cage.

"NOW FOR THE PUNISHMENT!" Slimwood intoned.

Robert heard a hiss from his left and turned to see that Silva had sidled close to him. "If they put you in with the animals," she whispered, "throw your arms up in the air and blow raspberries at them as loud as you can. It's the only thing that scares them."

Robert nodded in a horrified daze.

"You will walk the wire," Madame smiled, "over the cage. And if you make it to the other side, then you'll have learned your lesson."

"But I can't!" Robert glanced at the wire. It cut through the dark heights of the Big Top as sharp and taut as the fear inside him. "I'm afraid of heights. What if I fall?" The wild beasts paced about beneath it. "I'll end up in there!"

"*Quelle tristesse!* How sad! But then you will no longer be our problem. I hear the lions have been quite ravenous of late."

"Please," Lily cried, "don't make him go up there alone."

But Madame ignored her plea.

Lily pulled away from her and rushed through the crowd to Angelique. "You mustn't let him fall," she whispered tearfully to the winged girl. "I beg you. I'm sorry I didn't tell you the truth about my mama and Droz, but Robert has nothing to do with any of that, he's good and kind, and I know you are too. Don't let them harm him. Please."

Angelique's eyes flickered with fright and indecision. She didn't know what to do.

There was a screeching and a crunching sound from inside the cage. Robert quaked in his boots. He tried to remember Da's advice, what he'd said every time Robert had been afraid: *No one conquers fear easily. It takes practice to reach true heights; a brave heart to win great battles.*

He repeated those words carefully to himself as he climbed higher and higher into the roof of the tent, where a hanging platform led out onto the high wire strung out over the baying animals below.

Deedee was already on the platform, having just finished rehearsing her act.

Robert glanced dizzily down at the ground. Far below, the circus folk had gathered in bunches at the edges of the ring, watching in shock and horror.

Robert shuffled toward the edge of the platform and stared out along the wire, then down into the open cage of animals. If he fell, he'd land in there with them. He clutched at his chest for the Moonlocket, hoping it would bring him luck—but of course it wasn't there.

"I can't do this," he whispered to Deedee, who was standing beside him.

"It's all right." Deedee handed him the balance bar. "I'll help you. Take off your boots, so you can feel the wire beneath you."

Robert did as he was told, pulling off his boots and his socks. Somehow the cold of the metal platform under his feet and Deedee's soft and soothing voice helped to calm him.

"Keep your head up and your gaze steady," Deedee said. "When you take your back foot off the wire, swing it out and lean a little in the opposite direction—that way you'll keep your balance. And no matter what, always move forward, never back."

"But how do I know where to place my feet if I can't see them?" Robert asked.

"Put the heel of your front foot against the toes of

your back," Deedee explained hurriedly. "You can't go wrong that way." She balled a fist and placed it over his belly, then his heart. "Find your courage here and here. It's the only way you're going to make it."

Robert placed one foot on the wire.

"Don't think," Deedee whispered. "Thoughts are bad. Feel your way. Sense the wire beneath your feet, put one foot in front of the other, and walk the line step-by-step."

Robert's mind whirred, but he did as he was told, moving forward, feeling the open space of the ring yawning beneath him.

"And don't look down!" Deedee called to him.

But as soon as she said that, it was as if his eyes couldn't resist. It was like when someone tells you not to think of pink elephants, and then that's all you can think of.

Unable to stop himself, he glanced at the ground far below…and realized he was walking above the open top of the cage.

Then Robert lost his grip on the balance bar, and it bounced off the wire and toppled sideways into the cage. He reached for it desperately as it fell, lost his footing, tipped to the side and tumbled…

…grasping at the wire…

…snatching at it with his fingers.

And, miraculously, managed to get a grip…

Which is how Robert found himself swinging back and forth, gazing between his dangling feet.

Sweat slicked his palms. Hairs stood up on his back, and his arms stretched out in a sharp knife of pain, trying to wrench themselves from their sockets.

Below him in the cage, the lions and tiger leaped onto their boxes, huffing and roaring excitedly, while the bear scuffed the sawdust with his claws and snarled, rearing up on his hind legs.

Beyond the animals, Robert glimpsed dots of faces and splotches of colorful costumes—Lily in her sparkling outfit stood out amongst everyone else in their rehearsal clothes, entreating the circus players who were running about looking for something to catch him with. Madame and Slimwood looked on with detached amusement at the chaos their actions had caused.

"Hold on!" Deedee screamed.

"Leave him be," Madame shouted up at her. "Or else."

"It'll be a second strike on your record," Slimwood warned Deedee with a sneer.

Deedee ignored their commands and ran toward Robert, her metal feet clasping the bouncing wire with their whirring toes on each step. When she got close to him, she tried to sit down on the rope and haul him back up onto it. "Give me your hand," she said.

Robert shook his head. He didn't want to let go. The fingers on both his hands were loosening, about to slip. Each arm felt weary and weak. He didn't know which to let go with first. He took his left hand off the rope and reached out to her.

It was the wrong choice.

The other wasn't strong enough alone to hold him.

The dead weight of his body pulled him down…

And he fell…

CHAPTER 18

Robert tumbled through the dark, his heart a mush of blurry beats. A stream of red-and-white stripes, bars, and roaring beasts flew past. At least he'd missed the cage, falling just short of it. He closed his eyes, anticipating the bone-shattering oblivion of the crash.

But it didn't come.

Instead he was pummeled sideways, giving gravity the slip, turning and soaring, twisting and fluttering.

Feathers brushed his cheek, puffing past in a chatter of clockwork.

He opened his eyes.

Angelique had him by the waist. Her skin was slicked with sweat, her face a grimace of teeth.

She flapped her wings wildly, trying to keep them aloft, and swung about in slow motion, gliding gently downward to deposit him in the ring with a soft *thump*. She keeled onto the floor beside him. Her feathers dragged ragged shapes in the sawdust as she snatched mouthfuls of air.

The circus folk rushed over, gathering round.

Robert climbed shakily to his feet and helped Angelique up. The winged girl leaned against his shoulder.

The room spun.

His legs felt weak enough to bowl him over. Everyone around him looked like novelty figures on a merry-go-round. Robert wondered when he might get off. Fragments of conversation drifted to him.

"Did you see that—the freak-girl saved the boy!"

"Rescued him."

"Angelique, it was."

"One of our hybrids…"

"Who'd have thought?"

"Quiet, all of you!" Madame shouted.

"SILENCE!" Slimwood glared angrily about and raised his whip.

Lily stumbled through the crowd; her body was shaking. Her legs tangled beneath her, but she managed to make it over to Robert.

"Thank you," she whispered to Angelique. A torrent of relief rushed through her veins. She hugged the winged girl so hard in gratitude she could feel every feather in her twitching wings.

"It was for him, not you," Angelique said simply.

Lily didn't care; she was just relieved Robert was alive.

"Are you all right?" she asked him.

"I'm fine," he replied. "A bit shaken." He'd survived a scrape with death. Woken from a nightmare of falling into a dream of flight. The room had stopped spinning, and the earth beneath his feet felt solid and durable. He wondered if he should get down on the ground and kiss it.

"I haven't caught anyone before," Angelique was saying. "I'm not a catcher." She wiped the sweat from her face with the back of her hand. "You almost dragged me down!" She was laughing in relief as she spoke.

Luca joined them at the front of the crowd, Silva and Dimitri too. They began clapping for Angelique. And then, gradually, the other performers joined in—a friendly round of applause, their faces filled with warm smiles.

"They've never applauded me before," Angelique whispered. "Only their own."

Maybe, Robert thought, *there was still hope*. He could

bring the two groups together: humans and hybrids working in partnership to put a stop to this vile circus and to get out of it altogether.

But then Slimwood barreled through the crowd. "Enough!" he screamed, hitting everyone with his whip to break them apart. "Rehearsal's over. Get back to your cells. If one of you breaks the rules, YOU ALL BREAK THE RULES. There will be no dinner and NO PRIVILEGES—everyone's PUNISHED because of these two."

The mood darkened, and Robert felt the elation drain away. People had begun to stare at him accusingly.

Madame grabbed Angelique by the arm, and Slimwood grappled with Robert. "I warned you not to cause trouble," he hissed. "I can't have you trying to turn my crew against me. Three strikes. This isn't the end. Tomorrow, we'll decide on a new punishment for you both."

Despair rose up in Robert once more. He turned and looked for Lily. She was with the other hybrids, being corralled away by the Lunk, probably back to Room Thirteen.

The roustabouts had arrived too and were hustling the rest of the crowd of performers out toward the gondola. Slimwood let Robert go and signaled to Auggie and Joey.

"Take him back to his cell."

As he was being pulled away, Robert glanced over his shoulder at Angelique. She was struggling to free herself from Madame, but the woman kept a firm grip on her arm, leaning forward to whisper something into Angelique's ear. Angelique's eyes glistened with tears, and Robert wondered if she would be all right.

The hybrids huddled together as the Lunk maneuvered them up the stairs inside the hulking prison ship and along the corridor, back toward Room Thirteen. Lily could hear the other acts, who were being corralled by the roustabouts, gossiping behind them. She knew they thought she and Robert were the reason everything had turned out this way, the reason they were being slammed up early—them and Angelique. After that spectacular stunt to save Robert, Madame had kept Angelique behind in the Big Top. Lily hoped she wasn't being punished.

The Lunk unlocked the padlock on the iron gate and opened Room Thirteen, thrusting them inside.

Malkin jumped up at Lily, licking her face as the door slammed on them. "Lily, thank clank you're all right! Where's Angelique?"

"In the tent." Deedee paced the cabin, her mechanical legs clicking and clacking. Luca sat down on the end of his bed.

Minutes later, Angelique arrived back, her face streaked with tears, her hair a mess, her folded wings sticking out at odd angles, and her plumage tattered. "They threatened to pluck my feathers out one by one if I ever pulled a stunt like that again," she said. "And they said to warn you all that from now on we had better toe the line." She slumped into the chair and lay her head on the table.

"What happened in there?" Malkin jumped up at Lily's legs.

"Slimwood was mad at Robert, so he made him walk the tightrope," Lily explained.

"Good gracious!" Malkin said. "Is Robert…?"

"He's fine," said Lily. She glanced at Angelique. "Angelique saved him."

Angelique gave her a glowering look, and Lily wondered if she was still angry about Mama's papers. "I was always worried I wouldn't be strong enough to carry someone," she said. "And then I did. Though the effort and what happened afterward were…" She trailed off and stretched her wings out wide until they filled the width of the cabin. Lily could see some of the feathers

258

were damaged, and she didn't know if it was from Angelique's rogue flight or what Slimwood and Verdigris had done to her as punishment.

"I just don't know if it was worth it."

"Remember the faces of the other performers, Angelique," Luca said. "And their applause. They were willing you on—on your side. Perhaps they're not as bad as we thought? Perhaps you made them see us at last?"

"I hope so," Angelique said. "Even when we help one of them, Slimwood still encourages them to hate us."

"I don't think that's the case anymore," Luca said.

"Luca's right." Deedee sat down next to him on his bunk. Lily noticed she looked rather shell-shocked too. She'd been the one who'd tried to grab Robert and had been inches from him when he fell. She must've seen the startled look on his face. "Maybe we can work to change things."

"Why was Robert punished?" Malkin asked.

"He was hiding," Lily said, "so he could give me this." She pulled the wallet out from her sock. Inside it were eight lockpicks and a folded piece of paper, which contained a message that Lily read aloud.

"*Meet me at midnight. I'm with the Buttons in Room…*"

Lily turned the paper over.

"*Nine.* He's in Room Nine." She looked up at the three

hybrids. "Are you going to come with me?" she asked. "We could use your help."

"Especially Angelique's to fly us over the fence..." Malkin added.

Angelique shook her head. "We can't risk it. What if we get caught?" She folded her wings around her. "They went easy on the punishment this afternoon, but they can do far worse. Haven't you seen the wall of mementos? Besides," she whispered fearfully, "what is there for us hybrids outside? No one wants freaks like us in the real world. That's how we ended up here in the first place."

Deedee and Luca said nothing, but Lily knew they agreed with Angelique. What was wrong with them? How could they bear to remain here? Did they not trust her? Were they still upset that she'd lied to them about Mama and the notebook? She needed to persuade them to come with her. Perhaps it would help if she read them something Mama had written, something that proved she wasn't so bad...?

Lily pulled out the last few ripped pages of Mama's red notebook, but there were no more diary entries, merely a few small sketches of people with wings.

"Who are they?" Luca asked, peering over her shoulder.

"Daedalus and Icarus," Lily explained.

"Were they part of the Flyology experiments your

mama mentioned in her notes?" Deedee wanted to know.

"No," Lily replied. "They're from a story from long ago. Mama used to tell it to me at bedtime."

Angelique's nose had wrinkled at this discussion of Lily's mama. Nevertheless, she seemed interested.

"Is it a children's story?" she asked.

"Sort of." Lily decided to tell it to them. After all, they had hours to kill and bonds to rebuild if she was to persuade them to come with her at midnight.

"Daedalus was an inventor," she began. "He created a maze for the King of Crete—King Minos—called the Labyrinth. At the center of the Labyrinth was a horrible half-man-half-beast called the Minotaur, and every nine years, seven young men and women would be sent into the Labyrinth as a sacrifice to him. The King's daughter Ariadne fell in love with Theseus, one of the heroes sent into the Labyrinth, and Daedalus helped them both to kill the Minotaur and escape. The King was so angry when he discovered this that he locked Daedalus and his son Icarus in a high tower in the middle of the Labyrinth forever. He told them they would die in their prison and never escape."

The others were enthralled. Deedee and Luca leaned forward in their seats, listening.

"But Daedalus was a great inventor," Lily continued.

"And his son was clever too. They both knew that if they put their minds to it and worked together, they could find some way to get out."

"What did they do?" Deedee asked.

"They designed wings for themselves to be made from feathers, wax, and twine."

"That doesn't sound like the greatest design to me," Malkin said.

Lily ignored him. "It was so they could fly away from the tower and Crete and King Minos," she explained, glancing at Angelique. Her eyes were so big and childlike that Lily guessed no one had ever taken the time to tell her a story before.

"What happened next?" she asked.

"They built the wings," Lily said. "And put their plan into practice."

Luca leaped up. "And then they were free!" he cheered.

And it was only then that Lily realized she'd chosen a bad story to tell. "Not quite," she said. "When Daedalus created the wings to fly himself and Icarus out of prison, he warned Icarus not to fly too close to the sun. But Icarus was an impetuous boy and never did what he was told. He loved flying. He dived and swooped and flapped up to the sun, and its heat melted the wax on his wings, and his feathers blew away, and he plummeted into the sea."

"Bit of a downbeat ending," Malkin said.

Lily knew he was right. She'd completed the story, but it didn't feel very satisfying. The light had faded in the room, and she could barely see the faces of the hybrids, but Luca and Deedee were teetering on the edges of their seats.

"Did he drown?" Deedee asked.

"I...I'm not sure," Lily lied. Though she knew that the stories said he had.

"See," Angelique said, her face set in angry resignation. "I told you. Bad things always happen to hybrids out in the world."

In the half-light Lily could see the cogs and leather joints beneath the feathers of her plumage. Wires wove across her back, and when she raised her arms, the mechanical wings responded to her movement as if they were part of her. The mechanism was integrated into who she was, just like the Cogheart in Lily. They were like sisters. Lily wished she could give her some hope. But she couldn't lie about it. It had to be the truth.

"I'm sorry that Dr. Droz changed you," Lily said at last to all of them. "And I'm sorry if any of my mama's or papa's ideas had anything to do with that. They always meant for their work on hybrids to help people, not hurt them. And it did—I wouldn't be alive without it. Surely that's enough to prove their good intentions?" She paused and looked each of them in the eye. "But most of all," she said, "I'm sorry that Slimwood and Madame locked you away. You should know, despair isn't the answer. Despite the risks, we can still fight; we can still escape. That's what we need to do. And we'll take Robert with us."

"I think you're right," Angelique said finally. "We'll go with you."

The other two nodded.

"Thank heavens for that," Malkin said, "because I don't think I could listen to another of Lily's stories."

There was still a long wait until it would be quiet enough to make their escape attempt. Lily's stomach rumbled from a lack of dinner. She changed back into her red dress, coat, and scarf and left the circus outfit Madame had chosen for her bundled in the corner. She intended to leave this place with everything she'd brought with her, and that included Mama's notebook and the other things Madame had taken, even if she had to break into the ringmistress's office. She was sick with nerves at the thought of the risk they were taking and glad that she,

Robert, and Malkin wouldn't be taking it alone.

They counted down the time to midnight by listening for the Lunk as he made his hourly inspection rounds of the cell corridor. Even after twelve, when he came less regularly, it would be difficult to avoid him, but this was their only chance, and they would have to give it a try. While they waited for the allotted hour, Lily and the hybrids drew a chalk map of the layout of the gondola and the circus site on the tabletop, and Lily went over her plan.

Once they'd reopened the hatch, they would push Malkin through the gap, and he would slip between the bars of the gate outside, run to the end of the corridor, and keep an eye out for the Lunk while they opened the cell door itself—that would be down to Lily and her lockpicks.

Then they had to unlock the padlock on the barred gate across the hall, and then Robert's cell, to get him out. Then they needed to pick the lock on the comms room to send an SOS message, and Madame's office door to retrieve the rest of Mama's notebook. And, finally, they would have to unlock the hatch door out of the sky-ship itself.

If they got that far, they would have to sneak across the site and Angelique would fly them over the fence one by one. The final part of the plan was to disappear into the Bois de Boulogne and make their way to Paris, in the hope that they could find someone there who would believe their story and help them out or get them back to England.

The whole scheme was going to be nearly impossible to pull off. But if they failed, then Madame would go through with her dastardly plot for Lily in the show tomorrow. Lily shivered at the thought of it.

Finally, the hour had come. They'd gone over everything multiple times, and there could be no more stalling. It was a quarter to twelve and time to put the plan into action.

Luca and Deedee pulled the pins from the door hinges and undid the bolts on the outside, then they removed the hatch.

Lily picked up Malkin, ready to push him through again.

"Try to be careful with me," he warned. "I was nearly squashed to death last time!"

"Just make yourself thin," she instructed as she carried him toward the hole—though it wasn't as if he could breathe in to do that. "We'll need a quiet signal for you to use on the other side if you see or hear anyone coming. One that we'll recognize from this end of the corridor."

"How about my soft pining noise?" Malkin suggested.

"That'll do."

"And while I'm risking cog and limb for you," he asked, "just what exactly are you going to be doing?"

"I told you," Lily said. "Weren't you listening? Picking the lock on the outside of this door. Then the other five." She posted him through the door and waited while he landed on the other side softly and slunk off into the shadows.

She pulled the lockpicks from her pocket, selected what she guessed was the right pick, and furrowing her brow in concentration, put her hand out through the gap.

As she got to work on the first lock, she felt a small tingle in her chest. A tingle that could be only one thing: hope.

CHAPTER 19

Even with her lockpicks, rather than the hairpin she'd tried before, Lily found the first lock a tricky proposition. The dim throbbing electric bulbs in the corridor gave off barely sufficient light to see the outside of the cell door, but they were bright enough that if someone was to walk down the passage, they would spot her. She was glad Malkin was on lookout, but she would have to be quick if she didn't want to be caught, and the mechanism already felt like it was jamming.

She needed a second pick. She pulled her hand back through the hatch to select one and tried to visualize the lock's interior in her mind as she jiggled them both into place.

Slowly, steadily, she rotated the two picks sideways. A knot formed in her chest. It was a tricky task, and if she failed, they would never get out.

She heard a rattling far off, and she wasn't sure if it was just the night creaks of the ship or the Lunk returning. But there was no turning back. She had to keep going. She tried to ignore the noises and carry on with her work.

Eventually, the lock's cylinders turned with a low grinding noise. Soon they'd reached the halfway point—past forty-five degrees—and Lily knew all she had to do was…let go.

With a *click*, everything dropped into place. The lock was open. Silently, she blessed Tolly and his birthday present and Robert for recovering it for her.

She held her breath and pushed on the door.

It swung open with a horribly loud creak, reminiscent of the Lunk's limbs. The noise echoed down the passage, sending shivers up Lily's spine and making her heartbeat quicken.

Had anyone heard? She waited for one pulse-pounding minute for Malkin to give a signal from the far end of the corridor.

Nothing stirred.

No one was coming. A wave of relief washed over her.

They'd opened the first door and gotten away with it. Only five more to go.

The others crowded in behind her as she stepped through the doorway.

She was just about to beckon them out, when she heard Malkin's pine. He was dashing back down the corridor with his brush up and his nose pointing toward the stairwell.

"Someone's coming!" he called out quietly.

Lily pushed everyone back inside and replaced the hatch, throwing the bolts across to hold it in place.

Malkin squeezed through the barred gate, and dashed past her into the cell. "Quick!" he said quietly. "Shut that door!"

Lily did as he commanded, and the five of them stood behind it, clustered together in the dark. A sliver of light leaked through the thin gap in the hatch. Lily leaned against it to keep it shut, and the four children kept very still and listened.

CREAK-THUD! CREAK-THUD! CREAK-THUD!

Footsteps trod the hall. It was the Lunk, making his late-night rounds.

He tramped the passageway twice, before they heard the clang of the door to the stairwell at the far end.

Lily's back was wet with sweat. Her red evening dress

clung to her beneath her coat. She let out a deep hysterical laugh that she hadn't even realized she was holding in.

Then she put Malkin down and cautiously opened the door.

The pair of them stepped outside.

"Go and check again if he's coming back," she told her friend, and he skittered up the corridor.

Lily turned to the others. "Do you still want to come with me?"

They nodded.

"It was a close call," Luca said quietly.

"But we still want to risk it," Deedee whispered.

Angelique said nothing.

Lily felt a wash of relief. The four of them stepped out the door again.

Lily's Cogheart pounded loudly in her chest as they tiptoed the few steps to the iron gate that stretched across the corridor. Malkin returned from his scouting, flicking his brush from side to side impatiently.

Lily bent down. Her hands slicked with sweat as she fiddled with the padlock on the gate, almost dropping the lockpick through the bars...

"Hurry," Malkin muttered, giving Lily an encouraging nudge through the bars with his nose. "You're taking too long."

"Then stop your chatter," Lily whispered back.

"Move out the way," Luca said softly. "I'll do this."

Lily stepped aside, and he snipped through the padlock with his claws. "It's quicker this way since we're not coming back."

The lock on Room Nine was the same as the one on their cell door.

Lily chose the two picks that she'd used before and jiggled them about in the keyhole. This lock was easier than the first, and she was through it in a matter of minutes. With relief, she realized that she had become a better lockpicker now that she'd had some practice and could use the right tools.

She pushed open the door. "Wait here," she hissed softly to the others. And to Malkin she said, "Head off and stand guard."

Malkin grumbled under his breath just a little at being bossed around, but nevertheless positioned himself farther off down the corridor. Luca, Deedee, and Angelique huddled together in the next doorway along.

Quietly, Lily pushed open the door to Room Nine and stuck her head inside. She'd expected Robert and the Buttons to be ready to leave and waiting in the center of the room, but they weren't. Instead there were four sleeping bodies in bunks wrapped in blankets.

Perhaps they'd all drifted off while waiting? She peered closer into each berth and suddenly felt dizzy with fear. A fully grown roustabout was lying in each, breathing loudly, one even snoring. Lily exited the room as quickly as she could and shut the door noiselessly behind her.

"What's the matter?" Deedee asked when she saw her face.

"Robert's not in there, and neither are the Buttons. I don't understand what can have gone wrong!"

"Maybe someone got wind of your plan and moved them to another cell?" Luca said quietly.

Malkin's fur bristled. "Maybe this is a trap?" he suggested.

"It can't be," Lily said. "They would've stopped us already."

She took Robert's note out of her pocket, flipping it from side to side and peering at it in the throbbing yellow electric light. She felt slightly queasy.

9

"Wait a second," she said. "I read his reply up the wrong way."

"Of course," Malkin said. "He's in Room Six!"

The five of them edged along the corridor to Room Six, stopping in an alcove just outside and waiting to see if anyone was coming before Lily tried to pick this lock.

At once they heard footsteps, and in a panic Lily pushed the others back into the shadows and squeezed herself into the doorway beside them.

Everyone held their breath.

The footsteps did not stop, but they didn't seem to get any closer either.

"I think they're coming from the floor above," Deedee whispered, and Lily realized she was right.

As soon as there was silence again, she started in on the lock. Malkin took up his lookout position a few feet away once more, and Angelique and Deedee kept watch too. Luca offered to help with the lock again, but Lily shook her head. It was too fiddly for his claws. Besides, she found she was getting quicker, especially with these picks. In a matter of seconds, the door swung open.

And there inside was Robert, dressed in his work clothes and ready to go. Silva and Dimitri were waiting with him. Behind them in their bunks, Bruno and Gilda Buttons were sat up watching too. Their eyes almost popped when they saw Lily and the hybrids crowded into the doorway.

Robert pulled Lily into a hug. She could feel the waves of relief wash off him.

"What took you so long?" he asked.

"Trouble with numbers," Lily explained. "Nine turned out to be six."

"What?" he asked. Then, "Never mind. What's the plan?"

"We have to get going," Lily said. "Find the comms room and telegraph Papa, then steal back Mama's notebook from Madame's office and pick the lock on the exit door. Finally Angelique's going to fly us over the fence and out."

"We'll have to sneak through the Big Top on the way and get the rest of my things. I hid them on the costume rail, and we can't leave here without my ma's Moonlocket," Robert said. "Let's hope that's in Madame's office too."

Lily nodded. "All right then."

"The comms room is on the top floor," Gilda Buttons advised. "And Madame's office is opposite it, on the other side of the stairwell. Best of luck."

"Aren't you coming with us?" Lily asked the Buttons and Dimitri.

They took one look at the hybrids and shook their heads. "We can't," Bruno Buttons said quietly. "We have to see out the season. We've no money to go anywhere else."

"And I need to stay with my parents," Silva said.

Dimitri nodded. "Circus is family. We can't leave them."

Lily wondered if that was the only reason or if they had some residual mistrust of the hybrids that meant they didn't want to go with them.

"We'll telegraph the police," Robert said. "Bring them here to sort out this mess. At least then Madame and Slimwood will be taken away and held to rights, and you might get paid." He looked back at Silva and Dimitri. "Well, thank you for everything. I hope we'll meet again."

With that, he stepped into the corridor to join Lily and Malkin and the other three, and they hurried quickly along to the dimly lit stairwell.

The six of them climbed the stairs in a long line, taking care to keep to the edge of the walls to stop the steps from creaking. Deedee and Luca followed Robert at the front, Angelique behind them grasping the bannisters in one hand and her stick in the other. Her wings were folded against her back, twitching irregularly. Lily and Malkin brought up the rear. Lily's heart was pounding so loud she could barely think. They reached the top-floor corridor, and she heard a horrible scuffling coming from somewhere ahead in the dark. Everyone froze. A shiver ran down Lily's spine. She gulped back a wave of panic and stood stock-still, waiting…

Finally, the noise died down to silence.

"What was that?" Lily hissed.

"Probably mice," Deedee said.

Lily hoped she was right, because Madame's and Slimwood's quarters were up here, and the last thing she wanted was to be discovered by them. The punishment Robert had endured just for hiding in the Big Top had been bad enough—heaven knew what would happen to them if Slimwood and Madame caught them trying to break out. Though whatever it was, Lily couldn't imagine it would be worse than the terrible-sounding machine Madame had prepared for her in the show.

They passed a doorway, and Luca tapped her shoulder.

"This is the comms room," he whispered.

Lily nodded; her mouth was dry, and her throat ached. She wished she could have a drink of water, but there wasn't time. "Lock number five," she said to herself, putting a pick into the keyhole.

"Let's hope it's as easy as the oth—" Malkin said.

But he didn't even have time to finish the sentence, because she'd got it open.

Robert whistled softly in approval. "You're getting good at this, Lily," he whispered.

Malkin shook his head. "I don't know," he said quietly. "There's still the main door to go, and so far it almost seems as if it's been too easy."

"Don't say that," Lily whispered. "We're nearly out. Malkin, you're on watch again." She turned to the others. "The rest of you'd better come in with me. You can help

277

Robert get the telegraph machine working: we need to get a message to Papa and the French police about this place."

The five of them stepped through the door into the comms and navigation room. Lily turned on a desk lamp rather that the main light.

On the wall was a large map of Great Britain and Northern Europe with a string of X marks in prominent sites on the map.

"That's all the places we've ever been to," Luca said, staring at it.

In the center of the room was a swivel chair with a blanket folded on it and a wooden desk that was strewn with telegraph tape and message pads, and beside those were a headset and the brass telegraph key on its wooden base. Above them, fixed to the wall, was a shiny-looking machine—a transmitter and receiver box, with a brass plate screwed to its front that was imprinted with the words:

TESLA ELECTRIC COMPANY Ltd.
Patented Short-Range Wireless Telegraphic Device

On the floor beneath this, a large battery and a tangle of wires were wedged between two filing cabinets full of manuals. A set of instructions laying out the Morse code letter cypher was pinned to a noticeboard on the wall above.

"Crikey!" said Deedee, her eyes darting over this complex collection of equipment.

"Are you sure you can get this working?" Angelique asked.

"If anyone can, Robert can," Lily said. She smiled at him.

Robert didn't seem as certain. He connected up the battery to the positive and negative plates on the transmitter and pointed the others around the room, getting them to turn on brass switches and dials for the transmitter and receiver, while he checked their settings.

Lily could see that his hands were shaking. She hoped he knew what he was doing.

The battery began to give off an electrical hum as current passed through it.

Luca took the blanket off the back of the chair and threw it over the thing to muffle the sound.

"I may not be a trained telegraph operator," Robert said quietly as he sat down at the telegraph desk and put the headphones on, "but I read a book about it once."

"Hopefully, that will suffice," Lily said. "If you can't

get an answer from a book, goodness knows what the world's coming to," she added.

"We shall see," Robert said. He was about to brush aside a stack of paper on the table when something made him stop. He picked one up and turned it over. "Oh no!" he exclaimed.

"What's the matter?" Lily asked. It was a ticket for the circus, just like the one she had received with her book, only with a slight difference.

Etched on its front in silver and gold was an image of a girl in a crackling coffin-shaped box. She looked like she was around fourteen years old. From one end of the box an enormous yellow cone of light spilled up onto a screen, where there was a complex engraving of cams and cogs and springs, making up the image of a clockwork heart. Around all this, a set of curlicued words was arranged:

SLIMWOOD'S STUPENDOUS
SKYCIRCUS
presents...
Miss Cora Valentine — the world's only clockwork-hearted girl!

Witness a unique feat of heart-stopping entertainment!

★ Show also includes outstanding acrobats, animals and aerialists, funambulists, freaks, and clowns! ★ One-hour-long performance, 7.30 p.m. nightly. All month.

"Miss Cora Valentine must be you," Deedee whispered in shock.

"And there's more." Robert handed Lily a telegram dated yesterday. She read it.

Lily's head spun as she finished the telegram.

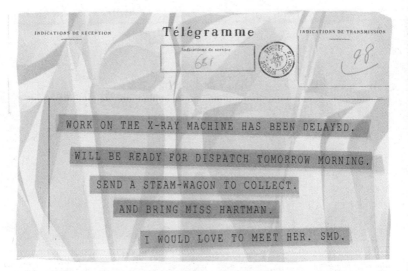

Télégramme

INDICATIONS DE RÉCEPTION — Indications de service — 681 — INDICATIONS DE TRANSMISSION — 98

WORK ON THE X-RAY MACHINE HAS BEEN DELAYED.

WILL BE READY FOR DISPATCH TOMORROW MORNING.

SEND A STEAM-WAGON TO COLLECT.

AND BRING MISS HARTMAN.

I WOULD LOVE TO MEET HER. SMD.

"SMD is Droz's initials," Luca said. "That X-ray device must be intended to reveal your Cogheart."

"I don't like the sound of it," Deedee said.

Lily didn't either. X-ray machines were a dangerous

281

new technology, barely perfected. Papa had told her that one dose of radiation from some of the early machines that had gone wrong had been strong enough to kill someone. She folded the telegram and put it in her pocket.

Robert flicked a switch on the transmission box and reached out with one hand for the metal transmission key, then began tapping out a telegraph code with it.

The key emitted a low intermittent beep, and Lily, who was good with codes, knew almost immediately what the first three letters he had tapped in were: SOS.

Robert tapped a long sequence of dots and dashes into the transmitter with the telegraph key.

SOS. POSITION 48.86 N and 2.25 E.
FIVE KIDNAPPED CHILDREN, INCLUDING
ROBERT TOWNSEND AND LILY
HARTMAN, REQUIRE IMMEDIATE
ASSISTANCE. HELD PRISONER IN
SLIMWOOD'S SKYCIRCUS, MOORED IN
BOIS DE BOULOGNE, PARIS. INFORM
PROF. HARTMAN OF BRACKENBRIDGE,
ENGLAND.
COME QUICK.
WANTED CRIMINALS ABOARD.
WE ARE IN DANGER.

He hoped he hadn't made a mistake in the transmission. He'd set the machine to broadcast on all frequencies.

When he'd finished sending the message, he, Lily, and the other hybrids waited for a reply.

Angelique stood leaning on her stick, with her ear pressed to the door, listening for a warning from outside from Malkin in case anyone was coming.

A good few minutes passed, but nothing came through the machine.

Robert couldn't understand why. He'd used the open broadcast frequency designated for emergencies—the message should've been read by now.

"I don't know what's wrong," he muttered.

"Maybe you didn't set the transmitter right?" Luca suggested.

Robert checked the dials. "It looks correct," he said. "We could try one more time?"

"We've spent too long doing this," Lily said. "We still need to break into the circus office and get our things. We can go to the police later, once we're out of here."

When Robert and the others had turned the machine and the light off, Lily opened the door.

"Lily," Angelique whispered, leaning on her stick as they were about to leave the room. "I have to tell you something…"

"What is it?" Lily asked.

"I...I—"

But, just then, Malkin appeared in the doorway.

"I think I heard a sound on the stairs," he interrupted. "We need to go."

"There isn't time," Lily said to Angelique. "Tell us on the way. We still need to get the notebook and Robert's locket."

They made their way to the circus office, stopping outside the door. Before Lily started picking the lock, she tried the door handle, as she always did, just in case.

Only this time the door swung open and the lights inside the room flashed on.

There, in the center of the space, sitting in a chair facing the door and waiting for them, was Madame. On the table beside her sat the Moonlocket, Robert's penknife, and the red notebook. Lily's heart skipped a beat, and the others behind her let out horrified gasps. All except Angelique.

CHAPTER 20

"Lily!" Madame exclaimed. "And Robert, Malkin, plus Deedee, Luca, and Angelique—I wasn't expecting the rest of you, what a pleasant surprise! I take it, Lily and Robert, you've come for your things?" She indicated the red notebook and the Moonlocket and the rest of the items on the table.

Such insincerity. Robert shuddered. He reckoned she'd been waiting in there all along for them to show up.

"I hope you weren't thinking of leaving us?" Madame said.

There was a creak in the hallway behind them, and the Lunk stepped across the doorway to block their path. Slimwood and Joey ducked under his metal arms. "Ah, reinforcements have arrived!" Madame said. "Come in. Join the party."

"What's this?" Slimwood asked, grabbing Lily by the shoulder. "Our two showstoppers and the troublemaker out of their cells!"

"Don't call me the troublemaker," Malkin barked.

"I was talking about Robert," Slimwood snapped.

"Children," Joey cried, snatching at Angelique's arms and folding them over her wings. "What a delight! To meet you all here on this beautiful night!"

The Lunk just made a horrible screeching sound as he gathered a growling Malkin up in one arm and Robert in the other, clutching them both with his enormous fists.

Lily tried to run, but Slimwood twisted both her arms up behind her until she winced and a sharp stitch of pain shot through her shoulders.

As Madame took the lockpicks and her pocket watch from her, Lily turned angrily to Angelique. "Is this what you were going to warn me about...? But how did you know?"

"She knew because she betrayed your plans to me," Madame explained as she patted Lily down in one final search. She ignored the ripped pages of the notebook, stuffing them back unceremoniously in Lily's pocket.

Everything else she put with the pile of stolen goods on the table.

Robert felt as if all the air had been knocked out of him. He couldn't believe Angelique had deceived them. Lily had turned white. Her eyes were glazed and confused. Luca and Deedee's faces were a picture of shock too. Malkin growled with disbelief at Madame.

"Why?" Lily whispered to Angelique. "Was it because of what you read in those pages from Mama's notebook?" She couldn't quite credit what Angelique had done—trusted Madame's word over hers. "Or was it because I didn't tell you my parents had known Droz?"

Angelique shook her head. "It was neither of those things—I didn't mean… It was after I rescued Robert. Madame threatened to make me vanish for good, and Slimwood said he'd pull my feathers out and pin them to his wall. Then Madame said if I told her your plans, she'd make sure I was safe, and she would never hurt any of us ever again." She glanced at Deedee and Luca. "They understand."

"And you believed her?" Lily asked.

"Why the crunk didn't you just come with us?" Malkin said.

"You could've been free," Robert added.

"I-I wanted to…" Angelique leaned heavily on her

stick, her eyes darting tearfully between them. "But look at me, I can barely walk. I'm broken. I would've slowed you down. We all would have."

"That's not true," Lily said. "You're strong. You can fly. What you think is your worst weakness is your greatest power."

Madame laughed. "Some people prefer the routine of a world they're used to, Lily, no matter the discomfort. You can open a door for them, but if they aren't ready, they won't step through it." She smiled at Angelique, Luca, and Deedee. "Especially when they know how cruel the outside world is. How badly it would treat them. Things may be awful here, but at least they are safe. They're home. Isn't that right, Angelique?"

"This place isn't a home," Lily said. "It's a hellhole." She shook angrily and gritted her teeth. "And you're wrong. Angelique tried to warn us. Which means she has the same hope in her heart that I have in mine. Hope that can lift her up, even on damaged wings."

"You always were a most disgustingly rude and stupid child, Lily," Madame said, stepping across the cabin. The electric lights on the walls flickered sickeningly, throwing soft circles of light from one corner of the room to the other. "Who knows why your papa gave you such a great gift as the Cogheart. He would've been better off saving

Grace." Madame tapped the red notebook on her table.

"You didn't even know my mother," Lily said.

"Not personally, no," Madame replied. "But a good friend of mine has told me all about her."

"Droz?" Lily said.

"How did you guess?" Madame glanced down at the notebook. "Oh, I suppose it was in there. Droz is giving us the X-ray machine in exchange for your papa's papers, and the good doctor has requested a meeting with you too, *ma chère* Lily. The pair of you will meet tomorrow, before the show."

Lily's brain scrambled to keep up. "And what are you planning to do with this X-ray machine of yours?" she asked.

"Oh, you'll find out soon enough," Madame said. "When you perform with it tomorrow, as our showstopper!" Madame chuckled until her earrings swung, their glass beads tinkling together. "You see, Lily," she explained, "your Cogheart makes you the greatest freak of all time. And with that X-ray machine, people will be able to truly see it."

"Then the Skycircus will be the biggest show ever!" Slimwood added. "Bigger than Cirque D'Hiver and the Cirque Fernando put together. It will make us hundreds of thousands of francs."

"Even if you don't survive the experience unscathed," Madame added.

Anger bubbled over inside Lily. She snorted. "What a pathetic plan! Use my heart to make you money. Is that all you care about?"

"Your heart makes you valuable"—Madame gestured to the other hybrids—"just like the rest of these half-and-halfs. You might, in a way, call them your brothers and sisters. Uncared for, homeless monsters, whereas you're a monster who's lost a home. But you're my perfect little circus freak, Lily, and soon I will be able to prove it by using you in the shows. Now that I have you, I can display to the world what a damaged and misshapen and beastly girl you are."

"I'm not misshapen or beastly," Lily spat. "And neither are they. We're not monsters. We're worthy human beings. If anyone's a monster here, it's you. I may have a metal heart, but yours is made of stone, and it's the ugliest, most unfeeling heart I've ever come across. And I'm not lost. I never was. Papa will be here soon to take us home." She tried to wrestle free from Slimwood's grasp, but he gripped her even tighter.

"And the police," Robert added. "They'll see to the lot of you, and this tin-can man." He gritted his teeth as the Lunk sunk his metal fingers into the bones of Robert's shoulders. Malkin snapped at the Lunk's other arm looped around his waist.

Madame smirked. "What are you children talking about?"

"They're on their way at the moment," Lily said. "Isn't that right?" she said to Angelique and the others.

They nodded.

"When they catch you, you'll rot in jail." Lily eyes watered as Slimwood twisted her arms tighter in his grip.

"Nonsense. I've no more time to argue." Madame turned to Slimwood. "We'll take them all back downstairs and lock them up. One of you will post yourself outside the cells and—"

Before she could finish speaking, Auggie stumbled into the office, clasping a strip of ticker tape.

"They tent a selegram!"

Lily held her breath. The tape must be a reply to their message.

"What?" Madame snapped. "*Je ne comprends pas!* Speak properly, you idiot!"

"A telegram! They sent a telegram and received this reply."

"*Mon Dieu!* This is terrible! Well, read it out. What does it say?"

"From the Critish Bonsulate: 'We have meceived your

ressage and contacted Hofessor Prartman and the gendarmes—they're on their way.'"

"*Sacrebleu!*" Madame cursed.

"What the clank?" Slimwood spouted, fingers burning into Lily's arm.

"Well," Lily said, "what are you going to do, Madame? You're a fugitive, already wanted for the theft of the Hartman papers, and now this kidnapping as well. You'll be in deep trouble if they catch—"

"*Silence!*" Madame shouted. "We must get them out of here at once," she instructed Slimwood and the others. "Joey, start up the steam-wagon." She pointed at Auggie. "Auggie, bring their friends from their cell. Those other circus children, Silva and Dimitri, or whatever they're called—the ones who helped them plan their escape."

The circus thugs press-ganged the children down the stairs. Slimwood bullied Lily and Deedee along. Madame had Angelique by the wings and had bound Luca's hands. The Lunk brought up the rear, carrying Malkin under one arm and holding Robert by the shoulder with the other.

As they passed the second floor, Auggie emerged, herding Silva and Dimitri in front of him like sheep. "Meep koving, you porrible hair," he shouted. They stared at Lily and Robert in alarm. Silva had tears streaming down her cheeks, and Dimitri's eyes were wide, his face a sickening yellow in the flickering lights.

Together the ruffians shooed the children down the last flight of stairs toward the gondola's open exit.

Madame pushed her way to the front and unlocked the door with her ring of keys. She was about to step out into the field when someone barreled through the group and threw himself across her path.

"What the devil's going on?"

It was Bruno Buttons, followed by Gilda. "You have to stop them!" Robert told the Buttons, pulling away from the Lunk's viselike grasp. "The police are on their way."

"Quiet that boy!" Madame shouted, and the Lunk's big hand came up and smothered Robert's mouth. Robert felt dizzy as the Lunk clutched at his face—it was like his head was being forced against a radiator. He peered through the Lunk's fingers.

"Where are you taking our children?" Gilda Buttons demanded tearfully.

"BUTTON IT, BUTTONS!" Slimwood snapped. "That's none of your business."

"Get back in your cells, *now*!" Madame yelled at them.

"NO!" Gilda Buttons yelled.

"We've had enough of taking orders from you," Bruno Buttons agreed loudly, standing beside her defiantly.

"Is that so?" Mâdame said. "Well, think on this—if you want to see your children again, you'd best do as I tell you. When the police arrive, you will say nothing of Robert or Lily, myself, or these freaks. We'll be back tomorrow for the show, and if anything prevents that going ahead, then you will feel my wrath, and your children will be long gone, never to return. You're to explain that to the rest of the circus folk too."

She pushed Bruno and Gilda Buttons aside and thrust Angelique out ahead of her through the door hatch. Lily, Robert, and the rest of children were herded out behind her into the fenced field. Robert was last out; he glimpsed the distraught Buttons as the doorway to the gondola closed behind him.

Madame waved the line of captured children onward, out past the kiosk and wooden fence, through the spiked entrance gate, and onto a dirt track that ran through the woods beyond.

Joey was waiting in the hearse with the engine running and the coffin compartment open.

Madame pushed Angelique into the coffin compartment at the back of the steam-wagon first, then ordered the rest of them to climb in behind her.

The children had to lie down side by side like sardines to hide them from view. Then the Lunk carried Robert and Malkin over and thrust them in. Robert was wedged next to Deedee—he could feel her shivering and her legs twitching. Malkin was thrown on top of him, and Robert got a brief face full of fur. He lay there with the others, shoulder to shoulder in the confined space.

Last in was Lily. Slimwood thrust her into the sliver of remaining space and slammed the hearse's back door. A narrow shard of light filtered through the window, illuminating their anguished faces.

Through the glass, Lily and Robert heard Madame's chilling final words with a sickly feeling of dread: "I'll deal with this lot. Slimwood, you and the Lunk keep an eye on everything here until I'm back."

Robert craned his ears desperately for more, but the rest of their conversation was lost as Madame strode around the side of the wagon. Then there was a rumble beneath them and the drone of the starting engine, and the trapped children were driven off into the night...

CHAPTER 21

Lily bit the side of her tongue. There was a metallic taste in her mouth, and her pulse beat hard in her ears. She lay flat on her back, squashed in with the others in the rear of the hearse, her coat and scarf wrapped uncomfortably around her.

There was no sign of other vehicles on the road, nor people on the pavement, just molting trees in circular metal cages and iron-scrolled gas lamps.

The lonely siren of one passing police vehicle echoed through the night. It must've been responding to the telegram, but it wouldn't find them at the Bois. They were now gliding through Paris in an unending nightmare in the back of a hearse, hidden in a city so sprawling it would be impossible for the detectives or for Papa to track them.

Somewhere far off, she heard a single chime of a clock. The hour had just passed one.

Robert shifted beside her; his face looked thin and ashen, drained of color. On his other side, Silva gave a whimper and clasped Dimitri's hand. Deedee shifted against Silva's shoulder, her legs creaking as she tried to keep them flat and together. Luca's claws twitched. They were still bound in wire to stop him from using them. Angelique was in the far corner. She couldn't lie down because of her wings, so she was folded up against the wall as tight as she could be. It looked as if she was trying to hold herself together or hold something in.

They turned a sharp corner. Malkin scrabbled around at Lily's feet, his claws scratching the steam-wagon's metal. "They're making a grave mistake if they think they can do this to us," he muttered over the sound of the vehicle's chugging engine.

"They *are* doing it, Malkin," Lily said.

"And there's nothing we can do to stop them," Robert added.

"It'll be their funeral in the end. You wait and see—"

"I've got something to say," Angelique said, interrupting them. She picked awkwardly at her feathers, grooming them between her fingers. Her eyes were full of tears.

They waited.

Finally the words burst out of her: "I'm sorry I betrayed your plans to them. I didn't mean to…I was scared. And I thought that if I did what Madame said, she wouldn't harm me…or any of you." She glanced around at everyone.

"That's all right," Lily replied. She wasn't really angry with Angelique—she couldn't afford to be. They were the same, the two of them. Trying to survive.

"I'm sorry too," she said, smiling at her friend. "Sorry I didn't trust you enough to tell you the whole truth about Mama as I knew it."

"So many bad things have happened in my life," Angelique said. "So many people tricked me and treated me unfairly. Even when I was a tiny girl, before I could fly, they would treat me differently because of how I looked… And I…I didn't know if I could trust you. I was scared, and so I made the wrong choice. I wanted to tell you in the hallway what Madame knew, but sometimes, when I'm scared, the words don't come." Her feathers shook. "But I've faith in you, Lily. I know if anyone can get us out of this mess, you can."

"Thank you," Lily said. But she wasn't sure if that was true.

She transferred Malkin to Robert's lap and sat up as best she could so that she might peer out of the hearse's rear window.

They were passing a gigantic arch lit by gaslight. The top of it was covered in crenellated decoration like icing on a cake, and the sides had large plinths that were dotted with statues of flying figures and baying crowds.

As they turned away down a side street, Lily caught a far-off glimpse of the spiked Eiffel Tower Airstation and the airships moored to its platforms. She realized she might be able to use its position to work out the direction they were traveling in.

But soon they pulled along a boulevard lined with tall houses and trees, and the tower disappeared.

Her stomach rolled, and her scars tingled on her chest as the steam-wagon turned onto another unknown street.

After they'd been driving for around twenty minutes, the city thinned out once more. The few dots of light they passed illuminated industrial-looking buildings and warehouses. The engine noise growled lower and flattened out, and Lily realized they were slowing down. Then the steam-wagon pulled to a stop in front of a long, low building that looked like an abandoned hospital.

"I recognize this place," Deedee whispered, peering over Lily's shoulder. "It's Droz's office."

"It doesn't look very homely," Malkin said.

"It's not." Luca shook beside him.

"They can't be taking us back," Angelique said, her voice sounding higher and thinner. Fretful. "They wouldn't dare."

"There's no saying what they'd do," Luca said.

They sat for a long time listening to the muffled voices of Madame and the two clowns, Auggie and Joey, coming from the driver's cabin.

"What do you think they're up to?" Silva whispered.

"Who knows?" Dimitri said. "They've some horrible plan."

Deedee's face was white. Luca bit his lip. Angelique had gone silent again, lost for words. Malkin shifted uncomfortably in Robert's lap. One of Robert's arms was stuck under him, and his fingers were starting to go to sleep.

Lily's pulse rattled like a sewing machine. She pressed her nose to the window glass and peered out. They were parked in front of a grand stone archway. A flickering coach lantern mounted on the wall above it illuminated two huge doors that must once have been the entrance to the coaching mews of what looked like a large derelict hospital.

If this really was Dr. Droz's office, that couldn't be

good news. She waited with trepidation for whatever was to happen next.

Click! The door in the driver's compartment opened, and Madame stepped out. She passed the window, approached the arched entranceway, and rang a bell on the wall. Then she waited, wringing her hands together impatiently.

Eventually, the door creaked open.

In the slit of light, Lily saw a tall and broad mechanical man. He was as large as the Lunk—if not bigger and more heavyset—and he had the same soulless lantern eyes. They gleamed in the darkness as they swept across the bonnet of the steam-wagon.

Finally, he looked to Madame, and they spoke back and forth before Madame gave him a curt nod and gestured to the rear compartment of the hearse.

"What do you think they're saying?" Robert asked, stroking Malkin, who was now lying across his chest.

"I don't know," Malkin said. "But I don't like the face of that mechanical. He won't be any help to us—he seems like another of those evil reprogrammed types."

Malkin was right. The mechanical looked like more of Droz's work. Lily shivered and pressed her ear against the window.

She could make out only a few words of their conversation, enough to know it was being carried out in French. She wished now that she'd paid a little more attention in her studies with Madame when the woman had been her governess and in Mademoiselle's French lessons at the academy.

Finally the heavyset mechanical man nodded and stepped back inside the doorway.

Madame turned to the steam-wagon and beckoned to Joey in the driver's seat. With a *phut-phut* and a hum and shudder, the vehicle started up again.

By this time, both the grand doors of the building were opening inward. The steam-wagon inched forward through the archway until the darkness swallowed them up in its devilish mouth.

"Get out, *tout le monde*!" Madame commanded. "And *vite*!"

The steam-wagon had juddered to a stop, and the doors to the rear compartment had been flung open. Madame was looming in the gap, with Joey and Auggie both clasping lanterns.

Lily, Malkin, Robert, and the other children scrambled down from the hearse and looked dazedly around. They were in a cobbled courtyard, walled in by the backs of various tall buildings. The exit to the street had been blocked by the mechanical man, who was closing the grand arched doors behind them.

Lily's scars tingled on her chest, beneath her coat and the silk of her red dress. She gritted her teeth and tried to calm herself. Beside her, Deedee whimpered uncontrollably, and Luca looked ashen-faced. Angelique had gone silent; her wings drooped, and she was gradually folding in on herself. Silva clutched her stomach with one hand and held on to Dimitri with the other. Robert cradled Malkin in his arms and flinched away from the clowns.

Madame led the children and the fox past a row of broken windows and through another archway into a gray concrete lobby filled with dripping pipes. She seemed to know the place well.

At the end of the lobby, a wide staircase of low stone treads, with a black metal bannister flanking one side and a flaking plaster wall on the other, ran up and up and up into the dark.

A column-like cage was wedged in the central stairwell, its sides rising up the full height of the building between the flights of stairs. Madame pressed a brass lever near the bottom of the cage. With a shudder, some pulleys inside it began to move. For a moment Lily thought it was some new and horrible torture device, but as a platform slowly descended from the top floor, she realized it was an elevator.

"Joey, Auggie, lock up the mechanimal and these children," Madame said, pulling back the lift's rickety gate. "Lily and I will take the *ascenseur* to the top floor to visit our host."

Where were they taking the others? Lily tried to pull herself free to stay with her friends, but she was too tired and disoriented, and Madame easily manhandled her into the elevator. She peered worriedly through the closing doors at Robert, Malkin, and the others being corralled away by the clowns down a long corridor.

As the tiny wooden box rose, the polished brass fixings stuck into Lily's side, and she found herself squashed against Madame's shoulder. The sickly stench of the woman's perfume made her dizzy, and the worry of being separated from her friends stretched inside her like taffy.

The elevator reached the top floor, grinding to a halt with a lurch that made Lily's stomach roll queasily. Madame shoved the metal gate aside and ushered her onto the landing, where a woman with deep-set staring eyes and silver-gray hair waited for them. She looked to be about sixty years old and was wearing a long woolen skirt and a velvet waistcoat and white shirt buttoned up to the collar.

"This is somewhat of an egregious interruption," she snapped at Madame. "What are you doing here at this hour? I thought we were to meet tomorrow? I'm in the middle of the delicate last-minute work on your machine."

Madame hailed her. "*Bonsoir*, dear doctor. *Désolée*, but there's been a change of plan. Lily, this is Dr. Droz, a good friend of your parents. And this, Dr. Shelley Mary Droz, is Lily Hartman, our *special* guest and the circus's new showstopper."

A terrible fear blossomed in Lily's chest. She felt suddenly stupid to not ever have considered that Dr. Droz might be a woman. She'd assumed that, like most mechanists, the doctor would be male. But then she remembered Droz had taught her mama at Histon Ladies' College all those many years ago.

She wondered how on earth she could've made such a stupid assumption. For now that she saw her up close, Lily *did* recall Dr. Droz. Her cloud of gray hair and the habit she had of sweeping it back from her face with that flicking gesture seemed awfully familiar. She remembered her coming to tea on that summer's day her mama had written about in her notebook.

"My dear Miss Hartman," said Dr. Droz, stepping forward excitedly and putting a hand on her shoulder.

"This is a surprise! I wasn't expecting to meet you until tomorrow." She turned to Madame then. "I think perhaps you'd both best come inside."

She turned and pushed open the door behind her, and Lily wondered, her heart sinking, what new shocking things lay beyond it.

Robert could hear Joey and Auggie pacing around outside the door. As soon as Madame and Lily had taken the elevator to the top floor of the abandoned hospital, the two clowns, along with the large mechanical man, had ushered them along a corridor filled with broken tiles and rotting equipment to this small room and locked them in.

A chill breeze invaded the space. The glass was smashed in one window, and a little jagged light drifted in from the coaching lamp outside. The walls of the room were lined with shelves full of broken dishes and jars of colorful liquids and powders, all of them labeled with chemical names.

"We appear to be in the hospital's abandoned pharmacy," Malkin said, sniffing at a pile of yellowing prescription pads on the floor. "I prescribe there will be trouble."

Robert strode past him and approached the window. His heart dropped as he saw that outside, the aperture was barred.

"I can't believe we're back in this building." Luca's eyes anxiously flicked from the room to down at his bound hands. "This is where I first got these terrible claws!"

"Me too," Deedee said. "It's where Droz gave me my legs."

"I was the last," Angelique said. It was the first time she'd spoken in a while. "The last hybrid Droz created." Then she went silent again.

"This place used to be an asylum," Deedee whispered. "But they closed it down around the time Dr. Droz came and began her experiments. She stayed on anyhow, to continue with her work. She hid out on the top floor, making new machines from the leftover equipment."

Robert felt sick. That was where Madame had taken Lily. What had she and Dr. Droz planned for his friend? He knew it had something to do with an X-ray machine. He wished he could be at Lily's side right now, looking after her. X-ray machines were a new invention, still being developed, and were very dangerous. Robert remembered how John had said the rays from them could kill you. He hoped the machine was only for the magic trick Madame was planning for tomorrow night, and that Dr. Droz and Madame wouldn't try anything dangerous on Lily now. He glanced at the others sitting around him. Silva and Dimitri looked scared out of their skins.

"What'll happen to us here?" Silva asked in a whisper.

"Don't worry," Deedee said. "Droz won't do anything to you. It's Lily she wants."

"Droz only takes orphans to experiment on," Luca explained. "Children no one will miss. You have parents, Silva and Dimitri, your family is the circus—she would never dare destroy either of you. That would be a step too far."

"Or," said Dimitri, "you may be wrong. Maybe we'll disappear, like those others who disobeyed Madame. Maybe they'll keep a piece of each of us for Slimwood's wall of shame."

Deedee shuddered at the thought of that, and Angelique crawled farther into her corner alone. Robert saw that she was barely speaking to anyone; it was like she had regressed to some former lonely state.

"I'll bite their ears off before I let them do that to any of you," Malkin proclaimed. "You know what they say: 'It's not the size of the fox in the fight, but the size of the fight in the fox.'"

"Malkin's right," Robert said. "We can't sit here and

wait for them to make the next move. We need to fight back."

"What with?" Deedee asked. "We don't even have a plan."

"If we band together, we can come up with something," Robert told them. "It's the only way. Together we can be strong." The faces around him nodded in relieved agreement. But Robert was thinking anxiously of Lily, who right at this moment was facing Madame and Droz on her own.

CHAPTER 22

Dr. Droz showed Lily and Madame into a warehouse-sized space lit by dim gaslights on brackets attached to the walls. In the center of the room was a chaise longue, an armchair, and a coffee table—an island of plush furniture at sea in an industrial space of concrete. An irregular ticking noise echoed from the walls at the room's edges, where bookshelves and display cases filled with jars lurked in the shadows.

In the far wall was a huge iron-barred window looking out over the whole of Paris. Houses spread out behind the reflections in the glass, and the Eiffel Tower Airstation skewered the distant sky, lights burning on each of its decks, illuminating the moored zeppelins.

"I would very much like to inspect my machine," Madame said to Droz.

"All in good time, Hortense," Droz replied. "First, let's have some tea and refreshments."

Lily wondered what fresh insanity this was. She'd heard of midnight feasts, but tea in an abandoned hospital at the unearthly hour of two in the morning? That seemed another level of erratic behavior.

Dr. Droz led them over to the chaise and bade them sit. Then, when they were both seated, she picked up a bell from a side table and rang it, summoning her mechanical servant.

He finally arrived, clattering through the doorway, and Droz spoke with him. "Mr. Creaks, I realize it's rather late, but could you possibly fetch our guests some tea?"

Mr. Creaks nodded and lumbered off.

When he was gone, Dr. Droz sat in the armchair opposite Madame. She folded her hands in her lap and stared at Lily as if she was a miracle the doctor was seeing for the first time.

Finally, she leaned forward in her seat. "Ever since I read your papa's papers," she said, "I've been dying to meet you again, Lily."

Lily did not reply, though Madame gave her a sharp kick on the ankle to try to provoke one.

311

"Say something, Lily. *Mon Dieu!* Anyone would think you had no manners. And after I recommended your father send you to finishing school!" She smiled apologetically at the doctor.

Droz shifted awkwardly in her seat. "She's probably quite tired. It's late, and you have brought her rather a long way in difficult circumstances to see me."

Lily wondered if Droz meant the kidnapping or merely tonight's excursion from the circus in the hearse.

Madame shrugged as if to say, *So what?*

"You probably don't recall," Droz continued, facing Lily, "but we met when your mama was alive." Her voice ran with a treacly sickliness, and Lily found her accent hard to place. It was not French like Madame's, but it also wasn't English. "I was working with your father and Professor Silverfish at the time. This was before my name was discredited in English scientific circles, and I left England. Since then, I heard of your reincarnation from Madame here and read of it in your father's scientific papers. And I gather it's something of a miracle that you're alive. Your father's notes had much to say both personally and professionally about the creation of the Cogheart."

"I don't know anything of that," Lily said nervously. She wasn't quite sure what to make of the woman. "Anyway," she added, "those notes don't belong to you. Madame stole them from Papa. And Mama's red notebook."

"They were only my due," Madame interjected.

Droz ignored this remark. "But your father has spoken of me, yes?" she asked Lily.

"Not really."

"Funny." Droz's face clouded with anger. "I discussed the concept of hybrids with him many times and with your mother too. My ideas are in both their papers, though I took their theories further than any of us could've imagined." She paused and pursed her lips. "They would never aid me with my projects. Only Silverfish offered help. And then solely because your father had disappeared with his clockwork heart, and Silverfish needed assistance in creating a replacement."

"You created Silverfish's heart too?" Lily asked. She was intrigued now, despite herself.

"Of course," said Droz. "After your father's betrayal, there was no one else he trusted to do the work. And it had become illegal." She rubbed her hands together as if they were cold. "That's also part of the reason your papa hid you, Lily. Although he would never have told you so himself. That, and the fact he had a lucrative reputation to protect."

"That's a lie," Lily said. "The real reason Papa hid me

was to save me from people like you, who wish me harm."
Although, she realized, it had never worked. Somehow
bad fortune always found her, no matter how far away
Papa tried to shield her from it.

Dr. Droz laughed. "I wish you no harm, Lily. I merely
want to look at the invention inside you. It's quite
sophisticated compared to my creations—my freakish
children that I made for the circus."

"They're not freakish," Lily said. "They're people. Just
because you made them into lab rats and Slimwood and
Madame treat them like prisoners, it doesn't mean they
don't deserve a proper place in the world. Everyone
should accept them for who they are."

"Nonsense," Madame said, pursing her lips.

Dr. Droz smiled. "And do you think everyone would
accept *you* for who you are, Lily? If you were honest about
yourself?"

"I…I don't know," Lily said. "Robert did. And Tolly.
And Angelique and the other hybrids."

"Lost boys and freaks need as many friends as they
can get," Madame muttered.

Lily felt her scars itch angrily beneath her shirt.
Would the world accept her if it knew about her hybrid
nature? Reflexively, she put a hand to her chest… Deep
inside her, she wondered if, perhaps, they would not.

"My papa made his machines to help people and do good, to save lives," Lily said. "Yours have only made people miserable, imprisoned spectacles."

"Then why, if he was so pure-minded, did he abandon his work? Ask him that." Dr. Droz's face was etched with fury. "I'll tell you why—because he was afraid to defy a system that banned such inventions. Whereas I bravely continued and was punished for it, my work curtailed by those meddling men at the Mechanists' Guild. I was forced to come here and sell my creations—my children—to the Skycircus to make a living."

Dr. Droz looked off angrily into the distance. Only the tinkling of teacups brought her back. The large mechanical man had returned, carrying a tray.

Her face brightened. "Ah," she said, "at last! Here's Mr. Creaks with the tea."

The mechanical man had arrived bearing a grand floral teapot, a jug of milk, a tea strainer, three china cups and saucers, and a plate of delicious-looking biscuits. Lily's stomach rumbled at the sight of them. The only things she'd eaten in the last few days were gruel and stale bread.

The mechanical man was about to set the tray down on the table when he started shaking awfully.

"Clank it all!" Droz cursed. "He's malfunctioning.

We need to reset him! Where's his winding key?" Dr. Droz searched around in her pockets, but she couldn't appear to find it. The mechanical's fit was getting worse. He was spilling tea everywhere.

"Here, use this one," Madame said, taking the Lunk's winding key from her pocket and handing it to Droz. "They're the same model."

"Thank you." Dr. Droz stood and placed the winding key in the keyhole on Mr. Creak's thick neck, then turned it once anticlockwise.

The mechanical came to a stop.

"There," she said, and she took the tea tray from him before winding him up again.

He sprang back to life soon enough and left the room in a haze of jitters and odd movements.

"Apologies for his malfunctioning," Droz said. "I'll open his head up later and see what's wrong with him, but I imagine one of the cogs in his primary motor cortex has gotten out of line. Now, Madame Verdigris," said Dr. Droz. "If you might do the honors?"

"*Bien sûr.*" Madame began pouring out the tea through the strainer into the three cups, and when she was finished, she added a drop of milk to each one and stirred them.

Dr. Droz leaned toward Lily conspiratorially. "I

316

gleaned a lot of useful data from your mama's notes, which helped me complete my most recent creation, Angelique."

Lily was horrified. She hadn't realized that Mama's notebook had helped Droz as much as that.

Dr. Droz took one of the cups of tea from Madame. "After I was finished," she said, "Madame here suggested I send you the notebook. I thought it was a good idea. We wanted you to have it. At least until I could meet you in person." She smirked as if she'd told a joke.

Madame laughed too, though mirthlessly. She took up the plate of biscuits and offered one to Lily.

Lily decided she hated them both. She worried about what was happening to her friends while she was up here having fancy tea in the middle of the night. Droz was acting nice, but her words seemed as much for Madame as for her, and Lily wondered if they were just trying to lull her into a false sense of security. She couldn't, however, refuse their hospitality. Even if the biscuit was drugged like the chocolates, she was too hungry to care. Though, perhaps not? The two women were eating them too. She balanced her teacup on her lap and took one, biting into it. It tasted of almonds and sugar.

"Tell me," Droz said, watching Lily's face, intrigued. "How did you like it, the notebook? And our little birthday card? '*What it is that makes you tick*'—I suggested that part. Madame thought it might tip our hand, but I suspected you'd find it interesting. She told me you love solving puzzles, and I thought, with a little persuasion, such a gift would encourage you to investigate its origin."

Lily folded her arms. She refused to reply. She felt angry and betrayed. Was the doctor trying to goad her?

"Your mother loved mysteries too," Droz continued. "She thought that behind everything there was a fundamental truth. She was interested in using science to search for that truth." She took a sip of tea. "Yes, Grace was a great mechanist and a good friend. Though, like me, she was hamstrung by a lack of opportunity and support. The guild actively discouraged her ideas, in the same way they did mine."

She waved that last thought away then, as if it was of no consequence. "But we have talked enough. Why don't you wait here? Have another biscuit, and I shall speak to Madame in private."

Dr. Droz and Madame stood up and walked across the large room to a set of double doors hidden in the shadows, opposite the ones they had come in by. As Droz opened the door for Madame and stepped through, Lily caught a glimpse of a stark, white room and heard a terrible humming noise. Then the door closed behind them.

Lily had no idea how long they would be gone for. As quickly as she could, she got up and stalked the circumference of the room—in case there was anything she hadn't yet spotted that might help her to get away.

The window was too high up to climb from, and the bars too narrowly set, and anyway, it didn't even appear to open. The walls beside it were covered with blueprints for various mechanical hybrid devices—combinations of human and machine that Lily had never heard of or seen before. Springs and engine parts wove in and out of the wall between these drawings, clicking and ticking loudly—the source of the sound Lily had heard earlier—as if the space itself was part of a massive living clock.

When Lily investigated the cabinets, her skin crawled with shock, for they were stacked with glass jars filled with preserved animal carcasses—each one with a tiny mechanical adjustment. She glimpsed a mouse with a mechanical ear on its back, a monkey with an extra metal arm, and a kitten with six spidery legs, each floating in milky white water. Their eyes stared out at Lily, goggled wide by the magnifying curve of their glass jars. They felt somehow horribly alive and inarguably dead at the same time. The rest of the shelves were filled with old, rotting books.

She could find little else of use in the room—no implements of any kind. When she returned to the chaise and table, she noticed the three teaspoons on the tea tray. She picked up two of them and hid them in her dress pockets, just in case.

Then she went to the door Madame and Droz had left through and peered through the keyhole. The hairs on her arm stood on end, for it felt as if an electric energy was dissipating from the space beyond in waves.

On the far side of the room was an iron machine the size and shape of a small coffin. Its outside, painted a faded medical green, was covered in conductor loops, screws, and levers. As Lily glimpsed it, the nervous drumming inside her chest grew louder and louder, until the noise of her heart had become an unbearable cacophony of anxious, clattering beats, mixing with the ticks and clicks that the room itself was making.

Dr. Droz stood beside the machine. She was in the middle of saying something. Lily listened as hard as she could. "…and I've been able to combine the Hoffmans and van Kleef X-ray with the Lumière cinematograph to create the device," she explained to Madame as she fiddled with various dials and switches on the machine's control panel. "I call it the X-ray-cinematograph."

The machine hummed, making a terrible atonal purring noise that echoed around the tiled room. Lily could barely understand what any of this meant, but the machine itself *felt* bad to her, as if it was emitting waves of pulsing, repellent energy that Lily could sense even through the door.

"I thought you said you were having trouble with it?" Madame said.

"Oh, it works fine now," Dr. Droz assured her. "And it's relatively simple to operate. Let me show you… First, you adjust the conducting rod." She wound a handle on an outer panel. "Then turn it on with the switch, here." Droz pushed a button. "And it's ready to use."

Lily heard a click of engaging clockwork. The horrible whine that had been emanating from the machine's guts ratcheted up a notch, and she felt her own guts drop in terror at the sound.

Madame leaned forward to inspect the machine. She seemed pleased with the invention. "*Très bien*," she told Dr. Droz. "You've done a marvelous job."

"The patient to be x-rayed is placed here." The doctor ran her hand inside the coffin-shaped compartment. "Above them is a lens that will focus the X-ray image through this box here." She tapped the far end of the machine. "Which will then project the tiny image through the front lens, much like a pinhole camera. But I've adjusted the standard so that, instead of making a photographic plate, the cinematograph projects a live moving image out of the lens directly onto a screen."

Madame ran a hand across the machine. "And we can use this now, in the circus show?"

The doctor nodded. "It will be a spectacular debut that will get people talking. Something new to the audience. Most have never seen an X-ray before or a moving image. The two together will jolt them from their seats."

"A *magnifique* combination," Madame said.

"And," said the doctor, "it will expose the inner workings of the Cogheart. Nature and machine working in unison, which will prove to everyone that hybrids are a viable and worthy area of study."

"People will come especially to see it," Madame added. "It will be the highlight of our show—the entire city will bear witness to it, and soon money and fame will flood in through the doors of our little circus!"

The doctor flicked a switch on the other side of the machine. Immediately, lightning flickered from a copper rod that ran down the machine's center, crackling off a metal plate and running through a glass tube, lighting up the gas inside. This threw out an eerie green glow that illuminated the room at short, steady intervals, pouring across the women's faces and throwing their shadows against the walls.

The sight made Lily squirm. She watched through the keyhole as the little shaft of lightning flickered between the rod and the plate of the machine, and thought of the terrible lightning storm she and Robert had survived on the Thames earlier in the summer—how frightened she had been that the lightning would hit her and how it could have destroyed her heart if it hadn't hit Jack Door instead. Could this machine do the same? Would it reveal her heart but destroy it at the same time?

Dr. Droz put an apple inside the coffin beneath a large glass magnifying lens. The lightning crackled; there was a smell of burning dust. Then from the pinhole came a flickering negative black-and-white picture, which was projected onto the wall opposite.

The X-ray image showed the inside of the fruit, filled with seeds.

Madame clapped her hands together in joy.

"It works!" she cried. "With this machine, Lily will be the *pièce de résistance*. Our masterpiece."

Lily stared at the ghostly image of the apple. Its gray skin was shriveling slowly in plain sight. If the X-ray-cinematograph did that to an apple, then surely it would do the same to her? She felt sick.

"I'm afraid with multiple exposures to this machine the girl will likely not live long," Droz admitted.

"How long?" Madame asked.

"I'd estimate about six months."

"That's long enough for us to make our fortunes."

"And for me to find out everything I need to know about the workings of her heart," Dr. Droz agreed.

The image on the screen flickered, and the bright light of the projector went out. Droz's eyes turned to the door, and before Lily had a chance to react, she walked over and opened it to reveal Lily crouched on the other side.

"One never hears good things eavesdropping at keyholes, Lily," she said. "Now you know what we have planned for you tomorrow night."

"My papa will come for me," Lily said. "The gendarmes will have got a telegram to him. He's sure to be in France by tomorrow, and when he finds me, either here or at the Skycircus, you will be arrested."

"It's too late for that now," Dr. Droz said.

"The world is waiting for you, Lily," Madame added.

Lily was about to reply when there was a knock at the door.

It was Mr. Creaks, bearing an envelope on a silver platter. "A wire has come," he said in a low monotone.

"Read it out then, Creaks," Dr. Droz commanded.

Creaks opened the envelope and began to read.

"The police searched the circus and found nothing, stop. We're in the clear, stop."

"Ah, splendid!" Madame exclaimed, clapping her hands together. "Did you hear that, Lily? The show will go on after all!"

Then Lily knew with a giddy certainty that Madame was right. Their plan would play out to the bitter end, and if anyone was going to save her friends and stop it, it would have to be her.

CHAPTER 23

Robert, Malkin, and Angelique sat together on the dirty floor of the abandoned pharmacy, hoping and waiting for Lily's return. The others had all fallen asleep on a pile of old blankets under a workbench in the far corner, so the three of them were the only ones who heard the commotion in the hallway before Lily was thrust through the door.

She collapsed next to them ashen-faced, her eyes red from blinking away the tears. "The police found nothing suspicious at the circus," she said. "Madame and the others are taking us back later, when the coast's clear. Along with the X-ray machine." Fear prickled in her chest. "I wish Papa was here to stop all this," she blurted out.

"The thought of being forced into that terrible machine of Dr. Droz's…" She couldn't hold her sadness in any longer and burst out crying. "They're going to put me in it during the show, Robert," she sobbed. "I've seen it—and it's so dangerous it might kill me."

Robert placed a steadying hand on her shoulder. "It'll be all right," he said. "We'll come up with a plan."

Malkin jumped up on her lap and licked her face. Lily sniffled and wiped her eyes. "What plan? Madame took everything when she caught us. The lockpicks, your note, even my pocket watch. All I have left is these." She took out the few remaining pages of Mama's notebook and the two teaspoons she'd stolen earlier, and showed them to him.

"They might come in handy," Robert said.

"Very." Malkin snorted. "If we decide to have a tea break or do some reading in the next few hours."

"Malkin's right," Lily said. "They're useless."

Robert shook his head. "No, we'll think of something."

Angelique shifted uncomfortably and folded her wings behind her.

"Maybe you should rest, Lily?" she suggested.

"I'm too churned up inside," Lily replied. "I can't think straight. I've no ideas left. Madame's always one step ahead. I don't know how I'm going to save myself or the rest of you, and I don't think I can sleep for worry."

"Panic never solves a problem," Angelique said. "Answers will come, I promise. Think of something else," she suggested. "Why don't you tell me the rest of the tale of Icarus?"

"What about it?"

"When you stopped, he'd plunged into the ocean, and I never got to find out what happened next."

"There was no next. That was the end," Lily said. "He drowned. That's it."

Angelique shook her head. "No," she said. "I don't think that's true. I think it's just one ending. That's the beauty of stories—they're like clay. You can mold them into whatever shape you like. They don't always have to be the same. They can change."

Lily leaned toward her. "No matter what words are written on the page?" she asked.

Angelique nodded. "If they're stories for telling out loud," she said, "then who's to say what the words are? You can rewrite the ending. Like with your mama. It's not her notebook that's her legacy, Lily, but you. Through you, she lives on and so does her story."

Lily sat up straighter. "But *this* story...it's been the same for thousands of years, so it must be right. You can't go changing stories like that, can you? Tweaking them as you see fit? Things are as they are."

"No, Lily, things are as you choose to see them."

"Who taught you that?" Lily asked.

"You did, when you forgave my betrayal. And when you opened the door to our cell, you gave us another choice—to go with you or to stay in our prison."

"I don't know if that's a choice anymore," Lily said.

"It is," Angelique told her. "You made me see what our choices truly are. That even if they lock us up, if we're free in here—" she put a hand to her chest—"if we're free in our hearts, they can *never* truly imprison us."

"You could be right," Lily said. But she still wasn't sure. Everything over the last few days had confused her, and she was so tired and afraid. Robert and Malkin were slumped down beside her and looked like they'd given up too. Only Angelique's deep brown eyes still contained a tiny flicker of hope.

"So what do you think happened next in Icarus's story?" Lily asked her.

"I think Icarus was rescued from the water by—"

"Fishermen?" Deedee suggested. It appeared she'd woken up and had been listening in on their conversation.

"Who nursed him back to health," Luca added. He was also awake, sitting up next to Deedee.

"Icarus got well again, in their village," Angelique

said, opening her wings wide like a feathered blanket around them all, and then Lily saw that Silva and Dimitri were awake too and listening. "But he never forgot his father," Angelique said. "And one day he decided he would go and look for him."

"Daedalus could've been anywhere," Lily said. "He thought his son had drowned, but he couldn't even stop to mourn Icarus until he reached land on the far side of the ocean."

"Icarus imagined his papa had gone home," Angelique said. "To their old house, where they used to live."

At this, Lily thought of Brackenbridge Manor and her own papa waiting for her and how much he must be missing her. She hoped he was on his way. She took a deep breath before she continued the story.

"His old home was a long way across the Mediterranean," she said. "Icarus would need a proper ship to sail so far or some other way of traveling... But the fishermen wouldn't let him go. They thought he was a miracle when he'd fallen from the sky. He'd brought them luck, fish, and money after a long period of hunger. So they tried to keep him prisoner."

"But he was the son of an inventor," Robert said. "He'd watched his papa make the wings in the first place."

"That's right," Angelique said. "They'd defeated one

prison together, and so Icarus knew he could defeat another."

"He'd been his papa's apprentice so long," Robert said, "helping out on bits of construction, he found he could probably make wings himself from memory, to fly high again like he had with his da."

Lily realized everyone was working together now to tell the story. "The only thing stopping Icarus," she said, "was that last time the wings had almost killed him. He'd flown too close to the sun, and they'd melted. A risk like that can be deadly."

Angelique nodded; she knew such things from her own experience. "But not always," she said. "Failure, especially a big failure—and surviving it—that can make you stronger. You learn from your mistakes. You make better plans. The bigger the mistake, the stronger you become. You come out the other side, and if it's bad enough, you adjust your path and *never* make that mistake again."

"It's like learning the tightrope," Deedee added. "Don't look back and don't look down. If you fall, pick yourself up and try again. But the most important thing is not to give up, to keep moving forward."

"So," Lily said, "Icarus had learned from his father how to make wings and fly, and he'd learned from his own mistake not to swoop too close to the sun. He'd everything he needed. He built his own wings, took off into the sky, and didn't fly too close to the sun this time—instead, he flew home to find his father."

Angelique smiled. "And that's the end of the story?"

"It is," Lily said. "Or maybe just the beginning?" She sighed. "Madame had the Lunk's winding key, as well. I wish I could've stolen it. We might've been able to force a stop on him, or at least make him malfunction somehow, but I just couldn't get it."

"Which pocket did she put it in?" Robert asked.

"What?" Lily said. "I don't know…the left."

"Her left or your left?"

"Her left. Why?"

"No reason." Robert clutched the pair of teaspoons in his fist. "I've had an idea that just might work."

He sounded hopeful. Lily was relieved. Telling the story to the hybrids and having them tell it back to her had somehow lifted all their spirits. It had pulled Lily from the ocean of despair she'd been falling into, deep inside herself, and brought her back to the here and now.

She hoped Papa had gotten the message Robert had sent in the telegram and was coming for them, but she knew that it was just as likely he had not, especially if the police had been to check the Skycircus site and found no evidence of her there. She thought of what Angelique had said about how people could change their own story while they lived it and how even failure made you stronger. And she thought about what Deedee had said about not giving up and moving forward.

The X-ray machine was so dangerous there was a strong chance it might kill her in the very first performance. But maybe, just maybe, the circus ring would provide an opportunity for her to speak out, to prove to everyone that humans and hybrids were really no different from each other...

As she looked at Angelique, Robert, Malkin, Deedee, Dimitri, Silva, and Luca, she knew that they would help her. She might not be able to rely on the police or Papa, but she and the other children here had worked together, and she knew they could do it again.

"We need to get away during the show tonight," she said. "Before they bring me onstage to start my performance. We'll need to use your wings, Angelique, Robert's inventiveness, my heart, Malkin's speed and agility." She looked to the others. "And the skills of each one of you combined to help make this escape happen. I think we can do it if we join forces and if we can persuade the others to as well—we didn't try that before. But we need to succeed, because I might not live to tell the tale if I get put in that machine, and you all deserve a better life than this. I don't want this to be my very last chance to prove that we hybrids are just the same as everyone else. I need to tell Papa how I feel, and I…I mean we…we need to make a stand."

CHAPTER 24

The wait was interminable. Lily had barely slept through the night and was hungry and tired. She, Robert, Malkin, and the other children spent the whole morning held captive in the abandoned pharmacy with nothing at all to eat or drink and no news of what was happening.

Then, late in the afternoon, Madame, Auggie, and Joey finally returned and unlocked the door, escorting them out of the hospital.

As Lily was thrust back into the hearse with the others, she caught a terrifying glimpse of the X-ray machine already tied to its roof. Then they set off.

Through the window of the vehicle's passenger

compartment, she could see the back of Droz's head. She was coming to witness the show that evening. Lily's mind flashed nervously forward to it and all that could go wrong, and she dragged her eyes away from the doctor and out to the streets instead.

The people of Paris gave them puzzled looks as they drove past in the hearse. As they approached the Bois de Boulogne, Lily felt a deepening trepidation. She watched the city recede and the woodlands get closer. Through the dust-spattered glass, she glimpsed bill posters pinned to the trees that advertised the evening's show. A terrible sense of dread leeched into her bones. She felt as if she was being transported to her execution alongside her own unique guillotine.

They approached the high, spiked wooden fence of the Skycircus site and pulled past the ticket kiosk through the open gate, which was shut behind them by roustabouts.

The Big Top and the gondola of the sky-ship loomed outside the hearse's window as it drove right up to the edge of the tent and stopped outside the artists' entrance. The Lunk lumbered over and opened the doors of the hearse.

"We've only an hour till showtime," Madame said, appearing behind him with the two clowns. "Get in there, all of you, and put on your costumes." Her gaze snapped to Robert. "You, boy, can help everyone else get ready." And then to Malkin. "As for that clanking, big-snouted mechanical rag rug, put him in a cage or something, but just keep him out of my sight."

She stepped aside as Auggie and Joey dragged Malkin and the children out. Robert was last. Lily saw how white he looked, dizzy and tired on his feet; as he was pulled from the back of the hearse, he stumbled into Madame.

"Get away from me, you fool!" she cried, pushing him off.

Lily grasped his arm to stop him from falling, and he righted himself with a strange look.

Joey and Auggie led them into the tent, while Madame disappeared to talk to Slimwood, who was waiting on the other side of the hearse steam-wagon.

In the backstage area, Auggie and Joey locked Malkin in a large holding pen at the back of the tent that looked big enough for all of them and as if it had been specially set up to stop them from escaping.

"Get changed now," they told Lily and the rest of the children, and they strode among them, along with the Lunk, keeping an eye to see that they didn't try anything. The atmosphere was quiet and subdued, for the Lunk was monitoring everyone closely, and the rest of the roustabouts were lurking around at the edges of the backstage area. Droz was nowhere to be seen—Lily supposed she must've joined the crowds in the front of house.

Robert set to helping Lily find her stage clothes. When no one was looking, he flashed her a grin, revealing something in his palm. It was the Lunk's winding key.

"How the tock did you get that?" Lily asked, quietly astounded.

"Magic," Robert said. "And a bit of sleight of hand—I picked it from Madame's pocket when I fell against her as we got out of the hearse."

"Won't she notice it's missing?"

"That's the clever part. I put one of your teaspoons in its place. They're about the same size and weight." He gave her another smile. "With this key, we can force the Lunk to a stop," he explained. "Then we can open him up and change his workings so he malfunctions during the show. Do you remember what part of his brain we need to move the cogs in?"

"I think it's the motor cortex?" Lily bit her nails. She was a little unsure.

"Are you certain?" Robert asked.

She brightened. "Yes. It was written in Mama's notebook too. But how are we going to catch the Lunk and do all that with everyone watching?"

Robert shrugged. "I don't know, but we've got an hour now and nearly an hour of the show to work it out."

Lily felt nervous and uncertain about Robert's plan—but it was the only one they had, and anyway, she'd no more time to discuss it, for she was supposed to be getting into her outfit for the show.

She put on the sparkly white dress Madame had chosen for her and a spare pair of lace-up boots that were almost the same color as Angelique's ballet shoes. She still had no idea exactly what she was supposed to be doing in her act, and she was filled with trepidation at the thought of going out there to face the X-ray machine and who knew what else. Even if her and Robert's plan succeeded, it would be a close-run thing.

She finished dressing and tied her hair with a length of ribbon she found at the dressing table. When she was done, she approached her friend at the mirror.

Angelique had already changed into her leotard and ballet shoes with white ribbons. She had braided her hair and threaded it with glass beads from the drawer in the dressing table. She was using a palette of makeup to paint her eyelids in shimmering colors and another palette of red to rouge her cheeks.

Finally she turned to Lily and took her hand.

"Let's do your eyelids too," she said, laughing nervously.

Lily shut her eyes, willing the soft touch of the brush to stroke away her worries. As Angelique applied makeup to her face, Lily could feel the winged girl's hands shaking.

When she'd finished, Lily opened her eyes and stared at herself in the mirror. It was a shock, for she looked somehow more grown-up. Angelique had used the same makeup colors on Lily as she had on herself, so that Lily's eyes had the same shimmer as hers, and her cheeks the same blush. She'd even threaded Lily's hair with the same bright crystals as her own. Side by side in the mirror, the pair of them looked like twins with their makeup and determined faces, just with different complexions. Lily felt as if someone else's impression of her had been made real. Edgily, she pulled her eyes away and looked around at everyone else.

They were all ajitter as they changed into their stage outfits: Dimitri in his high riding boots, Silva with her scarf knotted round her neck, and Deedee and Luca in their glad rags for the show. Only Robert remained in his rough work clothes, and Malkin in his usual scruffy red fur coat. Neither of them were in the performance.

When they were finished, the Lunk gathered the hybrids and the other children together and locked them all in the holding pen with Malkin.

A little while later, the rest of the acts were brought in from their cells and began making themselves up at the costume table. Their faces looked pale and nervous, and they glanced every so often at the children in their cage, uncertain of what the ringmaster and mistress had planned.

Finally, Slimwood and Madame arrived in their costumes. Madame leaned her parasol against the makeup table and began gluing her beard on at one of the mirrors. When it was attached, she was barely recognizable, and Lily remembered she was a character for the show—the person she'd been when they'd first met her in the circus: Madame Lyons-Mane.

Madame Lyons-Mane clapped her hands together, and Slimwood blew his whistle. "GATHER ROUND, EVERYONE!" he shouted.

The entire company stopped what they were doing and made their way to the center of the dressing room, giving him and Madame their full attention.

The Buttons and the other circus acts and show families were there. Robert watched them through the bars of their special enclosure. An all-consuming dread filled their eyes as they contemplated the caged children. It seemed as if they'd no idea what to do.

Madame spoke loudly, although her mouth was barely

visible beneath her fake beard. "I wanted to say how delighted I am that we managed to procure our new arrival, Miss Hartman, to be our *petite surprise* in the show tonight. I've decided her *nom de scène* will be Miss Cora Valentine, and she'll be the most heart-stopping act anyone has ever seen!" She paused and stared around at the group, daring anyone to contradict her—but no one did.

"The rest of you must be at your best, performing to the highest of your abilities to complement her star turn. I want this show to be *le plus beau* on earth. I want people to be talking about it in a hundred years' time! We're not going to achieve that unless everyone believes in my vision and listens to me." She waved her hands at them. "Remember, I keep this house. I tell you what to do. And you do as you're told."

There was a hushed murmur among the company. Robert remembered how his ma had told him that the time before a performance was for everyone to come together, but in the Skycircus it seemed this moment was reserved for threats and recrimination.

"As for these children"—Madame indicated Silva and Dimitri and the hybrids—"who tried to steal away before our very important premiere… there will be no reprieve for them—not tonight, not ever. I've decided they will do the show, just as I command, as always. Then tomorrow, we'll discuss their punishment."

"No, please!" Bruno and Gilda Buttons cried together, rushing up to Madame. "They've done no wrong. Let them go, they need to be with us, we can look after them, make them behave, we promise."

"They helped the hybrids," Slimwood said. "Fraternizing with freaks is forbidden."

Tears streamed down Gilda Buttons's face. She reached out to Silva and Dimitri in the cage, but Auggie and Joey grabbed her by the arms and pulled her away, pushing her back into the crowd.

Madame turned to the rest of the performers. "This is what happens to those who don't play by the rules. It's not just you who gets hurt, but the ones you love. Remember that, the rest of you." Madame pulled Lily's watch from the pocket of her dress coat and checked it. "Ten minutes to showtime. Now get out there and entertain the crowds, and let's make it the best show ever. If it isn't, then I swear something terrible will happen to everyone!"

The company dispersed in shocked dribs and drabs, whispering among themselves. No one dared approach the caged children, though their faces showed their concern.

Time was running out. With a sickening lurch of terror, Lily realized they only had about sixty minutes to put their plan together before she would be taken out into the ring for the grand finale.

She thought of Papa waiting for her at home in Brackenbridge, and Tolly and the friends who had been there on her birthday when she had disappeared, and how they had never had her birthday party and maybe now they never would. She thought of the torn pages of the notebook. She needed her mama's courage now.

There was only one page she hadn't looked at. She'd tucked it into the sash of her sparkly white dress, and she pulled it out now. It was, she realized, the last entry in the book, for it was written on the day her mama had died:

<u>Wednesday, 30th October 1889,</u>
<u>Riverside Walk, Chelsea</u>

Tonight we are going to dinner together to celebrate leaving London. I will wear my red taffeta dress, the one Lily likes so much. She is coming with us.

She insists on bringing the ammonite I gave her on the beach this summer. She carries it everywhere she goes. She likes to take it out and flip it between her fingers like a magic trick to make the fossil appear and disappear.

I'm worried about John's plan to relocate to

Brackenbridge. He's always running away from things. I think that's why he wants us to move. He has kept our destination secret from everyone we know, and I wonder why. Is he in some sort of trouble? I know he and Simon have been quarreling over business matters.

I have glanced at the window, and it is snowing! It rarely snows in London. And in October—it seems a strange omen. To think two months ago we were at the beach, and the weather was fine.

I have realized something John has not. He cannot run away from his problems. Wherever he goes, there they will be. Whatever road he takes to avoid them is the road they await upon. Tonight, at dinner, I intend to tell him as much. We shouldn't be fleeing London, whatever issues he has with Simon—we should stay and see them through.

A moment of conviction will be required on my part to say this. But I must. To speak the truth we carry deep inside us, within our hearts, no matter how difficult, is the only way we can be free.

And if we cannot learn this for ourselves, how can we teach it to our daughter?

I will write more later, when I get back.

But she never had, for that was the last day she was alive. The day everything changed. The day Lily received the Cogheart and turned into a hybrid.

Tenderly, she touched the scars from the accident that itched across her chest.

Mama was right—whatever Lily's troubles were, she couldn't run from them anymore. She had to learn to live with them, learn to live with what made her different— the things she'd lost, as well as those she'd gained.

Her ma's few written words were like water in the desert, and now they were over, finished, gone. But one phrase rang out from them: *"To speak the truth we carry deep inside us, within our hearts, no matter how difficult, is the only way we can be free."*

Robert couldn't stand the waiting. He got up and began pacing around like a hungry lion himself. The far side of the cage was pushed against the curtain wall, and he could hear voices filtering through from the other side— the excited babble of children and adults finding their seats. The familiar jaunty jig of the accordion, accompanied by flute and fiddle, drifted from the front of house.

There was a small hole in the canvas wall that butted up against the edge of the cage. Robert put his eye to it and looked through.

The Big Top was filling up. On the far side of the ring, Auggie was selling his wares from the sweetie cart to a long line of customers. Their happy faces in the colored lamplight smiled at Joey's clowning antics. More folk were filing in, and Robert wondered if he could cry out to them as they filtered through the tent, but then he realized they wouldn't hear him over the music and their own excited chatter.

The rest of the circus troupe stood in a line beside the backing cloth of the ring. They waved at the crowds, but their smiles were only pasted on, and every now and then they flicked worried glances to the backstage area, obviously thinking of Silva and Dimitri, the children of the whole circus, locked up in the cage. But Madame's threats were enough to prevent them from doing anything to help.

When everyone was seated, the performers drifted through the curtain to the backstage. As soon as they stepped out of view of the audience, their grins dropped and their eyes were full of concern.

Meanwhile Auggie and Joey went into their routine: putting out the oil lamps that hung from the tent poles.

As darkness fell, the children in their cage shivered in anticipation.

Soon, the last light was extinguished.

The butterflies inside Robert's belly fluttered sharply, as if they had wings made of broken glass.

For better or worse, the show was about to begin.

CHAPTER 25

Slimwood and Madame Lyons-Mane stepped through the curtains in a flash of limelight. Robert and Lily watched them through the hole in the backcloth. As they set off walking in opposite directions around the sawdust ring, Lily searched the faces of the crowds in the front row for Dr. Droz, but she couldn't see the woman anywhere.

Slimwood unbuttoned his red swallowtail tuxedo as he walked, and Madame shook loose her blonde hair and fake beard. She wore the same vermilion dress from the show in Brackenbridge and carried the same striped parasol.

As they had before, Slimwood and Madame met each

other at a point directly in front of the VIP section and threw their arms up in the air.

"*MESDAMES ET MESSIEURS!*" Madame shouted. "*Je m'appelle Madame Lyons-Mane.*"

"And my name is Slimwood!" Slimwood added.

"*Bienvenue dans notre cirque, pour un spectacle MAGNIFIQUE d'un qualité UNIQUE!*"

There was more talk in French, but Robert could barely listen. He had to do something while the entire crew were out there and engrossed in the show; he had to take a chance—perhaps if he spoke to the rest of the circus folk, they would help?

He scrambled away from the hole in the curtain and waved at the adult performers in the room, who were wandering around like dazed drudges.

"Please listen!" Robert whispered.

Malkin joined in, letting out a quiet yap to attract their attention.

Some of the circus folk stopped what they were doing, including Bruno and Gilda Buttons.

Their backs were to him, but he could see them shift uncomfortably as he spoke, so he could tell they were listening.

"You may have thought it'd be only Lily and me and the hybrid children who'd be punished by Madame and

Slimwood, because we weren't part of the circus family, but you can see for yourselves, it's your own children too."

None of them had turned. He tried again.

"If you keep silent, then you're complicit, and eventually, when they see you won't stand up for yourselves, they'll come for you."

Lily came to stand next to him and took his hand. "Look around," she said quietly. "You think you don't have it so bad because you're not the ones in here behind bars, like us. But ask yourself this: are you really outside the cage? Or are you trapped too?"

"What you do tonight could make a difference," Robert added softly. "We have a plan that could mean we all get out of here. If you're prepared to stand up and be counted by helping us, then you won't just be saving my life and Lily's, you'll be saving your own."

That was it—that was all he could think to say. He hoped they'd taken it in and that, when the time came to act, they would help. If they didn't, he and Lily and the other children would be on their own out there in the dark.

The jangling filler music from the band told them the introduction to the show was over, and everyone moved quickly to their places. Madame and Slimwood trooped back in from their opening speeches, followed by the Lunk.

Auggie and Joey were still in the ring, doing their clown act. When that was finished, the next few acts went on. Then Madame came over and let Silva and Dimitri out of the cage.

"Silva," she said. "You may join your parents. Dimitri, you're up after them. Get the horses ready."

Silva joined Bruno and Gilda Buttons, who were waiting behind the curtains. The music started, signaling the start of the acrobats' set, and Slimwood announced them as they entered the ring: *"MESDAMES ET MESSIEURS! Nous vous présentons…THE FABULOUS BOUNCING BUTTONS!"*

Madame, Joey, Auggie, and the rest of the roustabouts stepped out to join Slimwood in watching the performers, leaving only the Lunk guarding the children. This was it. It was now or never. And who knew how long they had before someone would return.

Robert signaled to Dimitri outside the cage, who was preparing his horses. Dimitri ducked down, and when he reappeared he had his length of lasso rope in his hand.

He crept round the front of the horses and threw it—watching it land, first go, around the Lunk's neck.

Quickly, he looped the rope round one of the cage bars, pulling it back through and tying the end round the horse's neck. Then he slapped the beast on its flank so that it leaped forward, pulling the Lunk off his feet. The mechanical man was dragged up against the outside of the cage with a *bong!*

Luckily, the sound was covered by the noise of the crowd and music from outside.

The Lunk struggled to get himself upright, but before he could, Lily threw her scarf over his eyes so he couldn't see and Robert inserted the winding key in the back of his head, jamming the mechanism in the wrong direction, hoping upon hope that Lily was right and this was the emergency method to switch a mechanical off.

The Lunk opened his mouth and let out a screech that luckily was muffled by Lily's scarf draped around his face. Then his limbs went still.

"He's stopped," Robert whispered to Lily. "Now we need to open him up."

He used the handle of the winding key to undo the screws on the back of the Lunk's head-panel and then wrenched it out of the way with the end of the teaspoon.

They peered in at the stopped internal workings of the Lunk's clockwork brain.

Between the hairspring, gear train, balance wheel,

fork pin, and escapement mechanisms, Robert found the part that he thought might be the primary motor cortex and set to work using the spoon and the key as his tools, pulling out cogs and making some adjustments. Before he finished, he reset some dials on the time clock at the center of the Lunk's mechanical brain.

"I've timed his breakdown to occur in fifty minutes' time," he explained to everyone, "when they come to get Lily for the finale. The Lunk should be walking with you across the ring at that point, Lily. When you see his eyes flicker, you should get out of the way quick as you can, because I don't know exactly what he'll do when his system malfunctions."

Luca and Deedee looked aghast and delighted at the thought. Angelique smirked. Dimitri glanced over his shoulder to check no one had heard them. The rest of the performers were whispering amongst themselves in shocked belief at what they were doing.

Quick as he could, Robert closed the panel on the Lunk's head and wound him up again. Then he, Dimitri, Luca, and Lily undid the rope around the Lunk's neck. With the help of Deedee and Angelique, they strained to tip the heavy mechanical man back upright and away from the cage.

Robert could hear Slimwood still narrating the act.

"See the Buttons jump like tiddlywinks! See them shine in their most daring acrobatic feat, on the seesaw!"

They were just in time—that was the Lunk's cue to bring out the seesaw. He sprang back to life, wavering around and clutching at his head as if he was drunk, before picking up the seesaw and creaking off to carry it onstage. Robert hoped that when the moment arrived, the timer would go off and his efforts to reprogram the Lunk would work. He'd done all he could.

Act by act, the show continued.

As it got closer to the end and Lily's moment in the limelight, the children in the cage and the circus folk and roustabouts milling around backstage got more and more antsy. Order was beginning to break down. The other acts had obviously taken in what Robert and Lily had said to them, and some of them were refusing to go on.

Lily could see them through the bars of the cage, arguing with Slimwood. He'd already had to axe some of them from the bill.

"It's no good," she said anxiously to Robert and Angelique. "The show's running short. The Lunk's not going to malfunction until the show's over; I'll already have been in the X-ray-cinematograph machine."

"Then we need to do something to slow things down," Robert said.

"I can stay in the air for as long as you like," Angelique said. "Elongate my act. Delay things so we're back on schedule for the timer."

"You'd do that for us?" Malkin asked.

Angelique nodded. "This may be my one chance to change things in this circus for good. To make everyone in the audience really see what's been going on here."

"Thank you," Lily and Robert whispered together.

Malkin nudged his nose into Angelique's palm to thank her too.

Angelique's music started to play, and out front, Slimwood began his introduction of her. "LADIES AND GENTLEMEN, WITNESS THE FIRST OF TWO ASTOUNDING FINALES! A monster so magnificent, a hybrid so hypnotic, that they call her the fairy-princess of England…"

Angelique shook as he continued speaking.

"At the end of your act, just don't come down," Robert said. "They'll have to let you carry on."

Angelique nodded. Her face suddenly looked very nervous, and her hands were shaking. Lily thought she should probably try and say something to calm the flying girl's fears.

"All you have to do," she said suddenly—to herself as much as Angelique—"is take a chance and step into the light."

Robert nodded. "Think of the story of Icarus," he said. "Once you've fallen, you pick yourself up and try again. Then you can finally be free."

"I suppose it's the only way to stop the torture and bullying…" Angelique said.

Robert smiled. "That was their plan all along—divide and conquer. Treat people differently, make one group fear and hate the others. If no one pulls together, then Slimwood and Madame will never be defeated."

"But now you have the chance to help do that," Lily said, and as she spoke she saw Deedee and Luca and Dimitri were listening too. "The adults believe in you, Angelique, since you saved one of their own. Slimwood and Madame, they're big bullies. No different from any other kind of bully. We can fight them together."

"You're right." Angelique nodded as she paced around the middle of the cage, leaning a little lighter on her stick. "I was already different before all this. They may have been the ones who made me a bird, but they were also the ones who put me in a cage, and they don't deserve my loyalty or my fear."

The color was already returning to her face, and Lily

felt a small amount of relief. But her thoughts were stopped as Madame stormed through the curtain and toward the cage with the Lunk. Unlocking the door, she pulled Angelique out and hustled her toward the arena.

Lily watched her friend go, her back a little straighter than Lily had seen it before. She glanced around the cage at everyone else—each of them looked a little less dejected now. They were all standing up, ready to take the battle into the ring as soon as Lily went out there. Her eyes alighted on Robert and Malkin, her best friends, who had been through everything with her, and she knew they would play their part when the Lunk malfunctioned to get her out.

She was up next after Angelique. And now there was nothing left to do but wait for her turn.

Angelique didn't return after her act. Lily could only think she was in the rafters, refusing to come down. She hoped that the winged girl would be able to swoop in and rescue her when the time came, just as they'd planned.

But there was no more time for her to dwell on that, for Madame was rushing over. She unlocked the cage and pulled Lily out, then she yanked Robert from behind the bars as well, handing him over to Joey and Auggie, who marched him away toward the back exit of the tent.

"What are you doing? Where are you taking him?" Lily screamed at Madame.

"Auggie and Joey will put your friend in the feeding chamber of the wild animal cage," Madame explained. "And if you try anything in the ring, like pulling away from me or alerting anyone to the fact you're a prisoner here, then he will be fed to them."

"You can't do that!" Lily said.

"We won't, if you do as we say," Madame replied.

"Your machine's dangerous," Lily tried to tell her. "It'll make me ill, shrivel me up, until I won't be able to work for you any longer."

Madame shrugged. "Not in one go. Droz said it will take at least six months for that machine to snuff out your life, and in that time Slimwood and I will have made enough money to leave this circus behind forever."

"I'm not afraid to die," Lily told her. "I've died three times already—survived a steam-wagon crash, a near-fatal shooting, and a drowning attempt in the Thames. I'm sure I can survive your feeble attempt on my life. And when I get free of all this, it'll be you who regrets the choices you've made."

The words were like a shield to bounce the danger off, but she didn't feel that way inside. Inside she felt small and tired, like a broken wingless bird, as if the last fight had already been pushed out of her, and she'd lost.

In the ring the band began to play a new tune. It must've been her introductory music, for over it she could hear Slimwood speaking to the audience: "LADIES AND GENTLEMEN, YOU ARE ABOUT TO EXPERIENCE A BRAND-NEW SHOWSTOPPER!"

She remembered hearing almost the same words from the other side of the curtain when she'd first seen Angelique—and now here she was, trapped just like her friend. Not a winged girl forbidden to fly free, but a girl with an invincible heart in a heartless show.

Madame guided her up to the curtains, and the Lunk joined them, boxing Lily in on the other side. Lily felt sick with nerves. She didn't want to set foot in that machine. She didn't want to face the danger of death alone, but she couldn't turn back. How could she let them carry out their threat to throw Robert to the wild animals? She wondered idly why Papa hadn't come. Or anyone, in fact. Was it because Robert's telegram had gone astray? Did nobody in the audience realize what was really going on?

Out front, Slimwood was still shouting. "The Skycircus's most fantastic freak!" he announced. "A MAGNIFICENT MONSTER! A hybrid so stupendous!

A MIRACLE of our modern clockwork age! A once-in-a-lifetime vision so HYPNOTIC, to ignore her would be HEARTLESS! A bewitching blend of humanity and clockwork! Witness her secrets revealed now beneath our brand-new X-ray cinematic device. Revel in the image of the TERRIBLE CLOCKWORK CREATION that lurks in her chest. You are about to see a FUSION OF BLOOD AND STEEL never before witnessed. I give you our very final spectacle, a heartless girl who yet still lives: MISS CORA VALENTINE!"

The curtains opened, and the spotlight swept toward them across the ring, blinding Lily to everything that lay ahead. Then Madame thrust Lily before her out onto the sparkling sawdust stage.

CHAPTER 26

Lily was led across the circus ring by Madame and the Lunk. The band played faster and faster, elongating each note. The fiddle swooped in anticipation, and the drums beat as hard as Lily's heart, while the accordion spat out jagged notes that mixed in with the chatter and whispers of the crowds filling the tent.

Lily glanced around at them. The place was packed to the rafters; they had even brought in more seats, and people were sitting in the aisles. She searched desperately for Papa among them, but the darkness and the mess of panic inside her made the faces blur.

With shock she realized that Dr. Droz was standing in the center of the ring, fiddling with the levers and dials on the X-ray machine, which buzzed like a mechanical bee. A crackle of lightning flashed in a tube attached to its lid, spreading a toxic smell through the air and eliciting hushed groans and mutterings from the audience.

Terror spread through Lily like rancid melting butter. Her scars itched on her chest, and the hairs on her arms stood on end.

This machine was going to take a photograph of her insides, but more than that, she remembered with horror, the radiation it emitted would probably kill her.

The audience shifted around uncomfortably in their seats and coughed restlessly, taking in Lily with wide, frightened eyes. Then the whispers started. Lily caught a few words in French that she couldn't understand, but the tone suggested fear and distress—as if they were unsure of what they were witnessing but understood enough to be horrified.

The X-ray box made a terrible humming noise, and the projector clacked and ticked as Madame and the Lunk escorted Lily closer to the machine.

As the Lunk forced Lily into the machine, she heard the cogs in his head ticking oddly. Why hadn't he malfunctioned yet? Shouldn't that be happening right about…now?

Nothing.

Lily felt nauseous. This was it then. The plan had failed, and they were going to use the machine on her…

Robert was crammed into a narrow metal feeding chamber that opened into the bigger area of the cage. As soon as Lily disappeared for her part in the show, Auggie and Joey had come and taken him from the holding pen and brought him to the cargo bay, where the wild animals' cage had just been returned after their act. The wild animals looked particularly angry, probably from their turn being poked and prodded by the Lunk in the ring.

"What's going on?" Robert squeaked as Auggie and Joey shut the gate behind him with a clang. "You're not supposed to be doing this! Only if Lily did something wrong!"

"Never mind that," Auggie said. "It's teeding fime. We always feed them after they've performed, and tonight they're going to fite your blesh and bind your grones!"

"These beasts haven't eaten since Brackenbridge or before," Joey explained. "They're starving and restless, and they need something raw. You're a bystander, Robert, not one of life's winners. You've outlived your usefulness—except as their dinner."

Auggie pulled a lever, and a metal door flew upward in front of Robert. Then Joey reached through the bars and shoved him from behind so that he tumbled into the main cage. The two clowns didn't wait to see the result of their actions; instead, they turned and stalked away, Joey jingling the keys to the cage in his hand.

As Robert got to his feet, he glimpsed the lions and tiger and bear in the far dark corner of the cage, their bodies stiffened into alert poses, and he realized with a fearful heart that they'd seen him too.

He turned and rattled the cage door, but it wouldn't open. The bars were solid. Unmoving.

The animals eyed him suspiciously, huffing and grunting in the dust. They were used to the humans in their cage having big sticks to hit them with. But soon they realized that Robert had nothing like that, and they commenced to stalk slowly and carefully toward him. Robert began shaking, the horror shivering through every bone and sinew inside him. His nerves jangled, and the sweat poured down his back in rivers, slicking the hairs on his skin.

He turned again and tried to push himself through the gap in the bars. They were wide enough for his body to squeeze through, popping the buttons on his shirt, but his head was too big to fit. He could feel the iron poles crunching against the side of his skull, scraping at his ears. He gave up and stumbled back inside the bars. There was nothing for it. He would have to face them. One of the creatures gave a horrible roar.

"Our technical assistant will now turn on the X-ray," Slimwood narrated. "Once it's on, the radiation will mean the machine is too deadly for any normal human being to approach. At the end of the act, our metal man here"— he indicated the Lunk—"will go to turn the machine off and remove the freak girl from its clutches."

Lily felt sick. Stuck beneath the heavy lid of the machine, her neck trapped in a metal ring at one end, she could barely turn her head and could see nothing except what was directly above her. She caught a brief glimpse of Dr. Droz as she flicked the switch on the machine and checked a few dials on its side before retreating from view.

The humming of the machine rose an octave. The hairs on Lily's skin stood on end, and a static shock, potent enough to make her teeth buzz, shot through her. She watched in horror as lightning bolts of electricity wound snakelike along the machine's brass conducting-pole suspended over her chest, flickered through a glass tube, and broke across a metal plate suspended somewhere above her feet.

Suddenly, with a jolt, the image of Lily's chest appeared on the billowing white sheet above her head.

The crowd gasped in shock at the sight of her mechanical heart, its cogs and wheels turning, pushing blood through each chamber like a cross between an organic pump and a carriage clock.

"See the tubes, gears, springs, wheels, pins, and cogs inside her heart," Slimwood continued. "They're not only parsing the seconds, minutes, and hours of her existence, but also the blood through her body, creating each beautiful beating moment of her life. We should be able to hear the freakish tick of the heart too, if we listen carefully."

As he spoke this last line, Dr. Droz placed a trumpet-like amplifier against her chest, and the sound of her heart ticking filled the auditorium.

BOOM-TICK-
BOOM-TICK-
BOOM TICK
BOOM—

The sound echoed around the canvas tent, hovering over the crowds. So loud and pure. A mix of the dark and deep interior heartbeat you hear when you press your head to someone's chest, and the tick of a watch when you put it to your ear. The noise from Lily's heart hammered in time with the ghostly image of it projected on the screen—part blood, part bone, part clockwork.

Lily's body was buzzing with energy; her head pounded, and her limbs shook; nausea grew in the pit of her stomach. The striped canvas and the bright characters around her were waving like a flag in the wind.

Finally she managed to shift her head and glance around the ring.

From up in the eaves of the tent, Angelique was trying to swoop down toward her as they had planned. Only the Lunk was in the way, his long arms snatching at her in the air, blocking her path. Why hadn't his malfunction happened?

Slimwood stood on the curb to one side of her, gesturing with his whip to the screen above. Joey and Auggie had arrived at this side and were gazing openmouthed in amazement at the moving X-ray. On the far side of the ring, Madame stood with Droz. The Lunk had seen off Angelique, yet now his eyes blinked weirdly, as if he wasn't there. He swayed from side to side. Lily wondered if finally he was about to malfunction, but then he recovered.

The longer Lily stayed under the eye of the machine, the worse she felt. And the more likely it was, she knew, to kill her in the end. Shrivel her up like the apple. It didn't matter what their plan had been, she had to get herself out of this right now. Madame's threat against Robert weighed heavy in her mind, but she didn't really believe the woman would be merciful even if Lily did as she was told. The best thing she could do for Robert was get out of here and go and save him.

She wrenched her arm free from beneath the hood of the machine and pulled the end of the amplifying tube away from her chest and toward her mouth.

Her throat was dry as she began to speak.

"My name's not Cora Valentine," she said, "it's Lily Hartman." The words echoed around the crowd. She wasn't sure how many of them could even understand, seeing as she was speaking English, but nevertheless, she persisted.

"Yes, I am a hybrid, but I'm not improper or impure. I'm just like you, and I don't deserve to be treated this way. I've been kidnapped. These people are holding me prisoner. Holding us all prisoner—hybrids and humans alike!"

Joey, Auggie, and Slimwood were rushing toward her, but the rest of the circus folk, led by the Buttons and

Silva and Dimitri, stood in their path to block them. Robert's speech must've succeeded in changing their minds, as Lily realized with relief that they'd decided to help. The old man who ate china hit Joey over the head with his tea tray. Auggie, meanwhile, tried to wrestle Bruno and Gilda Buttons to the ground, but they merely ducked and backflipped round him, then clonked him on the head with one of his own juggling clubs, knocking him out. Only Slimwood managed to scrabble away from the group, waving his whip to keep them at bay. He shouted for the roustabouts, who rushed from the backstage area and began to surround the rebellious circus performers.

The audience could see something was up, but they hadn't moved beyond shifting uneasily in their seats; they seemed unsure if all this was part of the show or if they should be stopping it. Perhaps they were too afraid to approach the flashing machine after Slimwood had told them how dangerous it was? Lily had to persuade them to join the fight. She had a voice; she had to speak her truth, as Mama had told her.

"*Aidez moi!*" she shouted to the crowd. "Help us!"

Her voice sounded hoarse and ragged.

A handful of people in the crowd stood and took a few tentative steps from their seats. Maybe the language barrier meant they couldn't understand her exactly, but she could see from their faces that they felt the heartache behind her words.

Madame had stood too, and was talking animatedly to Droz, while gesturing to Lily. Lily could see the anger in their faces, the desire in them to come and stop her speaking. Only the crackling noises and the flashing electric current pulsing through the X-ray machine and the dangerous radiation it indicated made them keep their distance.

"SILENCE MISS VALENTINE!" Slimwood called out to the Lunk, who was once again snatching at the swooping Angelique. The Lunk turned and lumbered toward Lily.

Lily kept on speaking, while struggling to free her other arm and climb from the machine.

"Some think only pure humans have feelings," she shouted. "That only pure humans love and suffer. But that's not true. My heart is made of metal, and yet I feel things just as keenly as you do."

The audience were on their feet now. They understood that she was in trouble, that this whole show was just a dangerous, torturous sham. Some of them were stepping into the aisles, wondering whether to try to stop the performance.

Speak your truth, she heard her mama say in her head.

"Some say only pure humans have souls," Lily continued. "But my soul came back when I became part clockwork. Back from the void. Back to this body—part blood, part machine."

She'd run out of words. The expanse of faces waited, expectant.

And then it came to her.

"I was a human for the first half of my life," Lily said, "and a hybrid for the second, and I know from experience they are both the same. We hybrids, we should be treated equally, not shunned or hidden away or shown as freaks in a circus, and you can help make that change happen if you unite with us."

The crowd nodded in approval.

Lily had almost freed herself from the machine. She pushed the lid aside and sat up, only to see the Lunk approaching like a deadly steam train. He reached the machine and grabbed for her, but he was slow. Lily slipped from his grip, and his head clanged against the metal lid. It must've been enough to dislodge something for, finally, the Lunk's rogue program was set in motion, as Angelique flapped down from above and gathered Lily in her arms, scooping her up into the sky.

The Lunk squealed and thrashed his arms about,

his body spinning crazily, thumping against the empty X-ray bed before he keeled forward into its crackling, flashing center.

The machine whirred unhappily. Its dials flickered, and its cogs twitched. It paused in silence for a fraction of a second, until…

KABOOOOOOOOOM!

It exploded, knocking the collapsed Lunk aside and throwing jagged flashes of electricity everywhere, scattering bits of metal around the ring.

The crowds screamed and ducked beneath their seats.

Lily and Angelique were blown from the air. They tumbled across the sawdust and struggled to their feet as smoke and a loud ringing noise hung around them.

Madame lay prostrate on the other side of the arena… but in seconds she was up and coming for them, Slimwood too, but he was waylaid by angry members of the audience.

Angelique opened her wings, sending flecks of sawdust skittering away from her in the dark. "Take my hand," she called out to Lily. Lily glanced down at her dusty feet, pinned to the earth, then she reached out and grasped Angelique's hand in both of her own, holding it tightly.

Madame staggered closer. Angelique flapped her wings and lifted up into the dark interior of the tent, pulling Lily along behind her.

Lily felt her arms stretch out to their full length, felt herself rise to tiptoes and lift from the sawdust. Angelique couldn't take off very fast, carrying someone else.

Lily was four feet off the ground, now six. Angelique wobbled in the air above like a moth drunk on gaslight.

Lily stared up at her flapping figure. She could sense a ball of self-belief inside Angelique growing. It was incredible that the power of her wings was enough to lift them both off the ground.

But at that moment Madame jumped for them. Her hand shot out and snapped around Lily's ankle, yanking them both downward.

Angelique dipped in the air, and her wings faltered. She glanced down at Lily.

Lily's muscles ached from the weight of Madame holding on beneath, but she couldn't let the woman win.

"Keep going," Lily called out, and Angelique redoubled her efforts, flapping harder.

The three of them were rising off the ground together now. Madame was gripping Lily's boot, pulling her leg so hard that it knifed with pain and felt like it might pop from its socket.

Madame screamed and kicked her feet in the air as they left the floor and climbed high into the rafters.

The crowd, and the rest of the battling performers and roustabouts, stared at them and gasped.

Lily let go of Angelique with one hand and, reaching down, started pulling loose the laces of her boot as Angelique struggled upward toward the roof of the tent.

The knot was tight, but Lily finally got it undone and tugged the laces and boot free…

Then, with a piercing scream, Madame tumbled down, down, down, smashing hard into the sawdust of the ring.

CHAPTER 27

Robert heard the deafening explosion and felt the ground shake beneath him. The lions and tiger and the big brown bear retreated in alarm at the noise, cowering in the far corner of the cage.

The X-ray machine must've exploded. He hoped their plan to tweak the Lunk's brain cogs had worked, and Lily had gotten away in time. But he didn't have much time to contemplate that, for there were four hungry carnivorous animals stalking back toward him!

The tiger was the closest. It seemed to be the leader—the alpha of the pack. Its orange-and-black striped fur gleamed in the light thrown between the cage bars, and the bib of its belly was white, like a fresh dinner napkin.

Saliva dripped from its mouth as it ran a tongue hungrily over its teeth.

Robert could smell the hot sweaty stench and hear the rasp of its breathing. He tried to remember what Silva had told him to do in this situation. What was it?

"Throw your arms up in the air and blow raspberries at them as loud as you can."

Robert tried it.

BBBBBBUUUUOOOUPPPPPFFFFTTTTTT!

The tiger didn't listen.

"HELP!" screamed Robert in a high screech instead.

The tiger flinched at that jarring noise, probably because it sound like the Lunk.

"SHOO!" he screeched as loud as he could this time. "BE OFF WITH YOU!"

It had nearly reached him…but it was withholding the moment of attack, playing with him. He narrowed his eyes and shrank back.

Then something orange streaked through the bars and took up position in front of him, growling and baring its teeth. It was Malkin.

"GET AWAY FROM HIM, YOU FILTHY FLAMING FLEABAGS!" Malkin shouted.

The tiger looked quizzically at the tiny orange

mechanimal fur-ball, then shrank back in alarm. The other animals followed suit.

Malkin snapped his jaws together like a rabid dog. Between his screeches and grunts, Robert could hear the fox muttering to himself to give himself courage: "They're no bigger than the cats I chase from the garden. They're no bigger than the cats I chase from the garden."

It was working. The tiger, lions, and bear were so discombobulated that they gave little moans and meows, and stepped back in retreat.

Malkin barked and brayed at them…but it couldn't last forever. Soon the animals began to realize the fox was no real threat; they regrouped and started stalking in from either side of the cage, the bear closing in down the middle.

Then, suddenly, Dimitri, Silva, Deedee, and Luca arrived. The four of them began bashing at the metal bars beside Robert with sticks, creating a crazed rattling noise that made the wild animals dizzily shrink back once more.

"Thank goodness!" Robert cried. "How did you get out?"

"Malkin snatched the key to our cage in the panic!" Silva yelled above the din.

Luca grasped two metal bars between his claws and

pried them apart, wide enough for Deedee to pull Robert through the gap.

Malkin hopped out after him.

"I heard an explosion. Is everyone all right?" Robert asked.

Silva nodded.

"What about Lily and Angelique?" Robert said. "We have to find them."

Dimitri led both the horses from the stalls at the back of the bay, then mounted the black horse, while Silva flipped up onto the white.

As they maneuvered round the cage, she ducked and grasped Robert by the arm, yanking him up behind her. When he dared open his eyes, Deedee and Luca were already mounted behind Dimitri on the black horse, trotting down the cargo ramp.

"Malkin?" Robert called.

"I'm perfectly fine down here," Malkin yapped. "Don't expect me to ride on that animal too." His brush up, he followed Silva's horse toward the door.

Dimitri and the others waited outside the sky-ship on the black stallion. Robert felt the bones of the white horse's back beneath him as Silva cantered it down the ramp to join its friend.

"Gee-up!" Dimitri shouted to both horses, and the

pair galloped across the yard with the five children on their backs, barreling into the tent and smashing their way through the backstage area toward the Big Top ring.

"This is fun!" Malkin barked, weaving along beside them. "I've never been in a horse race before!"

They ducked through the curtains and into the arena.

The rest of the circus troupe and some of the audience were hurrying the other way, but as they passed the two horses, they swerved and turned back.

Robert glanced over his shoulder to see that the lions and tiger had slunk through the narrow opening in the cage bars and were now bounding into the backstage area, knocking over tables and mirrors and racks of clothes.

Then they spotted the horses and the trail of people heading back toward the Big Top and began to chase them.

There was a scream as one of the roustabouts was taken down.

It was chaos. Smoke drifted everywhere, sharp and acrid in Robert's lungs. It mixed with the sweaty smell of the panicked audience trying to get to the exits and the lions and tiger stalking amongst them.

Silva swung her skittish horse around as Robert scanned the tent frantically for Lily and Angelique.

Suddenly, he caught a glimpse of Angelique perched on the wire above and a figure beside her who was sitting on the wire with her legs dangling, one foot bare. With relief, he noticed a flash of red hair and realized it was Lily.

He was about to yell to her when Slimwood stepped up beside them and yanked him from the back of the horse.

"I've not finished with you yet, boy!" he said, dragging him across the sawdust ring.

Malkin bit at Slimwood's heels, but it didn't stop him from clutching Robert by the neck.

Silva's horse whinnied and reared up, leaping away to one side.

"Look behind you," Robert warned Slimwood as outside the tent, police sirens chimed in the distance.

Slimwood chuckled. "Ha! I'm not falling for that cheap trick!"

But Robert wasn't playing tricks. The tiger was stalking toward them, its body slinking low to the ground as it prowled the ring. Its tail dropped straight, following the line of its back, and each muscle moved in a synchronized, assured motion. It crouched lower, coiling into a tight, powerful shape. Its ears flattened against its head, and its mouth was a wide black hole beneath its terrible, fearsome eyes.

Then the tiger leaped, bounding toward them, its tail flung out behind it. Its jaw was wide, displaying its sharp rows of teeth.

Slimwood's mouth dropped open; his grip loosened from Robert's throat.

Robert took his chance and scrambled free, vaulting over benches and ducking behind the front row of seats as the great cat ran toward them.

There was a roar, and then Slimwood screamed.

Robert opened his eyes and peered over the rim of seats. The tiger was dragging the red-tailcoated form of the circus ringmaster away, vanishing into the smoky striped recesses of the tent.

Robert turned away. He couldn't watch. But the tiger had finished with Slimwood; now it turned to come back toward him and Malkin.

It stalked closer, snarling at them. After being kept in that cage for all those years, it was finally free and ready to hunt…

It was nearly upon them when Robert heard the beating of wings.

Angelique dived down and nabbed him, sweeping him into the air. With a great flap of her wings, she made it to the platform beside the high wire and deposited Robert there, the sweat pouring off her as she breathed heavily. "Wait there!" she cried. "I'll get Malkin."

Robert and Lily watched as she plunged back into the fray to pluck up Malkin, who was already running as fast as he could, dashing away from the tiger.

"I could've faced it!" the fox blustered at Angelique as she swooped down over him and scooped him up in her arms. "But thanks anyway for the rescue! I appear to have become a flying fox."

Angelique carried him high above the ring, and Malkin felt bilious. Foxes were not meant to fly—not in airships or with winged girls or anyhow. He was glad when Angelique deposited him on the platform beside Lily and Robert.

The police sirens were closer now; they pierced the air right outside the tent.

Lily glanced down at the ground. Silva and the others had made their exit on horseback, along with the audience, circus folk, lions, and the roustabouts. Madame and Slimwood both lay like rag dolls, abandoned in the ring.

The sirens outside had stopped, and the tent was eerily quiet, except for the growls and grunts of the tiger as it wrenched down the red curtains, overturned the makeup tables and props stand, and ripped them apart. Lily could see Joey, Auggie, and a few stranded rousties huddled behind a rack of clothes in the far corner, hoping it wouldn't notice them.

Then, just as suddenly as it had arrived in the tent, the tiger turned and ran off into the night, disappearing through the exit of the backstage area as the first few gendarmes arrived through the audience entrance.

Lily glimpsed the tops of their helmets as they fought their way through the smoke, guns raised. Three plainclothes figures were with them. Even from above and in the half-light, Lily could recognize each of them from their postures and gaits, and her heart leaped at the sight of them.

It was Papa, Tolly, and Anna.

"Lily! Robert! Malkin!" Papa rushed around wildly in the smoke, peering beneath rows of chairs and behind poles. His suit was rumpled, and his posture sharp and worried. He, Anna, and Tolly splintered apart and began searching different areas, along with the police.

"PAPA!" Lily yelled down to him, and he stopped beneath her. He'd heard her voice, but he couldn't see her.

"Lily, where are you?" he called out.

"I'm up here, in the roof," she shouted.

More police swarmed through the entrance to the tent as Papa turned and gazed upward.

When he spotted Lily, then Malkin, Robert, and

Angelique on the high platform, his shoulders drooped in relief, and he pointed them out to Anna and Tolly.

Lily climbed slowly down the ladder from the platform and ran over to meet Papa.

He scooped her up in his arms, wrapping a blanket around her sparkly but now tattered outfit, and kissing her on the cheek. "Lily, my dear-heart, thank goodness you're fine! We were so worried about you… and Robert," he added, throwing an arm around Robert as, carrying Malkin, he reached them too. "I wish we'd arrived in time to stop this," he said, gesturing with a nod of his head to the mess of the tent around them: the broken, smoking X-ray machine and the remains of the big mechanical Lunk trapped inside it and scattered round the ring.

"What took you so long?" Lily asked, tears smarting in her eyes. She wiped them away, smearing the makeup and dust on her cheeks, then dropped her hand and felt a surprising tickle as Malkin licked at her fingers. She ruffled his ears and squeezed Papa and Robert closer in a grand hug. Her heart was filled with nothing but relief, and she hoped, deep in its ticking depths, that the four of them would never ever be parted again.

CHAPTER 28

The show was over, and in its aftermath Lily and Robert sat wrapped in blankets in the ringside seats. Malkin was resting, curled up at their feet.

Lily watched as the gendarmes busily rounded up the rousties and Madame, Auggie, and Joey, who were alive and only lightly mauled by the tiger. Slimwood was in the worst state, bleeding profusely and unconscious. He was placed on a stretcher and carried from the tent to an ambulance that was waiting outside. The rest of the motley crew were handcuffed together into a chain gang and led out from the main entrance in a long line.

Despite the chaos and general devastation, the circus folk seemed filled with relief. Their faces shone at last.

The pain and sorrow lifted from their eyes. The Buttons clasped their arms around their daughter, and the rest of the acts and families gathered about Dimitri, their son— the son of the circus.

As Lily watched this scene unfold around them, Papa sat down in the seat beside her. Then Angelique flitted down next to them too.

"Papa, this is Angelique," Lily said. "She saved us."

"Thank you, Angelique." Papa shook her hand. "You certainly are a most remarkable young lady."

"You're very kind, sir," Angelique replied. Then she spotted someone in John's shadow. "Bartholomew," she asked, "is that you?"

A broad grin spread across Tolly's face. "Angela!" he cried. "Angelique, I mean. You changed your name! And I did too—it's Tolly now. But Lily and Robert found you! I'm so glad! I'd no idea where you were since you left the Camden Workhouse."

"I was missing a long time," Angelique said. "But I'm back now." She folded her wings around him and gave him the most enormous hug, and Tolly blushed beetroot-red.

Lily was glad to see him and Anna too. There had been moments in this awful week when she thought she might never be reunited with Papa or her friends again.

"When I got back to your home and told them what happened, the entire party was in an uproar," Tolly explained to Robert and Lily. "Everyone vowed to help find you, Inspector Fisk included. The trouble was," he continued, "we'd no clue where you'd been taken."

"Or where the circus might be headed," Anna added.

"I was in despair," Papa said. He brushed a lock of hair from Lily's face. "The only thing we could do was wait and hope for news. Then, last night, Mr. Brassnose came to the house with a telegram from the French police saying the Skycircus had landed in Paris and that you were being held prisoner by Madame Verdigris on board."

He squeezed Lily's shoulder in relief. "We awaited an update, but after the gendarmes investigated and couldn't find you, they claimed the message was a hoax. Tolly insisted it was true, so Anna kindly flew us here, along with Inspector Fisk, so we could try and make them see sense."

"Thank goodness you did," Lily said. At that moment she noticed Inspector Fisk himself stood deep in conversation with the most senior-looking officer of the French police.

Inspector Fisk looked up and saw them, then ambled over. "If you could step this way with me for a minute, please," he said to Lily, Robert, and John, "the commandant wants a quick word."

Inspector Fisk led them over to the French police commandant. Malkin came too, though he hadn't strictly been invited.

When the French inspector saw them, he gave a tight little salute. "*Monsieur Hartman, Monsieur Townsend, Mademoiselle Hartman, je m'appelle Commandant Oiseau.* My men have recovered some things from the Skycircus ship. Are they yours?"

He showed Lily the penknife, the Moonlocket, and the red notebook.

"Oh, yes, *merci beaucoup*," Lily said. Her heart leaped, and she felt overjoyed to have the red notebook returned to her and the rest of her mama's words back at last. She took it and clasped it to her chest before handing the Moonlocket and penknife back to Robert.

Robert's face flushed with relief. "Thank you," he said as he put the penknife away and fiddled with the Moonlocket. The clasp was still broken, so he tucked it away carefully in his pocket. Then he remembered Da's coat was still hung on the costume rail backstage next to Lily's party clothes and coat, and together, they dashed off to get them.

They returned changed back into their old outfits and were ready to go when they found the inspector and the commandant with Papa outside of the tent next to a police wagon.

The commandant was speaking with Papa. "*S'il vous plaît*," he said, pointing through the bars of the van at Madame, who was sitting on the bench in the back of the wagon opposite Auggie, Joey, and the rest of the roustabouts. "For the record, could you identify the suspect before you?"

Madame's eyes flicked to the window and caught Lily's, then she looked away.

"Yes," said Papa. "This is my old housekeeper."

"And the others?" the commandant asked. "Do you know them?"

"No," Papa said.

"These are the people who kidnapped you?" the commandant asked, turning to Lily and Robert.

They nodded.

"I should say so!" Malkin added for good measure.

"And this lady stole your property, Monsieur?" he queried Papa.

"She most certainly did."

"They don't have the rest of your papers, Papa," Lily said. "Madame sold them to Dr. Droz."

"Shelley's involved in all this?" Papa looked shocked. "Where is she?"

"She was here," Lily said. In the madness of the show, she'd forgotten about the doctor.

She scanned the back of the van, searching for her face among the handcuffed figures. But the woman wasn't there. She must've slipped away with the crowd sometime between the explosion and the escape of the animals—that was, Lily realized, almost an hour ago.

The commandant consulted his pocket book. "One of these clowns has given us her address, sir. It's an abandoned hospital. We're going to visit it as soon as possible and apprehend her, right after we have dealt with the situation here." He put a hand on Lily's shoulder. "Do you remember the exact location of her apartment inside the building, Miss Hartman?"

Lily nodded.

"Then, if you might come to show us the way?"

"I'm not leaving Lily alone again," Papa said.

"And neither are we," added Robert and Malkin together.

"In that case, Monsieur, might I suggest that you all come with us too?"

"We most certainly will," Papa replied. "I have a thing or two to say to Shelley myself, if she's responsible."

"Very good. Take these lot away!" The commandant slapped the back of the police wagon with his open palm, and it drove off past the wreckage of the Big Top and out of sight.

"Your friend Angelique and the others will be perfectly fine with my colleagues here," he said to Lily. "The site must be shut down temporarily, but our officers will see to their injuries and take statements, while the three of you, and perhaps Inspector Fisk as well, come with your *père* and us to visit Dr. Droz."

The commandant blew a whistle that hung on a length of gold braid from the breast pocket of his blue uniform, and another police steam-wagon pulled up to transport them safely away from the circus.

They flew through the Bois in the police wagon with the siren raging, and then through the city, passing the gigantic arch, which Papa told them was the Arc de Triomphe, before swinging along the river and through a familiar-looking district. Only when they approached the street with the derelict hospital did they turn off the sirens and proceed more cautiously.

It was nearly ten o'clock when they finally arrived. The inspector knocked, but Lily ended up picking the lock for them, as there was no one to let them in.

"It's this way." Lily led Commandant Oiseau and

Inspector Fisk and the gendarmes up the stairs to the apartment. On the top floor, Fisk pushed the door open and led the way. Lily, Papa, Robert, and Malkin followed behind with the commandant and the line of police.

The group stalked from room to room, searching for the doctor, but the entire apartment was empty. Droz's belongings had all gone, and the ticking noises of the building that had been so evident the night before had stopped. There were shadow marks on the walls where pictures had hung, and circles in the dust on the empty shelves where the jars of specimens had been.

The place felt as if it could've been derelict for years, except that in the main room a flicker of a fire burned in the grate, stuffed with half-devoured papers.

"My notes!" Papa rushed over to them and pulled a handful of burning pages from the flames.

Lily, Robert, and Malkin stood to one side as the inspector and the commandant paced the room. Then Lily noticed something propped on the mantelpiece above the fire. It was a letter.

She reached out and picked it up. The envelope was addressed to:

Miss Lily Hartman, Brackenbridge Manor

It was written in the same hand as the letter Lily had

received a week ago, and Lily realized then that it had been Droz who'd penned the original. She was the one who'd been behind the whole plot, even more so than Madame. Before Papa or any of the policemen could stop her, she slit the envelope open and pulled out a single sheet of folded paper.

Dear Lily,

I have a simple question, and it's one that's not a trick:

I have always wondered what it is that makes you tick?

Of course, you have shown most profoundly that it is not just a clockwork heart, but a desire for equality amongst hybrids and humans. I cannot deny that your cause is a worthy one. You've proved yourself as strong as your mother and so many other women before you. We too deserve equality, especially in the male-dominated world of science, and I know you will follow in Grace's footsteps.

I wish you well in all you do. And I am sure that we will meet again in the future.

Yours, with sincere admiration,

Dr. Shelley Mary Droz

Even after all she'd been through, Lily felt rather proud to receive such a letter. It felt less a conclusion than the congratulations of an admiring adversary that she'd beaten in a chess game. She was about to put the page away in the pocket of her coat, along with the papers and Mama's notebook, when Commandant Oiseau appeared behind her.

"We will need that as evidence," he said, holding out a white gloved hand. "Naturally it will be returned to you after the conclusion of the investigation."

"Of course." With a heavy heart, Lily handed it over to him.

"*Merci.*"

The commandant read through the letter. "Well," he said, after he'd finished. "We'll try our best to track her down. And if you think of anything more that might aid us…"

He regarded Lily and Robert, who were visibly wilting. "These children look awfully weary. Perhaps you ought to check in to a hotel and find them a bed for the night? You needn't wait around here any longer; my car will take you wherever you want to go, and we can clear up any last queries we have in the morning."

"You're probably right," Papa replied. "Where and when should we call on you?" he asked as the three of them and Malkin headed for the door.

"We'll be at the Skycircus site first thing," the inspector replied. "And if you don't find us there, I will be at the commandant's office at the Police Prefecture in Place Louis Lepine in the afternoon."

"Very good," Papa said.

Fisk saluted goodbye to everyone, and the commandant tipped his hat to Papa and then to Robert and Lily. "*Au revoir, les enfants! À demain!*"

Lily nodded a sleepy goodbye in return. She felt the tiredest she'd ever been in her life. She glanced at Robert; his eyes were drooping, and as they stepped into the hall, she saw him give a proper great yawn. Malkin too was running very slowly and had been gradually winding down for the past hour. She hoped the hybrids and circus folk would be all right on their own, dealing with the chaos and the police. But, yes, she realized, as the three of them followed Papa past the policeman on guard outside and down the building's stairs, there was only one thing she needed right now—and that was a proper bed and a good night's sleep.

CHAPTER 29

They spent that night at the Grand Hotel, where the mattresses were as soft as clouds. Lily and Malkin shared a room, and Robert turned in next door.

Tired as she was, Lily found it difficult to sleep. She woke a number of times in the early hours, her thoughts filled with worry about the fate of the hybrids.

Would they be all right left alone on the site with the other circus acts? What would happen to them after tonight—especially if any trace of the old mistrust and animosity between them and the other human performers lingered? She needed to make sure that things were going to be better for them as she'd promised. She felt bad even to leave them for those few hours alone after what they'd all been through together, so she was relieved when Robert knocked for her first thing, with some croissants he'd snaffled from downstairs for breakfast, and told her that Papa and Anna and Tolly had already commandeered a carriage to return them to the Skycircus site as soon as possible.

When they arrived, Lily was cheered at once to see that the hybrids and the circus folk who'd stayed seemed to have made their peace with one another. They'd been working together to dismantle Madame and Slimwood's regime, and now that there were no roustabouts or Lunk to control what they were doing, or Slimwood or Madame to tell them how to think, everyone seemed to be getting on just fine.

The police had first broken into the forbidden rooms on the gondola and discovered a safe full of cash, hoarded away from all the shows, that was enough to pay everyone for their season of work and buy fresh food for the mess hall. It even turned out there would be enough money to refit the sky-ship.

There were fewer people aboard, and the hybrids and remaining families and circus folk had divided up the cabins so they each had their own space and had already begun the process of renewing the gondola, first by ripping out a few of the locks and bars and then starting to reorganize one or two of the main spaces. The tables in the mess hall had been moved about to make it feel less like a prison and more like a dining room, and plans were afoot to convert Slimwood and Madame's old rooms upstairs into a parlor space where people could sit together and relax after dinner.

When they'd finished their tour of the gondola, Lily and Robert visited the Big Top. There they found that the chaos of the show had been removed too, and Angelique, Deedee, Luca, and some of the other performers were busy sprucing up the tent for a new start. Angelique, Luca, and Deedee were full of hugs and happy to see them, and Angelique told Lily that things had improved so much that all three of them were thinking about staying. The circus folk had decided to begin performing again, and Lily learned that the plan was to mix the hybrids and humans together into new acts, to create a fresh bill of everyone's devising. The intention was to wow the audiences of Paris before the new, improved Skycircus went on to change the world.

Robert, Lily, and Malkin spent the rest of the week at the Grand Hotel. Papa thought a holiday in Paris was the best way to recover from the horrors of their kidnapping, so they spent their time in a blur of treats and sightseeing.

They bought new clothes in the shops of Passage Jouffroy and at Le Bon Marché—a fabulous department store in the center of the city—and ate in the finest restaurants. They saw the beautiful paintings in the Louvre, viewed the whole of Paris from the hill known as Montmartre, and visited the half-built Sacré-Cœur church—which Lily told Robert meant *sacred heart* in English.

They even visited Notre-Dame cathedral—Robert remembered reading about it in a novel by Victor Hugo—and the bird market, where the cages filled with chirping birds made Lily think of Angelique and their days trapped in the circus. She was glad that things seemed to be working out better for them. They hadn't run from their troubles, despite the pain they had faced in the past, and now that their oppressors were gone, they were making the circus a new home for humans and hybrids alike. Soon they would be changing the minds of audiences day by day and show by show.

On their last night in Paris, the circus folk threw Robert, Lily, and Malkin a party to celebrate the fact that they'd helped rid them of Slimwood and Madame. There was a great firepit built in the center of the site, and everyone danced and ate and drank to their heart's content.

"I'm glad that you brought us together," Luca said. "Now that Madame and Slimwood are gone, this place has finally started to feel like home. I think perhaps the circus might be destined to start anew."

"Although we'll have to give it a different name," Deedee said.

"Perhaps the Fabulous Flying Human Hybrid Circus?" Silva suggested.

"It's a bit of a mouthful," Tolly said.

"How are you going to fit it on the posters?" Malkin asked.

"You could come with us, all of you," Angelique said.

"I don't think so," Robert and Lily replied in unison. Though Tolly had to think about it. He'd taken quite a shine to Angelique in the days since they'd been reunited.

"We mean," Lily said, "that it's probably time for us to go home too."

"Well, traveling's not for everyone," Silva admitted. "Though I actually think it might be for you two."

"What makes you say that?" Robert asked.

"These adventures you keep falling into. It seems you've got a terrible case of the great unrest."

"What's 'the great unrest'?" Robert asked.

Silva smiled. "It's a malady common in circus folks.

We go where the wind takes us. Keep moving in a whirl around the world, like a spinning top, visiting new towns and cities, broaching new horizons, traveling from here to there, from A to B to C to Z, seeing the sights and getting into trouble."

Deedee raised an eyebrow. "You and Lily both have that in spades," she said.

Luca nodded. "Adventure's in your blood, like a fever."

"It's not that we *want* adventure," Robert said. "It just seems to keep happening to us everywhere we go. Sort of by accident."

"Nothing's an accident," Dimitri said. "And you two, you are meant to see the world together, through good and bad."

"You're like us circus folk," Silva added. "You love life too much not to live every second of it to the full, even in the times when bad things are happening. I think you should ask yourself, Robert, are the adventures really finding you, or are you finding the adventures?"

Robert still wasn't sure. But he knew that he was now a better, stronger, braver adventurer than when he and Lily first met a year ago. He'd helped save a circus, hadn't he? Helped save the hybrids. And he'd helped save Lily. To save someone else's life seemed the worthiest cause of all.

"May I speak with my daughter for a moment?" Papa asked, interrupting the conversation, and he took her hand and led her off a little way.

They sat together on a wooden bench by the fire. His face was lit by the flickering flames as he smiled at her. "It's beautiful here," he said.

"Beauty is found in the places you least expect it," she replied.

"Yes," Papa said. "You may be right for once."

"For once?" she said. "Papa, I'm always right."

"Not always. But sometimes." He paused and a clouded look crossed his face. "I've been thinking about how things have been between us, Lily. How I've treated you, this past year… These past seven years, even. I haven't noticed you enough. Who you are and how you've grown, and for that I can only apologize. Things have been difficult for me too. But you, you deserve more of a chance at life, I can see that, especially with the new friends you've made. And I promise I'm going to give you all of the freedom your heart desires."

"Thank you." Lily put an arm around his neck and hugged him.

"When you come of age," he added, warningly. "For still, right now, you must take care in the world. Life can be a complex and dangerous thing, as much as it can be beautiful."

"I know that, Papa, but you have to let me make my own mistakes. You can't worry about me flying too close to the sun. Failure is how you learn and how people grow. Angelique has taught me that much. People need to fly on their own—on the wings they make for themselves—not the ones their parents give them."

Papa laughed at that. And Lily saw that despite all those years of wanting to keep her true nature a secret, he had finally changed his mind about her. He could see her at last, like the rest of the world could, and understood that he didn't need to protect her every day of her life, not now that she'd learned to stand up for herself. Not now that she'd fought so many of her own battles.

"You realize, this is the first proper party I've had for my birthday since Mama was here," she said. "All those years in between, you were trying to keep the fact that I'd survived and become a hybrid a secret."

"It was only to protect you, Lily, to keep you safe."

"That's not really the case, Papa," Lily replied. "We've got into as much trouble this past year from secrets as we would have if we'd been honest, I think. It's like Mama said in her notebook: '*Truth conquers all. To speak the truth we carry deep inside us, within our hearts, no matter how difficult, is the only way we can be free.*'" She looked pointedly at him. "I wonder if it's time things changed? If

I can use who I am to help people, and you can use your knowledge to make them better, why should we keep what we've learned a secret? After all, when you wrap someone up in cotton wool to keep them safe, sometimes you can shield them from the good they can do in the world too. Not to mention all the fun things in life they miss," she added wistfully.

"Like birthday parties?" he asked.

"Like birthday parties," Lily said.

Papa shook his head. "I never supposed…I mean, I always hated birthday parties myself!" He was trying to make light of it. "But not the presents, eh? No one hates those…which reminds me…"

He pulled two packages from his pocket that were tied with red ribbon. One a long, thin rectangle; the other short and square.

"I meant to give you these the other day."

Lily opened the thin one first. It was a beautiful fountain pen. She took it out of its box, and it shone in the flickering firelight. The second present was a red leather-bound notebook with a golden ammonite embossed on the cover, just like Mama's, except this book was filled with blank pages.

"I thought you could write your story in it," Papa said. "Just like Grace did in hers. And maybe one day you will continue her studies; you might find other, better ways of helping hybrids than we did. Of helping yourself…"

"Thank you," Lily said. She leafed through it. The bare, cream-colored paper felt a little intimidating, waiting to be filled with words that would take her somewhere, like footprints in the snow. But then she thought of what Angelique had said, about how she could be the one to continue Mama's story, and she knew this book would be the place to do it.

She would begin when they got home. That would be her new start.

She closed the cover of the notebook and glanced up. The circus band was playing in the firelight, and everyone was dancing: Robert, Anna, Tolly and Malkin, Angelique, Luca and Deedee, Dimitri, Silva, the Buttons, and the rest of the circus folk. All spinning, twirling, and pirouetting together—Silva was even flipping into handstands and acrobatic poses, while Angelique flapped her wings and created new hovering dance steps. They looked like one big, happy family.

Lily took Papa's hand. "Come on," she said. "I'll introduce you to everyone."

Papa nodded. "Lead on, Macduff—let's meet them."

On their final morning, they woke early to find the sun flooding through the windows of the Grand Hotel. After a breakfast of croissants, jam, and *pain au chocolat* washed down with large vats of sugary black coffee that made Lily's brain itch, they took a chaise and four to the Eiffel Tower Airstation.

The glowing sky was reflected in the puddles of water along the street. Horse-drawn carriages, steam-wagons, and omnibuses wove willy-nilly around each other on the busy tree-lined avenues, and groups of smartly dressed women and gents paraded on the pavements. Robert thought about what an amazing week it had been, seeing the sights of the city and also getting to witness the circus folk coming together after all that had happened to them.

Anna was talking with Lily, showing her the headline of the morning edition of *The Daily Cog*, which she had picked up at the hotel's reception.

"I filed my latest copy last night via telegraph," she explained. "I wanted to get the whole story, plus the aftermath too. They've given it the entire front page. I wrote about your speech, Lily, and how you and Robert persuaded the hybrids and the others in the circus to rebel, and how the circus came together afterward. And how Madame and Slimwood were imprisoned and are being investigated for multiple counts of kidnapping and murder."

"That sounds a lot to get into one story!" Malkin said.

"And the Cogheart?" Papa asked. "Did you write about that?"

"I'm afraid so," Anna said. "I know you wanted me to soft-pedal that part, but I felt I had to include it somewhere. It was in the French papers and by now will be common knowledge. The story's creating quite a stir in London." She showed them the paper.

HARTMAN AND TOWNSEND'S
DAZZLING ESCAPE FROM SKYCIRCUS

"Crikey," said Tolly, reading it over their shoulders. "You'll be more famous than when we met the Queen!"

"I reckon we will be," Robert replied. He peered at a smaller article below the main one. It said:

CIRCUS TIGER STILL LOOSE IN PARIS,
LAST SPOTTED IN THE BOIS DE BOULOGNE

"And that can't be good news either," Robert added.

Lily folded the paper up and handed it back to Anna. "You know, I've just finished living this," she said with a wry smile. "I don't think I need to read all about it right now."

"Oh, that's a copy for you and Robert to keep," Anna said, giving Lily back the paper. "I've plenty more back at the office."

"Maybe I'll just save the front page for us then. What do you think, Robert?"

Robert smiled and nodded, and Lily ripped the front page off the paper and folded it up, placing it in Mama's notebook with the loose pages and the card with the *What it is that makes you tick?* poem written on it, which had started this whole adventure.

She gave the rest of the paper to Malkin to chew on.

The autumn sun beamed down from a clear blue sky, and as they passed through the Trocadéro Gardens and approached the Pont D'Iéna, Lily glimpsed the imposing silhouette of the Eiffel Tower Airstation. Small ornithopters were docked on its lowest level. Above, hot-air balloons, sky-ships, and dirigibles clustered on the mid-level docking platforms. A fleet of brand-new single-man Santos-Dumont airships and a large commuter zep were coming in from the east, and there, nestled near the pinnacle, was Anna's patchwork dirigible, *Ladybird*.

Anna pointed up at her. "As soon as we get to the top of the Tower, we shall be taking her home. I must say, she flew pretty well across the Channel, barely complained at all."

"Although your father complained quite a bit, Lily," Tolly added.

"Well, I'm used to piloting my own airship," John said. "I freely admit I still find it quite strange to be flown by someone else."

Their carriage pulled up in the square beneath the tower, where the gigantic metal supports stretched out above them like the legs of some looming colossus.

While Papa paid the driver of the chaise and unloaded their few bags, Lily, Malkin, Robert, Tolly, and Anna headed across the square. As they had promised last night at the party, Angelique, Luca, Deedee, Silva, and Dimitri arrived in a steam-hansom to see them off.

"Thanks for coming to say goodbye," Lily said as the three hybrids and the other two circus children climbed down to join them at the base of the Tower.

"We wouldn't miss it for the world," Deedee said.

"We'll be lost without you," Robert said. "So will Tolly."

"You can always visit," Angelique said to Tolly. "Anytime."

Tolly blushed. "Maybe I will," he said. "When I finish up my work in London, with Anna."

While Anna had been covering the story and Lily and Robert and many of the others had been off sightseeing, Tolly and Angelique had been spending a lot of time together, rekindling their lost friendship.

"Well, I suppose this is goodbye," said Robert sadly.

"We're coming up to the platform too," Angelique told him.

"It'll be the first time we get to see the city from so high," Silva said, "without being locked up in that prison ship."

"Funny thing with Slimwood's," Luca added. "We traveled the world but never got to see anywhere outside the sky-ship and the compound."

"And now we finally can!" Deedee said.

"Perhaps you should all come and visit us then?" Robert said.

"Papa says any of you are welcome—for as long as you like," Lily added.

"And I can come see you," Tolly added to Angelique.

Angelique shook her head. "Maybe some day, but for now we are staying with the Skycircus. Things are different there." Luca, Dimitri, and Deedee nodded in agreement. "The Buttons are in charge, and the rest of the acts are happier. Now that all of those old barriers that Slimwood set up are broken down, they accept us and treat us like family."

"Circus *is* family," Silva said.

Lily watched her papa at the booth paying for the cross-Channel fares and organizing for the luggage to be taken up to *Ladybird*. Anna waited a few feet from him.

"Do you remember when I said that when you're different to other people, they don't believe you're as good as them, and that you have to prove it?" Tolly said to Lily as the group hurried together toward the elevator that would take them up to the airship.

Lily tucked her hair behind her ear to stop it from blowing in the wind. "I remember."

"Well, I think you've proved it, Lily."

"It doesn't work like that," she said. "The trouble is, you have to prove it over and over again. You have to fight every day to be treated the same, and sometimes it gets so wearisome."

"It's like your story, Lily," Angelique said. "The one about Icarus. If you fail, if you fall short, you pick yourself up and make stronger wings for the next flight."

The elevator arrived. Its metal doors clattered open, and everyone crowded in. Angelique tapped Lily on the shoulder and pulled her aside. "I don't fancy being trapped in another cage, not even for a moment. I think I might fly up instead. Do you want to come with me?"

Lily nodded. "Of course."

The others were already being shuffled into the elevator by the crowds. The doors started to close. Papa beckoned to Lily and Angelique. "Come on," he said, his face a picture of concern. "We have a flight to catch."

Lily smiled. "I'm catching a different one first, Papa."

She and Angelique stepped away from the crowds. Angelique took off her coat and handed it to Lily. Then she spread her mechanical wings as wide as they would go, until Lily could see every length of wire crisscrossing in complex patterns between the feathers, just like in the gigantic tower behind her. The crowds of people near them stepped back to give them room, gasping in admiration.

"Are you ready?" Angelique asked Lily.

Lily nodded. Then Angelique picked her up and flapped her wings, and soon they were rising, soaring up the side of the Eiffel Tower. Lily felt herself slipping, but Angelique grasped her tighter, her grip sure and confident.

Lily glimpsed Notre-Dame with its crazy ribs and spiked spire, and the Seine curving like an eel past the Louvre, and the manicured Jardin des Tuileries, where the paths were laid out in patterns as complicated as a board game.

Angelique flapped her wings and whooshed them higher, and the view of the tower's metal girders ran together in the sky like some kind of aerial railway junction as they sped toward its very tip.

A crowd of people waiting on the platform watched with open mouths as they circled around, sweeping in over the clustered zeppelins and balloons. They touched down lightly in the center of the platform just as the elevator doors opened with a ping and the other circus children stepped out, along with Robert, Malkin, Papa, Anna, and Tolly, who were ready to board the airship *Ladybird* for England.

CHAPTER 30

Since their return from Paris a week earlier, the autumn nights were turning inky and the days had a scent of wet fallen leaves about them.

Lily sat in the old armchair in the tower room of Brackenbridge Manor with her feet up on the steamer trunk, staring out the east window.

Half-bare trees filled the landscape. Their branches were a patchwork of sparse yellow and russet foliage, like the last fading thoughts of a summer long gone. She put a hand to her chest and could feel the wealth of life running through her with every tick of the Cogheart. The weight of it, and the truths it had led her to tell, made her wonder where things would go from here.

She picked up her new notebook and ran her fingers across the ammonite on its front cover before turning to the first fresh page, which crackled in protest.

She took the cap off her fountain pen and in the middle of the page printed three letters:

L.R.H.

For Lily Rose Hartman.

At the top of the next creamy slice of blank paper, in her own strong, round handwriting, she wrote the date.

Friday. 8th October 1897. Brackenbridge Manor

After that, she had no idea what to write. She glanced out of the window and thought about Papa, Robert and Malkin, Tolly, and Anna, then all her friends in the circus and everything that had come to pass since she was last here.

Life had changed from the moment they had gotten back. The article Anna had written for *The Daily Cog* and the others that had appeared in the French papers about Lily had blown things up in a massive way. Since then, every other newspaper in Britain had taken up her story. Journalists had come daily and rung on the doorbell at all hours, wanting to speak to her about the Cogheart and Papa and Mama and the other hybrids.

She was so famous now, people looked at her differently in the street.

At least at home things were quiet. In the rose garden, she could see Captain Springer with his rake, collecting up the leaves, and Papa walking across the gravel path to speak with him.

She watched them for a moment, thinking of nothing much, letting her worries fade away, and then a cough echoed behind her.

Lily turned from the window to see Robert and Malkin coming up the stairs.

"What're you doing up here?" Robert asked.

"Thinking," Lily replied. "D'you want to know why? Because I've no idea what to write in my new notebook."

"What exactly is the problem?" Malkin said, settling down at her feet like a furry rug.

"Well," Lily said, "I'm not sure if I want to write about the past…or the strange things that have been happening since our return. I'm not even sure I want to write about the future."

"Then don't write about any of that," Robert said. "Write what your dreams are. What you wish for."

He sat down on the edge of the chair beside her, and Lily suddenly saw how different he was from the boy she'd first known. He was taller, braver, more hopeful. And he was beginning to hold himself like a man.

"What do you wish for?" she said.

He thought about it for a moment. No one had ever asked him that before.

"When I was little," he told her at last, "I wished I could be anything other than who I was. Anything other than the clockmaker's apprentice Da wanted me to be. I used to fantasize about running away, signing up as a cabin boy with air-pirates or joining a circus."

Lily smiled at that one.

"It's true," he said. "Back then I'd a notion I wanted adventure. But now, I've had a few, I've realized something about them…"

"What's that?" Lily asked.

"They can be overrated."

She laughed. "I quite like them," she said. "Even when they go badly, somehow I always feel that there's time to save things and turn them around."

"I suppose so," he sighed. "But at home, you've the people you love around you. Or at least," he said, thinking of his da, "you have a piece of their memory in the places and things that remind you of them." Robert touched the repaired Moonlocket around his neck. "But out on an adventure you don't have those things, and there are days when you feel so alone."

"You're right," Lily said. "Sometimes I feel the past is

too heavy. That the wounds never fully disappear—they may fade over time and heal, but the evidence of them is still there, like old scars."

"That's how you know you're strong," Robert said. "Those scars are the healing: the reminder that you survived and that you're powerful."

He glanced at Lily. She seemed—almost in the last week—to have grown into someone quite altered from the girl he'd first known, with her bluff and bravado—that old bravery on the outside that had covered the fear beneath of a little girl lost. This new Lily was not like that. She seemed clear and open, truly confident.

"Your scars, Lily, are the map of your past and the key to the future. A future where you can fly high. And you were born to do that, I know it! To be spectacular and unique. To be who you're meant to be." He put his arm around her. "Remember, you're not alone. You never were. And no matter what happens, as long as I'm around, as long as we're friends, then you never will be."

"Is that a promise?"

"I think it might be."

"Cross your heart and hope to die?"

"Cross my heart and hope to live!"

He took her hand and squeezed it until he could feel the tick of her heart, soft as a chronometer, her pulse reverberating with his own.

"Go on then," he said. "Write something."

Robert was right, Lily realized: she should write about her dreams and aspirations, what she wished for in the future. But to begin with, she would say a little about who she was.

She took up her pen and began.

The words, which had seemed small when she'd thought them, looked bigger on the page, and the truth they contained seemed so large, it filled her heart with unparalleled joy:

My name is Lily Rose Hartman. And this is the story of what makes me tick. The heart-stopping tale of my most remarkable life...

A dictionary of curious words

A glossary of words that may be uncommon to the reader

Automaton: a self-operating mechanical device.

Flattie: a "landlubber" in the circus world—someone who isn't used to the ways of the Skycircus. Like a fish out of water or a rhinoceros on a tightrope.

Funambulist: another name for a tightrope-walker. The word comes from the Latin term for rope—"funis"—and to walk—"ambulare"—and is absolutely delightful to say out loud.

Hybrid: someone who is part mech, part human.

Lovelace, Ada: the woman who inspired Grace Hartman's ideas, Ada Lovelace was a nineteenth-century mathematician and writer. She was one of the first, if not the first, person to consider the idea of "computer programming" and worked with engineer and philosopher Charles Babbage on his ideas for an "analytical engine": the first computer. There have been multiple attempts to discredit or write out Ada's part in the history of computers; however, Ada is now beginning to garner the credit she deserves.

Mechanimal: a mechanical animal, such as Malkin.

Perpetual motion machine: a machine that will run forever, without the need for an external source of energy.

Roustabouts: also known as "rousties," the people who put up and take down the circus. In Slimwood's circus, they're a slightly unsavory bunch.

Shelley, Mary: the author who inspired Dr. Droz's parents to name her "Shelley Mary Droz" was an astonishing woman who learned to read from her own mother's gravestone. She wrote *Frankenstein,* which was initially published anonymously in 1818, before Mary took credit in 1823, though many at the time did not believe that a woman could have written the book.

Spoonerist: someone who gets their words in a muddle, like Auggie. The muddle comes when the corresponding letters between two words are switched. For example, cookies and milk might become mookies and cilk, or jelly beans might become belly jeans.

X-ray: a type of electromagnetic wave, which was first discovered in 1895. The waves travel through many materials, including skin and body tissue, but are absorbed by others, such as dense bones. This difference in how they pass through materials means X-rays can be used to produce images of the inside of your body.

Zeppelin: a type of airship. It has an oval-shaped "balloon," beneath which is a rigid metal framework filled with bags of gas to keep the ship afloat. The passenger and crew area —or gondola—is usually situated under the main balloon and can be quite roomy. (Unless you're hitching a ride in *Ladybird,* in which case it's a little bit cozy.)

ACKNOWLEDGMENTS

We've reached the end of our spectacle, ladies and gents, so please give a warm round of applause to thank the following fine folk who've assisted me in its creation...

Showstopping editors Rebecca Hill and Becky Walker, slicing clauses, sentences, and paragraphs at their own risk, blindfolded and without the aid of a safety net! Enchanting agent Jo Williamson—a comic sensation and charmer of publishers—offering invaluable advice and ever-present good humor.

Virtuoso artists Katharine Millichope and Becca Stadtlander, whose breathtaking artwork always astounds. Sensational Sarah Cronin for her dazzling type design. The sparkling parade of Usborne staff and freelancers who've helped edit, market, and sell this book. A galaxy of stars that includes: Sarah Stewart, Stephanie King, Stevie Hopwood, Anna Howorth, Hannah Reardon Steward, Jacob Dow, Katarina Jovanovic, Liz Scott, and Nina Douglas—to name but a few. Mari Kesselring, Megan Naidl, and everyone at Jolly Fish Press. Barbara Fisch, Sara Shealy, and all at Blue Slip Media. Everyone at Antony Harwood. Katelyn Detweiler and all at Jill Grinberg Literary Management.

The remarkable reviewers, readers, and bloggers who've championed this series. Chiefly Jo Clarke, Scott Evans, Ashley Booth, and Matt Edwards for your ongoing cheerleading and support. The fine school library service staff who've featured *Cogheart* and *Moonlocket* in their awards and reading schemes and helped get the books into so many schools. School librarians and book-consuming teachers, you're angels of your schools and your contagious enthusiasm for children's fiction and reading is invaluable to the children you teach. Each and every smiling face I've met at events across the country: It's a joy to talk about stories with you, and your enthusiasm buoys my writing.

Crit group buddies Lorraine Gregory, Meira Drazin, Miriam Craig, Tania Tay, and Gail Doggett for being excellent dinner companions, garrulous gossips, and occasional emergency phone contacts. My sister Hannah for reading the first draft and offering feedback.

The National Center for Circus Arts, whose circus skills taster course gave me the vaguest idea of what it might be like to fly on a trapeze, climb the silks, or wire-walk for real. It was an exhilarating experience, but not an exercise regimen I'll be pursuing!

Everyone who visited circuses with me while I was researching this book. Matt and Kate who came to Gifford's. My goddaughters Paula and Georgia who graciously accompanied us to Zippo's. Plus Michael who came to Circus Fantasia and all the others, and has endured the daily circus of me writing this book with good grace and no knife throwing! Here's to another night in the Big Top with each and every one of you, even if this time it's only in print.

Find out where Lily and Robert's
thrilling adventures began in...

A COGHEART ADVENTURE

COGHEART

A STUNNING ADVENTURE
of DANGER and DARING

PETER BUNZL

Lily's life is in mortal peril. Her father is missing and now silver-eyed men stalk her through the shadows. What could they want from her?

With her friends—Robert, the clockmaker's son, and Malkin, her mechanical fox—Lily is plunged into a murky and menacing world. Too soon Lily realizes that those she holds dear may be the very ones to break her heart…

"An exciting, fast-paced adventure."
—*Booklist*

And follow their escapades
into the dark underworld of
thieves and trickery in...

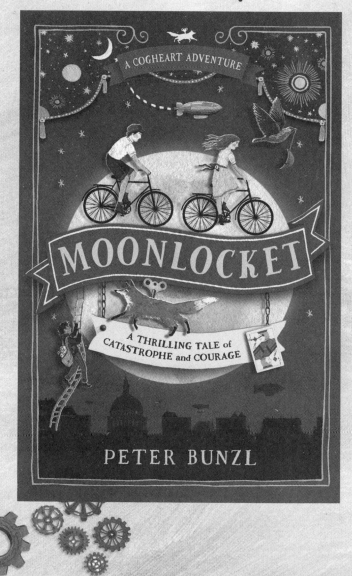

A COGHEART ADVENTURE

MOONLOCKET

A THRILLING TALE of
CATASTROPHE and COURAGE

PETER BUNZL